MURDER on BOARD

BOOKS BY HELENA DIXON

Miss Underhay Mystery Series

Murder at the Dolphin Hotel

Murder at Enderley Hall

Murder at the Playhouse

Murder on the Dance Floor

Murder in the Belltower

Murder at Elm House

Murder at the Wedding

Murder in First Class

Murder at the Country Club

HELENA DIXON

MURDER on BOARD

bookouture

Published by Bookouture in 2022

An imprint of Storyfire Ltd.
Carmelite House
50 Victoria Embankment
London EC4Y 0DZ

www.bookouture.com

ISBN: 978-1-80314-303-3
eBook ISBN: 978-1-80314-302-6

Murder on Board is dedicated to my dad who sadly passed during the writing of this book. He was always my biggest champion. When he wasn't busy telling people I was a nurse, he was busy telling them to buy my books. God bless until we meet again.

PROLOGUE

Torbay Herald, September 1934

Situations Vacant

Hotel manager required for immediate start at premier establishment. Must be of smart appearance and experienced in all aspects of hotel management. Apply for particulars with details and references to Miss K. Underhay, The Dolphin Hotel, The Embankment, Dartmouth, Devon.

Advertisement

The Kingswear Castle, *a luxuriously appointed paddle steamer, offers comfortable cruising on the River Dart. Leaving from Dartmouth twice daily and calling at the picturesque villages of Dittisham and Stoke Gabriel, why not spend a pleasurable morning or afternoon on the river? Also available for private hire for parties and evening dinner cruises. Contact our booking office at Dartmouth Quay for details.*

CHAPTER ONE

The September sunshine sparkled through the leaded glass panes of the large bay windows in Kitty's grandmother's salon at the Dolphin Hotel. Kitty's own mood, however, was not as sunny or hopeful as the weather.

'I fear that finding a suitable person for the job may prove rather more difficult than we had anticipated,' her grandmother observed, after the door had closed behind their last applicant for the position of hotel manager. 'Are there any more people left to see today?' She directed the last part of her question to Dolly, their young assistant, who had been seated in a corner quietly taking notes during the interviews.

'There's just the one gentleman left to come upstairs for interview now, Mrs Treadwell.' The girl looked at the paperwork in front of her. 'A Mr Cyril Lutterworth. He's come from London.'

'Is he the man who has been managing Porteboys Gentlemen's Club in Mayfair?' Kitty asked. She had been impressed by Mr Lutterworth's résumé when she had been reviewing the applications for the post.

It had been her grandmother's idea that they appoint a

manager for the Dolphin to work under Kitty's supervision. With her grandmother wishing to retire and Kitty's wedding rapidly approaching, the need to find a way to run the hotel effectively had become more pressing.

However, the first three applicants they had interviewed already that morning had proved something of a disappointment. One clearly had insufficient experience, the second had been very odd and the last applicant had smelt of alcohol – and it was not even eleven in the morning.

'That's the one, Miss Kitty. He's travelled quite a ways. Shall I fetch a tray of tea for you all when I brings him up?' Dolly suggested.

'Yes, please, Dolly dear, an excellent idea. I'm sure we could all use a little refreshment. I hope this Mr Lutterworth may be the person that proves suitable,' Mrs Treadwell replied with a smile.

Dolly flushed with pleasure at her employer's praise and left the salon to organise tea and to bring up their final applicant.

'Dolly is such a good girl,' Mrs Treadwell remarked, once the girl had gone downstairs.

Kitty murmured her agreement. Dolly was the younger sister of her own particular friend and maid, Alice. The girls were part of a family of eight. Alice at nineteen was the eldest of the Miller children and Dolly had not long turned fifteen, but was a very bright and hard-working girl.

'We are very fortunate to have her.' Kitty would make sure that whoever was appointed as manager would appreciate Dolly's contribution to the smooth running of the hotel.

After a minute or two there was a tap at the door of the salon and Dolly's bright-auburn head reappeared. 'Mr Lutterworth,' she announced, before vanishing once more. Presumably to collect the tea trolley.

Kitty's first impression was of a smartly attired tall, thin gentleman in perhaps his late-fifties. He removed his hat to reveal a narrow head topped by a shining bald pate. Long legs clad in black trousers with knife-edge sharp creases gave her the impression of a human clothes peg. A pink rose was at his lapel and his bright-blue eyes had an air of sharp intelligence.

'We are delighted to meet you, Mr Lutterworth. Thank you for coming.' Her grandmother had risen to shake his hand. Kitty followed suit, before her grandmother indicated a vacant seat and invited the man to sit.

'I am Mrs Treadwell, and this is my granddaughter, Miss Underhay. We are the proprietors of the Dolphin Hotel.' Her grandmother resumed her seat as Dolly re-entered the room with a tea trolley.

'A pleasure to meet you both.' Mr Lutterworth seated himself, while the girl bustled around serving tea and biscuits.

'Dolly tells us that you have travelled some distance to be here?' Kitty's grandmother remarked as she accepted a delicate china cup and saucer from her young assistant.

'Yes, I took the early train this morning from Paddington,' Mr Lutterworth agreed, before taking an appreciative sip from his drink.

'You were formerly employed at the Porteboys Club?' Kitty asked.

Mr Lutterworth inclined his head in agreement. 'Yes, I was the manager there for the last five years. It is a most respectable gentlemen's club for members of the engineering and scientific profession.'

Kitty's grandmother perused Mr Lutterworth's résumé. 'You have no direct experience in hotel management?' she asked.

'Unfortunately, no, but managing a club such as Porteboys is very much the same thing. There are room reservations to attend to, a restaurant and bar to manage, plus all the activities offered at the premises, fencing, bridge and so on. I am accustomed to dealing with all the problems that one might encounter when managing a high-class establishment.' He smiled gently at Kitty and her grandmother.

Kitty had assumed as much when she had received his application. 'May we enquire why you wished to leave your post?'

'I have enjoyed my position, but I felt the time had come for a change. The air in London is not good for my health and my doctor has advised me that living beside the sea would benefit me. I will be direct with you, I have asthma, no other conditions that might cause a problem, but the pollution in the city is not good for me as I have matured.' He set down his now empty teacup.

'Living here in Dartmouth will be quite a change after the hustle and bustle of the city. Do you have any family connections in this area?' Mrs Treadwell asked.

'A nephew in Paignton. My late sister's child.' Mr Lutterworth's expression became solemn for a moment and Kitty suspected that perhaps there was some personal story there.

Her grandmother continued to ask questions about Mr Lutterworth's knowledge and experience in the various areas of hotel management, before asking Dolly to take the gentleman on a tour of the premises.

'I take it from that you feel he would be suitable?' Kitty asked as soon as Dolly had led Mr Lutterworth out of the salon.

Her grandmother nodded. 'Yes, he certainly appears to have the requisite understanding of what the position entails. What do you think, my dear, could you work with him?'

Kitty nodded. Her impression had also been favourable and the day felt as if it had taken a turn for the better. 'If his references are good, then I agree. I think we may have found ourselves a manager. With his having recently left his post he can also make an immediate start.'

* * *

Kitty's fiancé, Captain Matthew Bryant, was also in Dartmouth that morning. Employed as a private investigator, his mission was far more furtive than Kitty's. He adjusted his position from the spot where he was concealed in the woods and raised his field glasses to his eyes once more.

His vantage point offered him a clear view of the River Dart lying below him in the valley. More importantly, it offered him a view of the German ship, the *Sigrid*, which lay at anchor not far from the training ship used by cadets from the nearby Naval College.

There seemed little activity on board and Matt sighed as he lowered his glasses. He had been in position in a hollow in the woods for a couple of hours and he was still no further forward in his mission.

To avoid his activity from arousing suspicion, he was attired in light-green tweed with matching cap. A copy of the *Birds of Britain* was in his pocket, along with a notebook. A folding pocket Brownie camera hung from a leather strap around his neck. All to add credence to his cover story that he was bird-watching, should anyone stumble across him.

Matt's former employer, Brigadier Remmington-Blythe, had commissioned him to 'keep an eye' on a particular man, Gunther Freiberg, who was believed to be connected in some way with the *Sigrid*. The brigadier hadn't given him too much information on why it was so important that they knew the man's movements and contacts. Just that it was a national security concern and Whitehall wished to be informed of any contacts the man made.

Matt had discovered that Freiberg had been in town for a few months working as a casual hire for a number of boat owners and publicans in the town. He appeared to have used a number of aliases in the past when he had lived at Plymouth, before his arrival in Dartmouth.

The *Sigrid* had arrived four days ago and was lying at anchor while the crew worked on an alleged problem with her engines. Dartmouth was a regular port of call for the vessel; however, Matt had learned that the brigadier had been following the movement of the *Sigrid* along the coast for some time before her arrival in the estuary.

Unlike the ship, Gunther Freiberg had proved to be a tricky character to keep under surveillance. Ostensibly, the man lived a quiet life in a rented room in the poorer part of the town. He was a tall, well-built individual in his mid-forties, with thick dark-blond hair and blue eyes. He took casual work as a labourer or a steward, but there had been gaps where he simply seemed to disappear for a day or so before returning to his work.

Up until yesterday Matt had seen little that seemed out of place and had duly reported this back to the brigadier. His former employer, however, had requested that Matt continue his surveillance for a few more days, at least until the *Sigrid* left port. With no sign of Gunther that morning, Matt had decided to watch the ship in the hope of seeing something useful.

Matt altered his position again and raised his field glasses once more. It was all very well for the brigadier to issue his orders. He wasn't the one camped out in a hollow in the woods getting cramp in his calves from sitting on the damp grass.

Movement on the deck of the *Sigrid* caught his attention and he adjusted the focus on the glasses to try to gain a clearer view. Two men had appeared on deck and appeared to be taking a cigarette break, leaning on the rails and looking towards Kingswear on the opposite side of the river.

He watched as the men appeared to smoke and talk while the passenger paddle steamer, the *Kingswear Castle*, chugged its way past with a party of day trippers on board. The boat was not as large as the American paddle steamers. Powered by a coal-fired engine it splashed and chugged its way gently along the river. Matt was about to lower his binoculars when he noticed a familiar figure on board the paddle steamer attending to the passengers. The very man he had been looking for.

The crewmen from the *Sigrid* gave a barely perceptible nod towards the paddle steamer and Matt saw that Gunther had picked up what was clearly a signal. A prickle of excitement raised the hairs in the nape of his neck. There was a connection between the German boat and his quarry, but what?

The men moved away from the rails and disappeared once more below deck. The paddle steamer continued on her way to her mooring not far from the Dolphin so her passengers could disembark.

Matt stretched out his cramped limbs before scrambling to his feet. He doubted he would gain anything further from remaining in the woods. There had definitely been a signal from the *Sigrid* to Gunther, but what did it mean?

He replaced his field glasses back in their brown leather case and started to make his way out of the woods towards the road where he had left his beloved Sunbeam motorcycle. A glance at his watch told him that it was almost lunchtime and he had promised to take his fiancée out for something to eat.

No doubt Kitty would update him on her search for a suitable manager for the Dolphin. He hoped that her interviews had procured a suitable candidate. Their wedding was rapidly approaching in December, and he knew Kitty's grandmother wished the matter settled.

He sat astride the bike and secured his cap firmly on his head. Out of the shade of the trees the sun was quite strong, and a gentle breeze stirred the bracken at the side of the road.

The town was busy as he rode down the hill towards the embankment. The paddle steamer was moored now, and he assumed that the next sailing would be after lunch, taking another party of day trippers upriver to Dittisham.

There was no sign of her crew, or of Gunther Freiberg. A rope was across the gangway leading to the boat and a sign advised that tickets could be purchased for the afternoon cruise from the booth near the boat float.

Matt rode further along and parked his motorcycle near the entrance of the ancient black-and-white half-timbered Dolphin Hotel. The painted sign creaked above his head in the gentle breeze from the river and seagulls called to each other as they wheeled overhead.

He stowed his field glasses and camera inside the leather bag at the rear of his motorcycle and brushed a few stray blades of grass from his trousers. He had no desire to arouse the suspicions of his sharp-eyed fiancée who would undoubtedly have concerns if she knew that his former employer had given him another mission. Especially as the one he had been involved with a few weeks earlier had led to several murders.

CHAPTER TWO

Kitty was in her small office behind the reception desk when Matt arrived. She heard the deep rumble of his voice in the lobby as he greeted Mary, the receptionist, and hastily tidied her short blonde curls.

She had just replaced her comb inside the drawer of her desk when the door to her office opened.

'Morning, darling, are you free now for a spot of lunch?' Matt appeared looking very much the country gentleman in his attire.

'Yes, all done for now. I've just finished telephoning Mr Lutterworth's referees and drafted a letter offering him the post. Dolly is typing it ready to take to the post. I'm hopeful that he can start before the end of this week as he has already left his previous position.' Kitty rose from her seat to collect her hat and handbag from the bentwood coat stand in the corner of the office as she spoke.

'Your quest was successful then? This Mr Lutterworth is the right man for the manager's job?' Matt assisted her into her pale-blue lightweight jacket.

'Yes, I believe so. Up until recently he was the manager of

the Porteboys Gentlemen's Club in Mayfair. Do you know of it?' Kitty asked as she led the way out of the office into the lobby.

A frown creased Matt's brow. 'Yes, I think so. A small, but well-respected establishment. I believe it's used by members of the engineering and scientific professions. I've lunched there a couple of times in the past as a guest.'

Kitty informed her receptionist that they would return in an hour's time and took Matt's arm as they stepped outside into the sunshine.

'Where are we going for lunch today?' Kitty asked as they strolled along the bustling embankment towards the boat float, a small marina just off the river.

'I thought perhaps the tea room near the Butterwalk.' Matt smiled down at her, the dimple showing in his cheek making her pulse quicken.

'And how have you been spending this morning? I see that Bertie has not accompanied you today, so I assume you have a case,' Kitty said.

Matt's blue roan cocker spaniel was invariably at his side. The dog had previously belonged to a victim in one of their cases and was notoriously badly behaved if left alone.

'Bertie is at home. I think my housekeeper may be softening towards him. She only scolded him when she discovered he had chewed her broom and I caught her slipping him a titbit of ham when she thought no one could see.'

Kitty laughed at her fiancé's response. 'That is good news. Let's hope he doesn't destroy anything else while you are out.' She noticed that Matt hadn't answered her question about what he had been doing that morning.

Normally he talked about the cases he was engaged on, knowing that she took a keen interest in his work. This reluctance to discuss his current case was concerning, still no doubt she would discover more over lunch.

The tea room was busy, and they had to wait for a few minutes for a table to be made available. Once they were seated and they had given their order for fish, chips, bread and butter with a pot of tea, Kitty drew off her white cotton gloves and prepared to quiz her fiancé.

The corner of a book was peeking out of the top of his jacket pocket and, before he could stop her, Kitty pounced upon it.

'*Birds of Britain*?' she asked, raising her eyebrows as she studied the cover. 'Is this a new hobby?'

Matt's feet shifted under the table. 'I've always had an interest in ornithology.'

'Really? I seem to recall you mistaking a crow for a magpie only a few weeks ago when we were walking near the castle.' Kitty was unconvinced by his reply. Matt was up to something that he knew she wouldn't be happy about. She was willing to wager her last shilling on it.

'Exactly, I decided that I should learn more about our native species.' He reached his hand across the table to retrieve his book.

Kitty passed it across as the waitress arrived with their lunch. Once the girl had set down the food and the pot of tea Kitty resumed her questioning.

'And where did you go for this birdwatching expedition?' she asked as she applied salt and vinegar to her chips.

'Not far, just above the town in the woods near the castle. I had been told that I might see a kingfisher there on the river.' Matt didn't meet her gaze as he took up his cutlery.

Kitty sighed. 'You were observing someone or something, weren't you?' She plucked a small leaf from the elbow of his jacket.

He raised his hands in a gesture of defeat. 'It's a commission from the brigadier.'

'I thought it might be,' Kitty said. She had guessed there must be an explanation why he had been so evasive. Commissions from the brigadier always tended to be shrouded in secrecy.

'It's simply an observation job. I don't know many of the details behind it.' His gaze met with hers. 'I didn't tell you as I know you weren't keen on my accepting more work from London, especially after what happened last time when Simon Travers was killed on the train.'

Kitty set down her knife and fork and picked up the chrome teapot to pour their tea into the modern brightly painted abstract-patterned cups. 'It's just that this work tends to be so dangerous. You left the service for a reason, and the brigadier always seems to find a way to reel you back in. I worry about your safety, that's all.'

Matt added milk and sugar to his cup and stirred. 'I know, darling, I'm sorry I should have told you. I just thought you had enough on your plate with appointing a new manager for the Dolphin and arranging our wedding. I intended to tell you about it once the case was closed.'

Kitty smiled. 'I'm still uneasy but I'll forgive you, just this once. Now tell me about the case.'

After taking care that they could not be overheard, Matt filled her in on Gunther Freiberg and his suspected connections with the *Sigrid*.

'I take it that you believe they were arranging some kind of assignation, or perhaps a collection if he is acting as a delivery man of some kind?' Kitty asked as she finished the last bite of her fish.

'It looked that way to me. The brigadier has been tight-lipped, but he seemed to think that there was some kind of flow of information that could compromise our national security.'

Kitty topped up their cups of tea, draining the pot. 'And you promise that your involvement is only to observe and report back?'

Matt flashed her a quick grin. 'I promise. No confrontations of any kind. All observations from a distance. The brigadier is keen to sweep in and net all of those involved when they least expect it. He was clear that I was to do absolutely nothing to arouse any suspicions either from the ship's crew or Herr Freiberg.'

The waitress came to collect their plates and they ordered a slice of apple pie, accompanied by clotted cream to finish their meal.

'Your grandmother must be relieved to have found a suitable manager for the hotel,' Matt observed.

'Oh, most definitely. I am a little worried about her, Matt. She really is quite tired, and I think the sooner she can step away from her responsibilities and take a proper holiday, the better.' Kitty smiled her thanks at the waitress as the girl set their desserts in front of them.

'Have you heard yet when you are to expect your father?' Matt asked.

Kitty sighed. There was no love lost between her grandmother and her father. Edgar Underhay had been absent from Kitty's life since she had been a child and had only reconnected with her just over a year ago.

He was currently residing in America and on receiving news of her engagement and the date of the wedding, had declared his intention to return to England in order to walk Kitty down the aisle. Unfortunately, his less than savoury reputation meant that the rest of Kitty's family, her grandmother, aunt, and uncle not so delighted by this news.

'He wrote that his ship is due about two weeks before the wedding and that he intends to return to America in the new year,' Kitty said.

Their wedding was booked for Christmas Eve at ancient St Saviour's Church in the centre of Dartmouth.

'And are you decided upon your bridesmaids?' Matt asked as he picked up his cup to take a sip of tea.

Kitty's shoulders drooped. 'The more I try to plan our wedding the more I understand why my parents decided to elope and marry in London. Everything is so complicated. Naturally I would like Lucy as my matron of honour.'

Matt nodded. 'Of course.'

They had attended Kitty's cousin Lucy's wedding to Rupert, Lord Thurscomb, only a few months ago in the spring.

'And I should very much have liked Alice as my bridesmaid,' Kitty said.

Matt looked questioningly at her. 'Why is that a problem?'

'Mrs Craven has pointed out that it would be most unsuitable to have my cousin, who is a lady, as matron of honour standing with my personal maid as a bridesmaid. "Think of the disparity in social class, my dear."' Kitty imitated Mrs Craven, her grandmother's best friend's disapproving tone.

'I wouldn't have thought that would bother you, or Lucy,' Matt said. 'Lucy loves Alice, and Rupert, despite his title, is hardly your typical stuck in the mud, keep to your own social station sort of a chap.'

Kitty frowned. 'Lucy has no problem with the idea at all. She was delighted when I suggested it and she is thrilled to be my matron of honour.'

'So then, what's the problem, old thing?' Matt asked as he gave her hand a gentle squeeze.

'It's Alice. Mrs Craven has seen fit to let it be known that Alice would be stepping above her station and would embarrass Lucy and I if she were to accept.' Kitty raised her shoulders in a gesture of defeat. 'You know what Alice is like. She is terribly proud. I still struggle to stop her from calling me miss instead of Kitty when we are out and about.'

Matt nodded thoughtfully. 'Perhaps if Lucy speaks to her, or perhaps your aunt Hortense? I take it your aunt and uncle have no objections?'

Kitty smiled. 'You know they are very fond of Alice. No,

they would not object at all. Our wedding is hardly some big society affair where it would be considered scandalous or avant-garde.'

Matt grinned. 'Then we will ask Lucy to have a word with Alice. Perhaps the next time she telephones you?'

Kitty nodded. 'Yes, you're right. Honestly, the fuss Mrs Craven is making you would think she was personally responsible for our wedding arrangements. If it wouldn't upset Grams so much, I would be sorely tempted to tell her to keep out of it.'

'She does love to be helpful.' Matt's grin widened.

'I have an appointment this afternoon about my wedding dress.'

'Let me guess, with the lady Mrs C recommended?' Matt chuckled at the slightly doleful look that Kitty knew had appeared on her face.

'At Mademoiselle Desmoine's in Torquay, yes, of course. I could hardly dare try anyone else, even if I knew of someone.'

'Then we had better pay the bill and I shall walk you back to the Dolphin.' Matt caught the waitress' attention and requested the bill.

'Shall I see you later?' Kitty asked as she took his arm once more to begin their stroll back to the hotel.

'Come for supper this evening when you have finished with the dressmaker,' Matt suggested.

'I may be a little late. You know that the chief constable, Sir Montague Hawkes, has booked the Dolphin for his daughter Serafina's twenty-first birthday party on Saturday, and I have a lot to arrange before then.' Kitty's grandmother was an old friend of the chief constable's wife, Lady Rose, and it was quite an honour to have been chosen to host Serafina's party.

Sir Montague had arranged a champagne supper and river cruise for the family and intimate friends aboard the *Kingswear Castle* paddle steamer to be followed by canapés, and a ball at the Dolphin immediately afterwards.

'I take it that all the great and the good will be in attendance at the ball?' Matt asked.

'Absolutely, Mrs Craven, of course, will be in attendance there too. As you know she is also a friend of Lady Rose's.' Kitty often wondered how Lady Rose had remained friends with Mrs Craven given how many times that lady had written letters of complaint about the police.

'I expect the hotel will be crawling with policemen. Our friend, Inspector Greville, will be there, no doubt, and his good lady wife?' Matt asked.

'I believe that everyone of inspectors rank and above from Exeter and locally has been invited,' Kitty agreed. 'There is such a lot to do. Lady Rose has been telephoning with instructions and requests at least three times a day ever since the booking was made. I swear this is partly why Grams is so exhausted. I shall be most relieved when Mr Lutterworth takes up his position to assist.'

They paused outside the entrance of the hotel. 'Poor you and poor Grams too. I shall expect you when you arrive then, darling. Take care and enjoy the dress fitting.' Matt kissed her cheek and waved as he set off back along the embankment towards his motorcycle.

Kitty waved back and blew out a sigh before squaring her shoulders and re-entering the hotel.

CHAPTER THREE

Her grandmother was waiting for her in her salon when she went upstairs.

'Did you have a nice lunch, darling?' her grandmother asked.

'Oh yes, it was lovely, thank you. We went to the tea room at the Butterwalk. Are you all set for our visit to Mademoiselle Desmoine's?' Kitty knew her grandmother was looking forward to accompanying her on the visit to the couturier.

Her cousin, Lucy, had offered her the use of her own wedding dress and her aunt had been pressing her to wear the family tiara to secure her veil. Generous though both offers were, and greatly appreciated by Kitty, she wanted to choose her own wedding attire. Lucy's had been a grand wedding as befitted her station, while Kitty intended hers and Matt's nuptials to be a much more modest affair.

Her grandmother was adamant that she would pay for her gown. She insisted that since she had been deprived of that privilege when Kitty's mother, Elowed, had eloped, she was determined to enjoy Kitty's wedding.

Kitty's father had mailed her a cheque shortly after she had informed him of her engagement plans. Her grandmother had advised her to bank it as soon as possible, remarking, 'That it is entirely possible that any cheque from your father might bounce as high as a tumbling act at the music hall.'

Much to her grandmother's chagrin, however, she had been proven wrong and the money now nestled safely within Kitty's account as her father's contribution towards the wedding expenses.

The couturier recommended by Mrs Craven was in Torquay, with an establishment and workshop just a little further along the street from Matt's office. Kitty drove herself and her grandmother there in her small red touring car. With the weather so fine, Kitty left the roof down and made leisurely progress in the sunshine along the coast road.

Her grandmother was still an uneasy passenger despite Kitty's driving skills and had hinted that they should travel via Mr Potter's taxi service. She shared her friend Mrs Craven's view that driving was really a man's job.

'Here we are then, Grams,' Kitty announced cheerfully as she pulled her car to a halt just outside the bridal shop. Her grandmother remained seated for a moment, her gloved hands still tightly grasping the bone handle of her ivory leather handbag.

'Thank you, Kitty.'

Kitty jumped out and crossed around the front of her car to open the passenger door, so that her grandmother could get out. The shop had a modest shiny black frontage, with one small plate glass window on either side of the entrance. Kitty had seen it several times before but had thought it to sell mainly formal gowns.

The establishment name, Mlle Desmoine, was painted in gold above the door. It was clear from the gowns in the window that evening attire was the mainstay of the business. Kitty hoped that for once Mrs Craven's recommendation would prove to be useful. If not, then she would end up having to travel to Exeter in order to acquire her wedding gown.

The brass bell on a curved spring above the door sounded as they entered. At first Kitty assumed the shop floor was empty. A large gilt-framed mirror on a stand was placed at the rear, rails of gowns were on either side and a small glass and gold counter displaying a modest selection of shoes, gloves and clutch bags was near the door.

Kitty's grandmother glanced around her as Kitty sucked in a breath and wondered where the proprietor of the store had gone. The pale-green satin curtain at the rear of the shop suddenly swished to one side and a tiny, fierce-looking lady clad from head to toe in black stepped forward.

'Miss Underhay? I am Mademoiselle Desmoine. You require a bridal gown?' the woman asked in a heavy French accent. Her sharp boot-button black gaze raking Kitty over from top to bottom.

'Yes, that's right, we were recommended by Mrs Craven. This is my grandmother, Mrs Treadwell,' Kitty responded.

'*Bien*, we are upstairs in the atelier. You will follow me.' Mlle Desmoine promptly disappeared back behind the curtain.

Kitty glanced at her grandmother and together they followed the seamstress up a narrow wooden staircase into a large sunlit room, which ran across the width of the shop. A cutting table occupied the one end and rolls of all kinds of material were stacked on shelving at the other end. A small group of worn, black leather chairs were grouped around a low table to the side. Several sewing machines were nearby, and a mannequin displayed an almost completed bridal gown in ivory silk.

'Sit, sit.' Their hostess waved her hand in the direction of the chairs, so Kitty and her grandmother dutifully obeyed the instruction. A young girl, not much older than Dolly, appeared as if from nowhere and their seamstress shooed her away downstairs to mind the shop.

Mademoiselle Desmoine's collected up a large notepad and some pencils and came to join them. 'Your wedding is on Christmas Eve?' She looked at Kitty.

'Yes, at St Saviours Church in Dartmouth,' Kitty confirmed as the dressmaker started to make a series of undecipherable squiggles on her notebook.

A series of rapid-fire questions followed. Long or short sleeves, satin or silk, lace, beading, style, veil. The woman nodded after each response, the tight black bun of hair on the top of her head wagging an affirmative.

'*Bien*. Now I measure you. Come and stand.' The woman drew a tape measure from around her neck and motioned Kitty towards a small, round wooden podium raised about nine inches from the floor.

Within minutes the dressmaker measured what seemed to Kitty every inch of her anatomy. All the time muttering unintelligibly to herself in French and making more notes on her pad.

Once satisfied, the woman permitted her to dismount and return to her seat beside her grandmother.

'I make a design for you.' The woman flipped over the page of her book and started to sketch, her fingers dancing nimbly across the page.

Kitty exchanged a glance with her grandmother who had seemed unperturbed by the whole business. They waited in silence while the woman drew and scribbled on the notebook.

'*Eh, bien*.' The dressmaker nodded in satisfaction and turned the book so that Kitty and her grandmother could see the design.

Kitty had been feeling more and more uncertain with each step of this extraordinary proceeding. However, a gasp of astonishment escaped her when she saw the drawing before her. It was as if the dressmaker had taken the vague vision from inside her head and transferred it to the page.

'Oh, that looks perfect. It's exactly what I had in mind.' Kitty blinked with surprise.

The dressmaker gave a small smile of satisfaction. 'Of course. Now we look at the fabrics, come.' She rose from her seat once more and led Kitty over to the rolls of cloth.

Kitty's grandmother came to join them as the dressmaker lifted out several rolls and spread them on the cutting table.

'This one would be good for your complexion. You are very fair and in winter it is a harsh light.' The seamstress spread a delicate ivory satin in front of Kitty for her to see. 'This lace would be good to trim the veil and you said a Juliet cap trimmed with perhaps flowers and greenery?' The woman looked at Kitty as she unspooled delicate lace from a reel.

'That is so pretty.' Kitty looked to her grandmother for approval.

'Perhaps also a small cape, trimmed with fur?' the dressmaker suggested.

'Oh yes, Kitty, I agree. That would be perfect.' Her grandmother smiled her agreement.

'Very good. I shall make a pattern and you will return in two weeks for a fitting,' the dressmaker said as she stowed the materials back in their place and made more cryptic notes on her pad.

'What about your bridesmaids, Kitty?' her grandmother asked as the seamstress wrote her estimate for the cost of the gown, cape and veil on the notepad.

Kitty's smile faltered at the thorny issue of her attendants. 'I'm not sure just yet, Grams. Obviously, Lucy is to be matron of honour. I thought a simple dark-green satin, bias-cut gown would be nice. As it's December then perhaps she could also have a stole or cape.'

The dressmaker nodded. '*Très bon*, for a winter wedding. There is just one attendant?'

Kitty's grandmother looked at her.

'There may be a second. I'm not certain yet.' Kitty's cheeks heated. Her grandmother had left it up to Kitty to decide upon her attendants. She suspected, however, that while she was fond of Alice that her grandmother was inclined to agree with Mrs Craven that it wouldn't be appropriate for a chambermaid to stand next to a lady.

The dressmaker asked a few more questions about the gowns before dismissing them from the appointment.

Kitty drew her cotton summer gloves back on as she accompanied her grandmother outside into the late afternoon sunshine. 'That was all very intense. Shall we call for a cup of tea at the seafront before returning home?' Kitty asked as she opened the passenger door.

'Why not, my dear? We seem to get very little time to enjoy ourselves nowadays.' Her grandmother climbed into the passenger seat and Kitty closed the door before running around to jump behind the wheel.

She drove the short distance to the seafront and parked near the Pavilion tea room overlooking the gardens with their ornamental fountain and flower beds on the seafront. Once installed at a table with a view of the bay and their order placed, Kitty started to relax. It was good to know that her wedding dress was in progress so at least that was one thing she could cross off her huge to-do list.

'How are the arrangements progressing for Serafina's birthday ball?' her grandmother asked.

'Quite well, I believe. I am hoping Mr Lutterworth will be able to start this Friday so that he can be on hand to assist with all the arrangements. He did say at the interview that he had already resigned from his post at the Porteboys Club,' Kitty said.

'Yes, I'm so pleased his references were suitable and the

letter offering him the position with an immediate start should reach him by morning. A room is ready for him on your floor, and he can obviously upgrade into your quarters after your marriage when you have moved out.' Her grandmother appeared a little wistful as she nodded to the grey-and-white uniformed waitress as the girl delivered their tea.

'I think he should be a real asset to the Dolphin once he's learned the ropes,' Kitty agreed as she lifted the lid on the white china teapot to stir the brew inside.

'A gentleman on the staff will be most helpful. I'm so sorry, my dear, if Rose is being rather tiresome over this party for Serafina. I think she hopes that Serafina's beau may propose during the evening.' Her grandmother inspected the small plate of biscuits that had accompanied their drinks.

'Oh, is Serafina courting?' Kitty couldn't help the note of surprise that had crept into her voice.

She had only met Serafina a couple of times before but recalled her as being a rather stout girl with something of a permanent frown and a hint of a moustache. Serafina also had a sharp tongue.

'It seems so, yes. I don't know much about the young man in question, but it appears to have taken them all by surprise. The girl resembles her father's side of the family, poor thing, none of them great beauties, I'm afraid, and Serafina can be, well... quite difficult.'

Kitty placed the tea strainer over her grandmother's cup and poured the tea. 'Lady Rose also said that Sir Montague intended to present Serafina with some kind of family heirloom during the evening?'

Her grandmother nodded. 'Ah yes, the famous Firestone necklace. It's always given to the eldest daughter on their twenty-first birthday. The diamonds are quite remarkable, so I'm told. I think I last saw it when Rose wore it at a wedding anniversary ball a few years back. Sir Montague keeps it in a strong box at his bank.'

'I presume it must be very valuable then? It's a good thing the hotel will be teeming with policemen.' Kitty added milk to their cups.

'Oh yes, my dear, Rose said it's priceless. It belonged to her great-grandmother, then her grandmother, her mother and then, of course, it came to Rose. I believe she's only ever dared to wear it out in public a couple of times.'

Kitty took a sip of her tea. 'At least we only have the ball to worry about. Well, that and providing the paddle steamer with the food for the champagne supper once they are moored again on the embankment.'

'Such a novel idea, an intimate champagne cruise and supper before the party. I believe Rose had the idea from a French friend of Serafina's. She had been to a similar event in Italy, and it seemed to be quite the thing over there.' Kitty's grandmother drained her cup and set it back on her saucer. 'Let us hope that Sir Montague doesn't drop the necklace overboard before it's safely placed around Serafina's neck.' She gave a chuckle at the idea.

'Well, I for one refuse to go paddling about in the river mud, diamond necklace or not, so I do hope the catch is strong.' Kitty grinned back at her as the rather absurd image of the chief constable's party all wading into the water popped into her head.

CHAPTER FOUR

Much to both Kitty and her grandmother's relief, Mr Lutterworth telephoned on receipt of the letter and pronounced himself happy to accept the position of hotel manager. He then duly arrived shortly after breakfast on Thursday complete with his trunk.

By the lunchtime he had unpacked, looked around the town and was already familiarising himself with the workings of the hotel. While Kitty found it somewhat strange sharing her responsibilities with a stranger, the relief on her grandmother's countenance that she could finally relinquish her responsibilities was clearly visible.

Kitty arranged a private welcome dinner for Mr Lutterworth with herself, Matt and her grandmother for that evening in her grandmother's quarters. She was keen for Matt to meet her new manager to gather his opinion.

'Mr Lutterworth, may I present my fiancé, Captain Matthew Bryant.' Kitty made the introduction while her grandmother poured them all pre-dinner drinks.

'I'm delighted to meet you, sir.' Mr Lutterworth extended his hand.

'You too, welcome to Dartmouth.' Matt shook the older man's hand, before accepting a whisky and soda from Kitty's grandmother.

'Thank you. I must say it seems a most delightful town. I walked around earlier this afternoon after I had unpacked, just to get my bearings and it all seemed very pleasant.' Mr Lutterworth accepted his drink and took an appreciative sip from the cut crystal glass.

'I imagine it must feel quite provincial after living in Mayfair for so long,' Matt observed.

'I shall welcome the change, I assure you,' Mr Lutterworth affirmed.

'Kitty said that you had some family connections locally?' Matt leaned his elbow against the corner of the marble mantelpiece.

'Yes, my late sister's child. We are not close, I'm afraid. The boy was quite wild in his youth. I hope he might be more settled now. I haven't seen him for some time.' A faint frown creased Mr Lutterworth's forehead.

Kitty sipped her sherry thoughtfully. 'Perhaps you may be able to become better acquainted now you will be residing here,' she suggested.

Mr Lutterworth gave a small smile. 'Perhaps, Miss Underhay.'

'If we are to be working together, I insist you call me Kitty.'

'Then you must call me Cyril.' His smile widened, and he raised his glass in her direction.

Dinner proved a delightful affair. Cyril had many amusing anecdotes about his time at the Porteboys Club and it seemed that he and Matt knew some of the same people. Matt's previous work for the brigadier meant he had met some of the Porteboys' members. Kitty was reassured that Mr Lutterworth would be the right choice for the Dolphin.

Her grandmother too seemed to enjoy Mr Lutterworth's

company. 'You have joined at a busy point in our year. The season does not start to quieten down until mid-October and I'm sure Kitty has informed you of the party this weekend for Miss Serafina Hawkes' twenty-first birthday?'

'Indeed. I can see that it will be a most prestigious event for the hotel,' Cyril replied.

'I must confess, I shall be relieved once it's over. I know Lady Rose is a friend of yours, Grams, but she has been most trying this past week,' Kitty grumbled.

Her grandmother smiled. 'I know, my dear, but I think she feels this is a very important event for Serafina. Let us hope that it goes the way she wishes, and that her young man proposes.'

'Hmm.' Kitty wondered if the sight of the valuable diamond necklace Serafina was to inherit might assist in speeding up the young man's proposal.

Kitty woke early Saturday morning ready for a full day of preparing for the evening's events. She glanced at her bedside clock and sighed. Alice had been avoiding her all week, ever since her friend had declined her invitation to be her bridesmaid. Usually if she was on duty and she knew that Kitty was facing a busy day she would have brought her a tray of tea.

Kitty missed their early morning chats. She hadn't even thought when she had suggested to Alice that she be her bridesmaid that her friend would refuse and she felt terrible that Alice had been made to feel uncomfortable about it. In Kitty's eyes there was no one better suited for the role. Her cousin, Lucy, had agreed with her when they had talked about it on the telephone.

It seemed that it was only Alice's belief that she would be stepping out of her station that had led her to refuse. Now though there was this awful rift between them, with Alice reverting back more firmly into her place as an employee of the hotel rather than Kitty's friend.

Kitty drummed her fingers on her pink-satin counterpane. She couldn't allow this to continue. Once this wretched ball was over and Cyril was more firmly settled into his new post, she had to make amends with Alice.

Cyril was already in the office when Kitty went downstairs. A fresh pale-yellow rosebud was in the lapel of his grey pinstriped suit and he was familiarising himself with the hotel paperwork with Dolly's assistance.

'Good morning, Kitty. I hope you don't mind that I have already started? Miss Miller here has been most helpful.'

Dolly's cheeks turned as red as her curls at Mr Lutterworth's praise. 'I thought as I should show him how the bookings and invoicing works.'

'That's an excellent idea. I'm sure you'll find that Dolly is a marvellous assistant.' Kitty beamed at her young friend and noted with amusement that Dolly's cheeks turned an even brighter shade of crimson.

The morning passed speedily and harmoniously. By the time Mr Lutterworth left to take his lunch Kitty already felt as if a great weight was shifted from her shoulders. Cyril had even fended off two more telephone calls from Lady Rose about the evening's events.

The Hawkes' party were due to arrive at the hotel at three. Since they were to be staying overnight, several of the best riverfront rooms had been reserved for them. The plan was that they would arrive and unpack, then take tea before dressing for the evening and boarding the paddle steamer for a short champagne cruise along the river.

The boat would then return to dock, and Kitty's kitchen staff would deliver the evening's dinner to be served on board. Once dinner was over the party would disembark and return to the hotel to greet all the guests who would have been arriving whilst the family dined.

Canapés would be served throughout the evening and then there would be a toast to Serafina and her father would present her with the famous Firestone necklace. A large, iced birthday cake would be cut and served before the ball ended at around one a.m.

Kitty's grandmother had made her personal safe available to Sir Montague for the safe keeping of the necklace. Mickey, who was in charge of maintenance and security at the hotel, had also arranged for a lad to keep watch on the suite. With something so valuable in the building Kitty was determined that all precautions should be seen to be taken.

The Hawkes' party arrived on time in two gleaming, black large Rolls Royce cars. The first car contained Sir Montague, Lady Rose, Serafina, and her younger brother, Theodore. The second vehicle carried Serafina's friend, Flora Rochelle, Flora's father, Baron Rochelle, and the young man who was courting Serafina, a Mr Edward Forbes.

Kitty joined with her grandmother and Cyril in greeting their guests and arranging for their luggage to be taken to their rooms.

'My dear Kitty, it's been a while since I last saw you in person, my dear. I think it must have been at least two years ago now in Exeter. Thank you so much for all your help with the arrangements for this evening. Your grandmother tells me you are to be married at Christmas. I've been so taken up with the plans for the party I've been quite remiss with my congratulations.' Lady Rose swooped on Kitty.

She was a tall, handsome woman with an aquiline nose and dark hair swept back in a bun at the nape of her neck. Sir Montague was also tall with silver hair and moustache and erect military bearing. Theodore was a handsome youth of around eighteen. He had his mother's dark hair and his father's height.

Serafina had not improved in looks since Kitty had last seen her. She was inclined to be short, stout and surly.

'Yes, I think it must have been in Exeter when we last saw you. Thank you, Matt and I are to be married at Saint Saviour's on Christmas Eve,' Kitty answered Lady Rose.

'How delightful to have a Christmas wedding. Serafina is also courting.' This last piece of conversation was added in a lowered voice and a quick glance around as if to ensure that the rest of the party did not hear her.

Kitty smiled politely. 'That's nice.'

Serafina's purported beau, Edward Forbes, was a good-looking, blond-haired man in his mid-twenties. He was dressed in the latest fashion and his watch and shoes were expensive. Kitty couldn't help but think that in looks at least he and Serafina were an unlikely couple.

Flora Rochelle on the other hand was dark haired, petite and very pretty. Her father, the baron, was a small rotund man with a florid complexion. Kitty's grandmother had explained that the baron had once saved Sir Montague's life in a boating accident and the incident had sparked a lifelong friendship between the two men.

With the formalities of booking in observed and the luggage dispatched to the rooms, Cyril took Lady Rose to inspect the ballroom, while Kitty's grandmother took Sir Montague to her suite to deposit the Firestone necklace safely within the safe for later.

This left Kitty to escort the rest of the party to a small lounge that had been reserved for their exclusive use during their stay to take afternoon tea. Dolly was dispatched to the kitchen to ensure that the refreshments would be ready.

'You must be looking forward to this evening, Serafina?' Kitty remarked as the group took their seats around the low, round polished oak table.

'The river cruise yes, but not the ball. That was all mother's idea. Father has invited all his colleagues and there will scarcely be anyone there that I know and certainly hardly anyone under fifty.' Serafina pulled a face.

Kitty was at something of a loss how to reply. She knew Serafina's parents had gone to a great deal of trouble and expense for their daughter's birthday.

'Oh, don't mind Saffy, she's always miserable.' Theodore grinned at his sister and dodged out of reach as she attempted to hit him.

'I'm sure it will all be most delightful, and you and Edward at least will be able to dance together at the party,' Flora attempted to soothe her friend.

'Absolutely. We can cut the rug and have a jolly time,' Mr Forbes also hastened to assure the disgruntled Serafina.

'And don't forget that your father is presenting you with the Firestone necklace, my dear. I'm looking forward to taking some photographs of the evening,' Baron Rochelle added his weight to the conversation, smoothing his silk-patterned waistcoat over his belly as he settled back in his armchair.

'A necklace that is too valuable to wear,' Serafina scoffed. 'It will be placed around my neck, then I shall be paraded about like a racehorse in the ring for everyone to admire. After that it will be whisked away and locked back in the safe until presumably the next heir to receive it will get it out.'

Kitty was relieved to hear the distant jingle of crockery on the approaching tea trolley at this point.

'I think refreshments are in order. You all have such a busy evening ahead,' she said brightly and opened the door ready for the maid to enter.

CHAPTER FIVE

By the time evening had come around Kitty was more than pleased to see the Hawkes' party depart dressed in their finery to board the paddle steamer. The gentlemen looked distinguished in evening attire, Lady Rose in silver-grey lace, Flora pretty in rose satin and Serafina in a low-necked loose fitting gown in a rather unflattering shade of purple.

Matt had arrived to join Kitty for the evening since they were both invited to the ball. He stood next to her at the window of the hotel lobby, and they watched together as Mr Lutterworth escorted them aboard.

'Phew, I had forgotten how trying Serafina could be. I used to see a lot of her when we were very young and she was annoying then too,' Kitty said as she allowed the heavy velvet drape to fall back into place.

'Oh dear, then let us hope this champagne cruise goes well before they return for dinner,' Matt remarked as he gave Kitty a sympathetic glance.

'Grams is in the kitchen now ensuring that the chefs have everything set so the minute the steamer returns the food will be ready to box and take on board.' Kitty wished the party had agreed to dine in the hotel's dining room. It would have been so much easier and more comfortable for everyone. However, Lady Rose had felt it would add to the romantic ambience of making the day memorable for Serafina if they dined on board the paddle steamer.

She realised that Matt had continued to gaze out of the window through a gap at the side of the curtain, a thoughtful frown creasing his brow.

'What's wrong? Please don't tell me something has happened already?' Kitty tried to follow his gaze, peering around his shoulder, but could see nothing untoward. The party appeared to have embarked safely. Cyril was returning to the Dolphin and the *Kingswear Castle*'s steward had commenced seating the party on deck prior to departure.

'It's nothing really and certainly nothing to do with your party, I'm sure.' Matt's frown deepened as the paddle steamer cast off and started to make its way upriver towards the pretty village of Dittisham.

'Matt...' Kitty warned.

'The man I have been tasked with observing, Gunther Freiberg, is aboard the steamer. He seems to have been employed by the captain as a steward. I'd lost sight of him since the day I saw him receive a signal from the crew of the *Sigrid*, but he seems to have resurfaced.' Matt turned away from the window and captured his fiancée's hands in his. 'Please don't worry, Kitty darling. He seems to have been picking up a lot of work from the various boats and companies that use the moorings. I'm sure there can be nothing significant about his being aboard the boat this evening.'

Kitty wished she felt more reassured. It was troubling enough trying to make sure that everything was as the Hawkes' party had requested without this new added complication.

'All safely aboard, Kitty,' Cyril called out cheerily as he re-entered the hotel lobby. 'We have an hour or so now until the boat returns.'

'Thank you, Cyril. You're doing a sterling job today.'

Her new manager beamed happily at her. He, like Matt, was in formal evening attire and a fresh pink rosebud was in his lapel. 'I shall carry on to the ballroom as I believe we are almost ready for the arrival of the first guests. The band has just arrived and will be here in a moment.'

The ballroom had been decorated with additional pots of fronded palms and the tables around the edge of the dance floor decked with pale-pink cloths and elaborate white and pink floral table centrepieces. Kitty had hired a well-known local band with a female singer to provide music for the dancing. She had also arranged for a professional compère as requested by Lady Rose in one of her many telephone calls.

Once her employee was out of earshot Kitty turned back to Matt. 'I hope this Gunther is not out to cause trouble this evening. The chief constable is a very important person.'

Matt shook his head. 'I'm certain it is merely a coincidence that he is on board. He has worked on the *Kingswear Castle* before. I doubt that he wishes to draw any attention to himself if his mission here is to gather intelligence.'

Kitty was somewhat mollified by Matt's response. If this man was some kind of spy, he would not wish to expose himself, especially in front of the chief constable. She checked the delicate gold watch around her wrist.

'I'm sure you're right. I doubt the Hawkes' party will be discussing any national secrets this evening.'

Kitty and Matt were both kept busy until Cyril reported that the paddle steamer had been spotted approaching its mooring. She left Cyril to continue greeting guests who had started to arrive for the ball and she and Matt began to supervise delivery of the evening meal to the paddle steamer.

Kitty was aware that Matt was keen to use the opportunity

to observe his quarry at close quarters. For herself, she only wished to ensure that the wooden boxes insulated with straw containing the main course was taken safely on board.

The menu had been arranged so that the first course was a freshly prepared prawn and crab salad, followed by veal cutlets with baby potatoes and greens, with a dessert of trifle. This all to be followed by coffee and petits fours. Lady Rose had felt this combined simplicity with elegance to set them all up for the ball.

Matt assisted the hotel chef to carry the food the short distance along the embankment to the boat. A tall blond-haired man dressed in steward's attire received it from them. Kitty could see that the Hawkes' party appeared to be relaxed and enjoying the evening so far and some of the tension in her shoulders eased.

'That's everything safely on board,' Matt reported on his return.

'Was that the man you are observing? The blond man?' Kitty asked in a low tone. The light was rapidly fading, and the paddle steamer's lights had come on. The street lamps along the embankment too had been lit and motor cars and taxis were arriving further along the narrow street.

The party appeared to have all taken a seat around the dining table that had been set up on deck and the man she was referring to appeared to be serving the first course. She wondered if Serafina's beau would propose before the evening was out. With the pinkish-purple sky lit by the setting sun and the sparkle of light from tabletop candle lanterns sat on the crystal of the place settings, it certainly appeared a romantic enough setting.

'Yes.' Matt risked another glance at the steamer. 'Everything seems to be perfectly all right though.'

'That's good, I shall be glad when this evening is over, I

must admit,' Kitty said, before turning away to greet more of the Hawkes' guests as they arrived for the ball.

'Doctor Carter, and Mrs Carter.' Kitty was delighted to see that the doctor, who had been involved in so many of the cases she and Matt had been caught up in, had arrived for the party.

'My dear Miss Underhay, Captain Bryant. This is a refreshing change, to see you both unaccompanied by a corpse.' Doctor Carter always reminded Kitty of a plump, genial cherub. He was unfailingly cheerful despite the rather morbid circumstances that often prevailed whenever they met.

'Hush, dear,' his wife chided him and gave an apologetic smile.

'It is rather, you both look very splendid tonight,' Kitty agreed. 'Please go on through, the cloakroom is just along the corridor and my staff will show you to the ballroom. Have a wonderful evening.'

Dr Carter was swiftly followed by another of Matt and Kitty's close acquaintances. 'Inspector Greville, is Mrs Greville not with you?' Kitty looked around for the inspector's wife.

'Toothache.' Inspector Greville's moustache drooped. 'Her cheek is swollen like you wouldn't believe. She thinks it was a walnut that did it. Cracked her tooth.'

'Oh dear, that is such a shame, poor Mrs Greville,' Kitty sympathised. 'Doctor Carter and his wife have just arrived. If you would care to carry on to the ballroom my staff will be serving canapés shortly.'

As she had expected, the mention of food brightened the inspector's expression and he followed the rest of the guests to the ballroom. The lobby was busy with people arriving and she could hear the strains of music coming from the ballroom.

'I hope no crimes will take place anywhere in the area tonight. I think all of the county's police force are here. I just greeted Inspector Pinch of the Exeter force,' Matt said.

'I believe the dinner party should be ending shortly. Shall I stand by ready to escort the party back to the hotel?' Cyril appeared out of the small crowd.

'Yes, thank you.' She looked along the embankment and saw that her new employee was correct. The gangplank had been lowered once more ready for the party to disembark. Once the Hawkes' party were all safely back inside the hotel, she could send her staff to retrieve the used dishes and boxes from the boat.

Since the sun had started to set the air had grown a little cooler and Kitty shivered a little in her thin pale-blue chiffon evening gown as she waited patiently beside Matt outside the front entrance of the hotel for Sir Montague and Lady Rose to lead their group off the boat.

From the bright flashes of light she spotted on the deck of the boat, she guessed the baron was making good on his promise to take photographs of the evening. She pasted a welcoming professional smile on her face as Cyril duly escorted the group the short distance along the embankment.

'I hope you all had a lovely cruise?' Kitty asked as they reached her.

'Splendid, my dear, absolutely splendid.' Sir Montague's cheeks were slightly flushed, and Kitty guessed from the slightly glassy look in his eyes that he had partaken generously of the on-board champagne.

'Delightful, my dear Kitty,' Lady Rose agreed.

Behind her mother's back Kitty saw Serafina roll her eyes, making Theodore giggle and smirk at Kitty.

Mr Forbes followed behind with Flora, with her father bringing up the rear of the party.

'An excellent dinner, Miss Underhay. I'm sure I have captured some wonderful memories for Serafina,' the baron said, patting the expensive-looking camera around his neck as he re-entered the hotel.

Kitty breathed a silent sigh of relief that the trickiest part of the evening appeared to be over. She waited until Cyril had escorted the group inside to the ballroom where her grandmother was managing the staff and socialising with the guests.

'Right, it's time to go and collect the boxes from the crew, then we can join the festivities,' Kitty said to Matt.

As she spoke one of the kitchen staff came around from the rear of the hotel with a small wooden handcart painted with the Dolphin's name and sign. Together they made their way to the *Kingswear Castle* where she lay at anchor.

'Stay here, darling. Your shoes are not the most practical for boarding the boat. You can check the boxes off as we bring them down,' Matt said.

Kitty waited at the foot of the gangway while he and the kitchen boy boarded the boat. She could see that the dinner table had been cleared so hopefully the boxes would have been repacked ready to bring off the vessel.

Another shiver ran up her back as she waited for Matt and her staff member to reappear. She really should have thought to pick up her evening shawl and she scolded herself for her lack of forethought.

She wondered where Matt and her kitchen boy had disappeared to. Surely it shouldn't be taking this long just to collect the used serving dishes and the crockery the paddle steamer had borrowed. Perhaps this Gunther hadn't completed repacking the borrowed crockery.

Matt reappeared at the top of the gangway. 'Kitty, go back to the hotel and send Doctor Carter and Inspector Greville here as quickly and discreetly as possible.' His expression was grim.

'What is it? What's happened?' A feeling of dread seeped through her. If Matt wanted the doctor and the police inspector, it could only mean that someone must have been killed or badly injured.

'It's Gunther. He's dead, and I don't think it's an accident,' Matt said.

Kitty turned on her heels and hurried back along the embankment and into the Dolphin. Her heart thudded against the wall of her chest as she tried to move as quickly and discreetly as possible in her evening wear. It took her a moment once inside the crowded ballroom to spot Inspector Greville standing on the far side of the dance floor, chatting to Dr and Mrs Carter.

Kitty made her way through the guests as swiftly as she could without attracting undue attention to herself.

'Miss Underhay, are you come to join us?' the doctor asked as she drew near.

'I'm afraid not. Instead, I'm most dreadfully sorry but I need to interrupt your evening.' Kitty kept her voice as low as she could over the music from the band and the sound of the chattering guests. 'Please could I ask you both to come with me for a moment. I'm terribly sorry, Mrs Carter,' she apologised to the doctor's wife.

The inspector's eyebrows raised, and he met the doctor's gaze. 'Of course, Miss Underhay, do lead on.'

Mrs Carter took her husband's glass from his hand. 'Your medical bag is in the car, dear.'

CHAPTER SIX

Kitty led the way out of the ballroom with the doctor and police inspector following closely behind her. Once they were through the still busy lobby and back out into the cool night air, the doctor hurried over to his car, parked a short distance away, and retrieved his black leather medical bag.

'Matt needs you both on board the paddle steamer,' Kitty explained as the doctor rejoined them. 'A man is dead and Matt suspects foul play.'

'Isn't that the boat the chief constable's party was on?' Inspector Greville's moustache twitched, and he fell into step beside her, his longer strides causing her to almost trot in an effort to keep up.

'Yes, sir, the very same,' Kitty said.

They reached the foot of the broad gangplank and Kitty stood aside to allow the two men to ascend first. The candle lanterns had been extinguished and the electric lighting on the deck had been shut off. Only a glimmer of light from the wheelhouse betrayed the fact that the boat was still occupied.

The river water slapped against the large round wooden paddles on the sides of the boat, inky black in the moonlight, and Kitty shivered again as she followed behind the doctor and the inspector. In front of them a narrow flight of stairs led up to the white-painted wheelhouse and the boat's funnel.

'Down here!' The call came from Matt in response to the sound of their footsteps on the wooden deck.

Doctor Carter went first down the small flight of wooden stairs leading below the deck, with the inspector close behind him. Kitty followed at the rear wondering what they were about to discover.

The passageway was lit but fairly narrow, and wood panelled. Kitty's view ahead was limited thanks to Inspector Greville's broad shoulders. On each side she saw that there were doors marked as public lavatories.

A moment later she entered the room at the very end of the corridor where the large coal-fired engine that drove the boat was housed. Doctor Carter was crouched down over the crumpled form of the man sprawled on the floor of the room. Matt was squeezed to the one side next to another man whom she assumed was the boat's captain. Inspector Greville was to her left silently surveying the scene. There was no sign of her kitchen boy and she assumed Matt must have sent him back to the hotel with the boxes.

A single electric light bulb illuminated the scene and the air in the small space was warm. Coal was stacked in a bunker at the end and Kitty hoped no soot would attach itself to her gown.

'Who found him?' the inspector asked as Doctor Carter continued his examination.

'That were me, sir. This gentleman and the boy from the Dolphin come aboard to collect the boxes and I shouted for Gunther to fetch the things. When he didn't come, I thought as perhaps he hadn't heard me, so I come along here to look for him,' explained the captain, a wizened-looking man with a thick, dark bushy beard.

'Was anyone else down here when you entered the passageway?' the doctor asked as he straightened back up.

'No, sir. The chief constable's party had all gone ashore, and as far as I were aware, Gunther were finishing packing up all the crockery and suchlike ready for the hotel to collect. I were up in the wheelhouse filling in my papers.' The captain fidgeted with the blue-spotted neckerchief tied around his throat.

'You didn't see anyone come aboard, either during the party or after Sir Montague's group had left?' the inspector asked.

The man shook his head. 'No, sir, not to my knowing. Only this gentleman and the boy when they come for the boxes.'

The doctor looked at the inspector. 'This gentleman has been killed by a blow to the back of his head. There is a large wrench nearby which may well be the murder weapon.'

Kitty peered around the inspector to see that the doctor was indicating a large metal monkey wrench lying on the floor beside the body. It looked as if there might be blood and a few hairs on the one side. She suppressed her instinct to shudder at the sight.

'What was the man's name?' Inspector Greville asked.

'Gunther Freiberg. He were German, or Austrian. He worked for a few of the boat owners as a casual labourer. I think he were lodging in a room in town. He'd only been with me for a few odd days just when I was busy. He was a good worker and experienced as a steward.' The captain looked at the late Herr Freiberg as he spoke, his bewilderment at this unexpected turn of events showing in his eyes.

'Thank you, sir. Do you know if he had any family here?' the inspector asked.

The captain shook his head. 'Not so far as I know. He never said much about anything except his work. Kept hi'self to hi'self he did.'

Matt looked at Kitty and gave a faint shake of his head. Kitty knew he didn't wish to say anything about his mission to observe the late Gunther at this point in time. Although she knew he would have to tell the inspector later, presumably once Brigadier Remmington-Blythe had been made aware of the situation.

'I'll go and telephone for someone to come and take photographs and retrieve Herr Freiberg and this wrench.' Doctor Carter looked at Inspector Greville.

'Yes, of course, do go ahead. I expect Miss Underhay will be happy for you to use the telephone at the Dolphin?' The inspector turned to look at Kitty.

'Oh, absolutely,' Kitty said.

The captain suddenly appeared to become aware of her presence for the first time. 'Here, Miss Kitty, you hadn't ought to be down here. 'Tis bad luck.'

'Forgive me, Captain, but I don't think your luck could be any worse than discovering that someone has murdered your crewmate,' Kitty said.

Doctor Carter chuckled as he squeezed past Kitty and the inspector to make his way back off the paddle steamer. 'She's quite right there, Captain.'

'Can this room be locked until my men arrive?' the inspector asked.

'Yes, sir. I've the keys on me now.' The captain produced a large bunch of keys from his pocket.

'Then I suggest we lock this room for now. Captain Bryant, Miss Underhay, may I use a room at the hotel to coordinate my enquiry?'

'Of course,' Kitty agreed as she led the way back out of the engine room and into the passage. 'I'll speak to Mr Lutterworth, my new manager.'

Behind her she heard the clink of metal as the captain locked the engine room behind them. She was suddenly glad of the fresh night air greeting her as she climbed the steps onto the deck. The faint tang of salt helped drive away the heavy smell of engine oil, smoke and coal from her nostrils.

'Please remain on board until the body has been collected. My constable will also take a formal statement from you,' Inspector Greville told the captain.

A gust of wind suddenly blew around the deck making the metal fastenings on the ropes clank and clang. Kitty rubbed the tops of her bare arms.

'Come along, old thing, let's get back to the Dolphin before we're missed. Sir Montague should be presenting Serafina with the necklace soon.' Matt removed his black dinner jacket and placed it around Kitty's shoulders.

He kept his arm around her as they walked back in sombre silence. Kitty's mind raced as she walked along, glad of Matt's steadying embrace and the warmth from his jacket. It seemed to her that if the captain's testimony was to be relied upon and no one else had boarded the vessel since Sir Montague's party had disembarked, then Gunther had to have been killed by one of that group.

She could tell from Matt's expression and that of Inspector Greville that she was not alone in this unhappy idea.

Once back inside the hotel she unlocked the door to her office behind the reception desk, telling Bill, her night porter, that the inspector wished to make some telephone calls. She returned Matt's jacket to him and asked him to find Cyril to appraise him of the situation.

Loath as she was to tear herself away from the enquiry, she knew she had to go to the ballroom to see Serafina be presented with the Firestone necklace. If she wasn't there, her absence would definitely be remarked upon. Not least by Mrs Craven, who had arrived earlier in the evening resplendent in imperial purple satin and black beading.

She slipped inside the ballroom just as the professional compère for the evening was calling for Sir Montague to come to the stage. Her grandmother was standing with Lady Rose and Mrs Craven at the side of the room, and she could see a large burgundy leather jewel case in Sir Montague's hand.

He joined the compère at the front as Kitty indicated to her waiting staff to ensure that all the guests' glasses were charged with champagne ready to toast Serafina. Sir Montague signalled to Serafina to come forward to join him.

Despite her earlier grumbles Serafina had clearly made a special effort with her appearance for the party. Her dark-purple chiffon gown had silver beading and trim that matched the diamond barrette clips in her dark hair. The colour was not especially flattering to her complexion, however. She joined her father in front of the large silver microphone and the compère moved aside to allow Sir Montague to take his place.

The ballroom filled with an expectant hush.

'My dear friends and colleagues, my family and I would like to thank you all for joining us on such a special occasion. That of my lovely daughter Serafina's twenty-first birthday. As many of you know, it is a family tradition that the eldest daughter inherits the famous Firestone diamond necklace when they come of age.' Sir Montague paused and opened the lid of the box as a ripple ran around the audience.

'Tonight, I am delighted to bestow the necklace on Serafina.' He lifted the necklace free of the velvet-lined case and murmurs amongst the crowd grew louder as the stones sparkled under the light from the crystal chandeliers. The compère stepped forward to take the empty case so Sir Montague could fasten the diamonds around Serafina's neck.

Serafina raised her hand to touch the end of the necklace as it was secured. Her expression seemed resigned rather than delighted and she appeared to force a smile.

'And now, dear friends, I must ask you all to raise your glasses. To Serafina.' He took a champagne glass from the compère and raised it into the air. The watching throng followed suit and murmurs of 'To Serafina', rang around the room.

Kitty took a sip from her own champagne glass, which she had acquired from a passing waiter and looked around to see where Serafina's beau might be. She spotted him partly concealed by one of the potted palms, deep in conversation with Flora, Serafina's friend.

Sir Montague led his daughter off the stage and stood with her as they began to circulate around the room so that people might admire the necklace and congratulate Serafina.

Matt reappeared at Kitty's side. 'I take it the necklace presentation has gone off all right?' he asked as he too acquired a glass from a passing waiter.

'Yes. Serafina is duly showing it off.' Kitty's tone was dry as she recalled the girl's earlier remark that she was to parade around like a racehorse in the ring.

'Inspector Greville has roused the constable and also telephoned to Torquay for reinforcements.' Matt's breath was warm on her cheek as he murmured in her ear. 'This is a bad business. I'm sure you have thought of the implications?'

Kitty inclined her head. 'Of course. I don't envy poor Inspector Greville.'

'My dear Kitty and Captain Bryant. Where have you two been hiding?'

Kitty's heart sank as Mrs Craven bore down on them, her lavender and black plumed fan in her hand.

'I'm sure you're aware there is a lot to do on such occasions, Mrs Craven,' Kitty replied politely.

'Oh, I know, my dear, your charming new manager, Mr Lutterworth, was telling me how hard you had all been working to make dear Serafina's party a success. I know Lady Rose is most appreciative, she just remarked how splendid the trip on the paddle steamer was.'

'Speaking of Mr Lutterworth, I think he is in position,

Kitty.' Matt nodded his head towards the entrance to the ballroom where Cyril was now poised beside the light switches.

'Thank you, Mrs Craven. I rather think that Serafina's cake is about to make its appearance.' Kitty stood on her tiptoes and checked to see that the chefs were ready with the large pink and white iced birthday cake.

She signalled to the compère who immediately recalled Serafina and her father to the stage as the crowd fell silent once more.

'Ladies and gentlemen, please join with wishing Miss Hawkes the most happiest of birthdays.' As the compère gave the instruction the lights were dropped, and the chefs entered bearing a masterpiece of the confectioner's art ablaze with candles.

They placed the magnificent cake in front of Serafina as the crowd finished singing the birthday song. The Firestone necklace glittered in the candlelight as Serafina leaned forward and blew out the candles, temporarily plunging the ballroom into darkness.

There was a scream from the stage and a shout. Kitty wondered why the lights had not immediately come back on. All around her she could hear people murmuring and the rising sounds of panic.

'Something has gone wrong. Why are the lights not on?' Kitty looked around the dark ballroom in confusion. Her own anxiety rose with every second of delay.

CHAPTER SEVEN

The words had barely escaped her lips when the lights blinked and came back on, eliciting a wave of chattering relief from the assembled company. Kitty's own relief was short-lived, however, when she looked at the stage and saw a furious-looking Sir Montague with his arm around an ashen-faced and bare-necked Serafina.

'The necklace has gone.' Matt started to push his way through the crowd towards Cyril at the doorway.

Kitty's stomach plummeted towards the floor as she realised that Matt was right. The magnificent Firestone diamonds were no longer around Serafina's throat.

Lady Rose had rushed over to join her husband and daughter on the stage and the murmuring of the crowd was interspersed with shocked gasps as others began to realise that something untoward had occurred.

The compère moved swiftly to recall the band back to the stage as Kitty's grandmother steered her friends off to the side.

'Whatever is going on? Kitty, what's happened?' Mrs Craven's cultured tones broke Kitty's shock at this strange turn of events.

'I'm not quite sure, Mrs Craven. Please excuse me, I need to speak to Sir Montague.' Kitty made her way through the crowd to where she had last seen Serafina and her father. After all her careful planning she couldn't believe the turns the evening had taken.

When she reached where they had been standing, she realised her grandmother must have taken them through to a small room behind the stage, which was used as a dressing area for any entertainment acts. Out in the ballroom the compère was announcing the band, and the music recommenced.

From her raised vantage point at the back of the stage she looked around the room hoping to see Matt's tall, elegant figure amongst the crowd. Eventually she saw him talking to Inspector Pinch of the Exeter police force and guessed he must be asking for his assistance.

Cyril was still at the door, and she could see that he was ensuring that no one was entering or leaving the room for the moment. He was swiftly joined by some of the inspector's men. Kitty set about making certain that her waiting staff were on the alert for any sign of the missing jewels. If whoever had taken them had not escaped from the room in the blackout following their theft, then they had to still be inside the ballroom.

Whoever had planned this must be most audacious. To attempt to steal the Firestone necklace in a room bristling with policemen took a high level of nerve. Matt joined her once more.

'Inspector Pinch and a couple of his colleagues are searching the ballroom as discreetly as possible. I don't think whoever took the necklace managed to get past Cyril. He says that no one left the ballroom while the lights were out or just after,' Matt said.

'My staff are also on the lookout. Do you think the necklace could have been dropped out through one of the windows to a waiting accomplice?' Kitty asked.

'I think that's unlikely; the street outside is busy now, thanks to our late German friend and I would have thought having uniformed constables beside the building would deter anyone from making such an attempt,' Matt said thoughtfully. 'I will go outside and check though, just in case.'

'I had better go and find Serafina and her family and discover exactly what happened when the lights went out,' Kitty said.

She spotted Mrs Craven bearing down upon her once more and slipped off towards the dressing area backstage, intent on discovering exactly what had happened before Mrs Craven could interrogate her.

* * *

Matt made his way along the corridor leading from the ballroom. Cyril remained at his post, having confirmed that he would not permit anyone to exit from the room until he received more instructions.

Inspector Greville had just emerged from Kitty's office behind the front desk when Matt reached the lobby. Matt quickly appraised the inspector and Bill, the night porter, of the events in the ballroom.

'Somebody took them jewels in a room full of policemen?' Bill asked incredulously.

'I'm just going to look around outside and along the embankment beside the hotel. Kitty wondered if anyone could have thrown something from the windows or handed something to an accomplice while the lights were out,' Matt said.

'I doubt as they could have passed anything over with all the police that's outside heading to the paddle steamer,' Bill observed.

'That was my instinct too, but they could have thrown

something out with the intention of retrieving it later,' Matt said. 'Bill, do you have a torch there I could use?'

Bill opened the desk drawer and pulled out a large metal torch. ''Tis pretty well-lit out there but here you are, sir.'

Inspector Greville accompanied him outside and the two men used the torch to scour the margins of the riverbank and a couple of small wooden rowing boats that were moored just at the edge of the embankment.

'Nothing out here, not a sausage,' Inspector Greville declared somewhat gloomily after a fruitless search of a flower bed.

'Then the necklace must still be inside the hotel.' Matt switched off the torch.

'We had best hope so. I have yet to break it to the chief constable that his party may be involved in a murder, let alone see a valuable necklace get stolen right under our blooming noses.' The inspector sounded deeply unhappy, and Matt couldn't blame him.

* * *

Kitty opened the door to the dressing room to discover a dramatic tableau. The baron and his daughter were stood to one side, their heads together. Serafina was seated on a low chair being urged to sip brandy from a crystal goblet being proffered by her mother. Sir Montague, his cheeks crimson with rage, was being soothed by Kitty's grandmother. Theodore was sprawled out in one of the other armchairs seemingly uninterested in the evening's drama, while Mr Forbes stood near the window smoking a cigarette.

'Kitty darling.' Relief spread over her grandmother's worried face as Kitty entered the room. 'Do you have news?'

'There had better be news. That ballroom is full of my finest officers. One of them had better have recovered the necklace and apprehended the villain by now,' Sir Montague thundered.

'Our manager has ensured that no one has left the ballroom since the lights went out. Matt is searching out on the embankment in case the thief tried to dispose of the jewels through the window. Inspector Pinch has rallied the officers and together with our staff they are searching the ballroom as we speak.' Kitty kept her tone calm.

'It all happened so suddenly,' Serafina wailed. 'I leaned forwards and blew out the candles. The lights went out and I felt someone snatch at my neck. I screamed but was too shocked at first to realise exactly what had gone on. Then the lights came up and I realised my neck hurt and the necklace was gone.'

Kitty could see a red line around the girl's neck, which she assumed must have been caused by whoever snatched the jewels.

'The audacity of it. In a room full of policemen. If this gets out, we shall be a national laughing stock.' Sir Montague looked like an angry turkey cock. 'After all the precautions we took.' He slammed down the empty leatherette box that had contained the necklace.

'Perhaps it is some kind of prank,' Flora suggested.

'Prank! Prank!' Kitty thought Sir Montague was about to explode. 'What a shambles.'

Kitty's gaze met that of her grandmother, and she decided it would be wise to remain silent.

There was a tap at the door to the dressing room and Mr Lutterworth's shining pate appeared.

'Good news, Miss Serafina. It seems the jewels have been recovered.' In his white-gloved hand he produced the glittering string of diamonds.

He had scarcely uttered the last syllable when Sir Montague snatched the necklace, glanced at it briefly and dropped it safely back inside its casket, snapping the lid tight shut.

'Thank heavens for that. Where was it? Who was the thief?' the chief constable demanded.

'I believe one of the inspectors discovered the gems concealed in the soil of one of the decorative palm pots. He noticed the soil appeared disturbed and investigated. Unfortunately, it is unclear who may have placed them there,' Cyril explained.

'Thank you, Mr Lutterworth, please convey the family's thanks to all of the searchers,' Kitty's grandmother said before Sir Montague could interrogate the man any further.

Mr Lutterworth smiled gently. 'If you will excuse me, several guests are anxious about missing their ferry.' He withdrew as swiftly as he had arrived.

'Now, I suggest that the jewels are returned to the safe until you depart tomorrow, Monty. Perhaps, Serafina my dear, you may like to return to the ballroom for the remainder of your party and try to put this unpleasantness behind you,' Mrs Treadwell continued. 'No doubt your many friends will wish to be assured of your well-being and there is still time for a few more dances.'

'That seems like a wise suggestion, come, my dear.' Lady Rose escorted her daughter out of the room with the baron and Flora following behind them.

Kitty's grandmother took Sir Montague's arm. 'Come, let's get that wretched necklace safely locked away and then I have a rather fine port you might care to try. It will settle your nerves splendidly.'

Mr Forbes extinguished his cigarette in one of the large onyx ashtrays that were placed on the different tables around the room. 'I had better go and see if Saffy has recovered enough to dance.' He too took his leave and Kitty realised that she was alone with Theodore.

'It seems as if Mademoiselle Flora was correct. The taking of the necklace must have been some kind of misguided idea of a prank,' Kitty said. Either that or the thief had lost their nerve when they realised they could not get out of the ballroom with the stolen jewels. She wouldn't mind a cocktail herself to settle her own nerves after everything that had happened.

Theo shrugged. 'Who knows. It was probably Saffy herself. She secretly loves a bit of drama, being the centre of attention. She may have staged it to stop that ass Edward from proposing,' Theo said with a smirk.

'I thought from what your mother said that Serafina was hoping for a proposal this evening?' Kitty was confused. Lady Rose had been very keen to ensure that the scene was set for a proposal during the evening's celebrations.

Theo rose from his seat. 'Mother and Father would like nothing better than to get Saffy married and off their hands. I don't think Saffy is quite so keen.'

Kitty frowned. 'Really?' It was true she hadn't seen much evidence of romance between Serafina and her beau, but then she hadn't spent much time with them.

Theo advanced closer to Kitty and she realised that the boy had evidently partaken generously of the evening's champagne. 'Now, a girl like you, one could easily propose to.'

Kitty took a neat step backwards. 'I am already engaged to be married, Theo.'

She could smell the stale smell of alcohol on his breath as he came closer, and she realised she had backed herself into a corner.

'That's a shame,' Theo slurred, and Kitty could see he was about to try and kiss her. She ducked her head and stepped forward making sure she put all her weight on top of his foot.

'Oof, oi, what's that about?' Theo winced and went to try and catch her as she slipped around him.

'Kitty darling, is everything all right in here? I wondered

where you had gone.' Matt's suave tone didn't betray that he had witnessed anything of Theo's clumsy drunken advance.

'Everything is perfectly fine, I was just coming to find you.' She slipped her arm through that of her fiancé and walked back out into the ballroom, leaving Theo behind in the dressing room to cool his ardour.

CHAPTER EIGHT

'That was rather nifty footwork there, Miss Underhay. I do hope that little twerp wasn't bothering you?' Matt asked once they were clear of the dressing room.

'I think the champagne has gone to his head. I dare say he will feel the most awful ass in the morning.' Kitty gave her fiancé a reassuring smile.

Matt patted her hand where it rested lightly on the crook of his arm. 'I'm sure you are more than capable of handling him, but if he does become troublesome then do let me know.'

'Of course. They should all return home tomorrow but after what has happened on the paddle steamer, I'm not at all sure that will be possible now. Has Inspector Greville informed Sir Montague of the murder yet, do you know?' Kitty asked.

Matt shook his head. 'There has been no time. The theft of the necklace was rather distracting, and I think the inspector wished to be certain of all of his facts before approaching his superior officer.'

Kitty frowned as she observed Serafina accompanied by her mother laughing and chatting with a group of their guests. 'I suppose the news that the brigadier is involved also makes it rather more complicated?'

The corners of Matt's lips lifted in a wry smile. 'I think Freiberg's death is not a matter that can be brushed under the carpet. I really don't envy Inspector Greville having to investigate this case.'

'And the attempted theft of the Firestone necklace? Are you inclined to believe it a prank or a theft gone wrong?' Kitty asked.

Matt's expression sobered. 'I don't really know what to make of it, to be honest. At least the necklace was recovered.'

Kitty told her fiancé of Theo's theory that Serafina had organised it herself to avoid Edward's proposal and to focus attention on herself. 'She didn't wish to receive the necklace or to show it off. She was making no bones about that earlier this afternoon. Serafina has never seemed to me to be an attention-seeking kind of girl in that way.'

'Hmm, it's all very strange. It looks as if she and her mother are passing it all off as a prank gone wrong to the guests,' Matt said as Serafina was claimed by Mr Forbes for a turn about the dance floor. 'I rather think we should dance too. Mrs Craven has her beady eyes upon us, and it would probably be as well to try and allay any suspicions that something is wrong.'

Kitty agreed and stepped into his arms before Mrs Craven could approach them to start asking questions.

'Grams is mollifying Sir Montague with her finest port,' Kitty murmured as she swayed to the music secure in her fiancé's hold.

'I see the baron is still making inroads into the champagne and Theo has emerged to dance with Flora, although he seems to have developed a slight limp.' Matt gave a chuckle as he twirled Kitty around so she could see Theo and Flora at the edge of the dance floor.

Kitty swiftly averted her gaze when Theo sent her an

injured look. 'Oh dear, he is only a boy and is clearly not used to drinking. I feel rather as though I've kicked a puppy now!'

She felt the rumble of suppressed laughter in Matt's chest and couldn't help smiling back up at him in return.

'You are far too soft-hearted, old thing. Look, let's just enjoy ourselves for a couple of turns then we'll go and see how Inspector Greville is faring. The ball should be wrapping up soon, shouldn't it?'

'Yes, the birthday cake is being dispensed and everything appears to be settling down. I see several guests have drifted away already. The last ferry is due to leave soon for those not staying here or in the town.' Kitty could see that the room looked less crowded than previously, and the hour was growing late.

Mrs Craven was now deep in conversation with Lady Rose, and Serafina appeared to be happily dancing with Edward Forbes. Satisfied that all appeared to be relatively calm and back to normal Kitty allowed herself to relax and enjoy a couple of dances with Matt. She suspected that this brief interlude might be the last bit of peace they were going to get when Sir Montague learned of the murder aboard the *Kingswear Castle*.

Sir Montague returned to the ballroom to rejoin his wife. The baron was now dancing with his daughter and Edward Forbes was still dancing with Serafina as Kitty and Matt set off back along the hall to the lobby to find Inspector Greville.

'The inspector has gone back to the boat, Miss Kitty,' Bill informed her when they reached the hotel entrance.

'Wait, let me just get a coat.' Kitty pressed Matt's arm and darted into her office to retrieve the lightweight linen jacket she knew was hanging on the coat stand inside the door. She shrugged it on quickly and then slipped out into the street with Matt to walk down to the paddle steamer.

The embankment was busy with guests leaving the ball. Taxis and private chauffeur-driven cars were stopping to collect guests and others were on foot heading for the last of the night's ferries to recross the river.

Even wearing her jacket, Kitty shivered slightly in the night air, and the wind had begun to whip up small wavelets on the river, the white foam caps just visible in the inky darkness. The paddle steamer was only showing a couple of lights on the prow and in the wheelhouse. A uniformed constable stood at the foot of the gangplank.

'No entry, I'm afraid, sir.' The constable held out a leather-gloved hand to stop them when Matt attempted to board.

'We're looking for Inspector Greville. Perhaps you could let him know that Miss Underhay and Captain Bryant are here,' Matt suggested.

Kitty could see indecision playing across the man's face. 'We promise we will remain here until you return,' she offered.

After a brief moment's consideration the constable retreated along the ramp and disappeared inside the paddle steamer, before returning to where they were waiting.

'The inspector says as he is in the aft saloon.' The constable stood aside and permitted them to board, before returning to his station.

Matt led the way down the flight of stairs they had taken earlier in the evening when they had headed to the engine room. This time, however, Kitty noticed that the doors on the opposite side to the lavatories were marked fore and aft saloon in painted gold letters.

'Inspector Greville?' Matt pushed open the polished wooden door to the aft saloon and Kitty followed him inside.

The inspector was seated at a low round rosewood table that still displayed some debris from the earlier dinner party. Empty champagne glasses and small dainty white coffee cups and saucers had been left on the tabletop scattered around the pink and white floral centrepiece.

'I see Herr Freiberg had not finished all of his tasks when he met his demise,' Matt observed.

'Indeed no, the box for these pieces is still over there.' The inspector indicated the small packing case filled with straw at the side of the room. 'I take it these are some of the hotel's, Miss Underhay?'

'Yes. We supplied the crockery and glassware for the party, as well as the food for the evening. The paddle steamer's were quite utilitarian, and Lady Rose wished to have something more elegant for Serafina's celebrations,' Kitty explained.

'The captain says that the party were all on deck when Gunther came down here. He'd waited for them to finish and go up top before clearing this area. He packed up the dinner things while they took coffee in this saloon.' Inspector Greville looked around at the tastefully upholstered chairs and comfortable arrangements of the room.

'Do we know what time they finished and went up on deck?' Kitty asked.

'The captain put it at just before eight thirty. Does that fit with when you both came to escort Sir Montague's party back to the Dolphin?' the inspector asked.

'I think so, sir. Kitty had worked out a schedule with Lady Rose beforehand. Mr Lutterworth came to escort the party back to the Dolphin, then Kitty and I took one of the kitchen staff to retrieve the boxes.' Matt glanced at Kitty for confirmation.

'The party started dining shortly after seven and were due back to the hotel between eight thirty and eight forty-five to greet their guests. We arrived at eight thirty to collect the crockery and to ensure they were happy with the evening so far.' Kitty frowned as she looked about the cabin. 'Is the captain quite certain there was no one else aboard the boat except himself, Gunther and Sir Montague's party?'

'There was the mate, but he was either with the captain or attending to the engine the whole time. The steamer is coal fired. He left the boat when they arrived back in Dartmouth as his job was finished by then, and we know Gunther was alive and serving dinner after that time. No one else boarded or left after that until it was time for the party to disembark.' Inspector Greville sighed heavily. 'The captain appears a good and reliable witness. He was in the wheelhouse watching all that time. I have been unable to shake his testimony or to find a loophole that could allow a stranger to enter or leave the ship.'

'And no one could have already been hiding on board when the vessel set off? Someone who could have gone ashore after the body had been discovered amidst all the kerfuffle?' Matt asked.

Inspector Greville gave a sorrowful shake of his head. 'The captain did a full inspection of the boat from stern to stern before the chief constable and his party arrived. He was most anxious that everything should be perfect for the party. I think he hoped this might lead to more of these cruises as it would be quite a lucrative event if successful.'

'Did the captain notice if any members of Sir Montague's party returned below deck before they disembarked?' Kitty was almost afraid to ask the question, knowing that it may well be that the captain could have seen the murderer.

Inspector Greville turned his gaze towards her, his moustache appearing more depressed than Kitty had ever seen it.

'All of them it seems at some point, for one thing or another. I shall have to cross-check it all when I interview them in the morning.' The inspector sounded most unhappy at this prospect.

'You do not intend to speak to Sir Montague tonight, sir?' Matt asked.

The inspector shook his head. 'Everyone has had a drink this evening and it is the young lady's birthday. I also need to take some direction from the brigadier before I approach Sir Montague. I need hardly tell you both of the delicacy that will be required in this matter. This strange furore over that idiotic prank with the necklace too has made it all much more complex.'

Kitty glanced at the dainty gold watch on her wrist. 'The party should be ended by now and I need to return to see if anyone requires coffee or hot chocolate before retiring.'

The inspector nodded. 'A few hours' sleep may aid us all. I shall return to the hotel in the morning after breakfast. Do you know at what time Sir Montague intended to return home?'

'I rather think they planned to stay until just before tea. Grams had offered to serve a light luncheon and then I think they intended to leave some time after then,' Kitty said.

'Very good, thank you, Miss Underhay.' The inspector gave her a faint smile.

'What do you think the brigadier will have to say on the matter?' Kitty asked Matt as they set off on the short walk back to the hotel.

The embankment was almost deserted again now, and she guessed that the majority, if not all, of the guests who were not staying overnight in the town had set off for home.

Matt looked across at her. 'I don't know, Kitty. We think that Herr Freiberg may have been a spy and he clearly had some kind of connection to the *Sigrid*. The puzzle is what, if anything, that has to do with any member of Sir Montague's party and was that connected with his murder?'

Kitty shivered as a gust of wind tugged at her curls and she snuggled closer to her fiancé. 'Perhaps we shall know more tomorrow, but I do feel for poor Inspector Greville. His will not be an easy or pleasant task.'

CHAPTER NINE

They found Cyril busy supervising the hotel staff as they cleared away empty glasses and used crockery, restoring order to the ballroom. The large room was now empty of guests and the band was packing away their instruments.

'Your grandmother has taken the Hawkes' party for coffee and chocolate to the small residents' lounge,' Kitty's new manager informed her.

'Thank you so much, Cyril. You've done a sterling job here this evening.' Kitty then turned to her fiancé. 'Would you care to come and join the party for a nightcap?'

He glanced at his watch. 'Much as I would like to, I really should return home. If I leave it any later, I shall not be able to cross the river till morning. It's a long drive around if I have to go via Totnes, and you know Bertie will destroy the house if he is left to himself all night.' Matt kissed her cheek and smiled regretfully at her. 'I'll be back just after breakfast. I think the inspector may need our support.'

Kitty watched her fiancé walk back along the corridor to collect his Sunbeam motorcycle from his parking space near the hotel. She hoped Bertie the spaniel wouldn't have done anything really bad in Matt's absence. Even with the housekeeper's grandson watching him he could still get up to mischief.

She left her staff to finish the clean up and went to find her grandmother and Sir Montague's party in the private lounge.

'Kitty darling, has Matthew gone home?' her grandmother greeted her as she entered the cosy room, discreetly lit by side lamps.

'Yes, he thought he should get back before Bertie destroyed anything in the house and while he could still get over the river.' Kitty slipped off her jacket and took a seat near her grandmother. She was careful to avoid sitting anywhere near Theo.

'Bertie is Matthew's dog,' her grandmother explained to Lady Rose who was looking puzzled. 'Hot chocolate, Kitty?' Her grandmother was poised with the silver pot and a bone china cup.

'That sounds heavenly. It's been such an eventful day,' Kitty accepted gratefully. With any luck the soothing drink would help to settle her busy mind and assist her to sleep.

'Have you had a good birthday, Serafina?' she asked, looking at the birthday girl.

'Of course she has, haven't you, darling?' Lady Rose answered before Serafina could speak for herself.

Baron Rochelle added his thoughts. 'A marvellous day.' He then returned to his coffee cup.

'And have you enjoyed the day, Edward?' Lady Rose turned her attention to Mr Forbes who was seated between Flora and Serafina on the long sofa.

'Oh yes. It was quite wonderful,' he agreed. 'Most memorable.'

Kitty thought she detected a slightly sour expression on Lady Rose's face and wondered if she was disappointed that Mr Forbes had not proposed.

'Could have done without that dashed funny business with

the necklace. However, no harm done since it's safely back in its case and locked up tight,' Sir Montague said.

'Quite so, my dear. I told everyone that it must have been some dullard's idea of a practical joke.' Lady Rose drained her cup and placed it back on the saucer.

'No doubt you are correct, Lady Rose. It was in very poor taste,' Flora agreed.

'Well, I think it's time to turn in. Thank you, my dear Mrs Treadwell, for all of your hard work today.' Sir Montague rose from his seat with the rest of his party following suit.

'Not at all. It was our pleasure for such old friends,' Kitty's grandmother assured him as she wished the party a goodnight and they took their leave. Theo still giving Kitty an injured glance as he trailed after his sister.

With Sir Montague's party having departed, Kitty closed the door to the lounge and pulled her chair close to her grandmother.

'Kitty, my dear, is there something wrong?' Her grandmother's eyes widened in alarm at Kitty's actions.

Kitty quickly told her about the discovery of Gunther Freiberg's body on the paddle steamer and the inevitable conclusion that Sir Montague's party must be involved in some way.

'Inspector Greville is returning to talk to Sir Montague after breakfast, once he has received directions from London,' Kitty concluded.

'Oh, my dear, this is most shocking. There must be some mistake surely?' Her grandmother's complexion had paled as she had taken in the enormity of what Kitty had told her.

'The inspector has explored every eventuality that he could think of.'

Her grandmother shook her head slowly. 'This as well as that stupid incident with the Firestone necklace. I'm afraid poor Serafina will remember this birthday for all the wrong reasons.'

'True, and no proposal from Mr Forbes either, despite Lady Rose's best intentions.' Kitty finished her cup of hot chocolate and placed it back on the tray.

'Indeed, poor Rose. She is most anxious to see Serafina settled. She always was a difficult child and I think her mother feels this Edward Forbes is her best chance of making a match. I understand from Sir Montague that he is well connected in the business world.' Her grandmother placed her hand in front of her mouth to stifle a yawn. 'I'm so sorry, my dear, it's rather late.'

'It's been a long day,' Kitty agreed as she leaned forward to kiss her grandmother goodnight. 'Time we retired to bed ourselves.'

A tap on her bedroom door accompanied by the clink of crockery roused Kitty from her sleep the following morning. She scarcely had time to rub her eyes and sit herself up in bed before Alice entered bearing a tray of tea and toast.

'Alice, I'm so happy to see you.' Kitty immediately moved over and patted the satin counterpane to invite her friend to take a seat.

Alice placed the tray on Kitty's lap before turning her attention to the rose-patterned bedroom curtains, drawing them back with a swish.

'I thought as you might be needing some fortification after all of last night's goings on,' the maid declared as she carefully poured Kitty a cup of tea in the fine china cup, before pouring one for herself in the more utilitarian plain-white earthenware cup she produced from her white apron pocket.

'I take it that you've heard about the business with the Firestone necklace?' Kitty asked before taking a bite of the hot buttered toast from the tray.

'Mr Lutterworth told our Dolly all about it first thing this morning when we come in. A bit of a rum do that, if you ask me.

Then there's that other business too with the foreigner being killed on the paddle boat,' Alice said composedly.

'How did you hear about Mr Freiberg's murder?' Kitty often marvelled at the speed in which news and gossip could spread around a small town.

'From the constable a-guarding the gangway. And there was a big sign on the booth nearby saying as there would be no day trips on the paddle steamer today due to unforeseen circumstances,' Alice replied.

'It was all rather shocking. Inspector Greville is returning here this morning to tell Sir Montague about the murder.' Kitty licked a smear of butter from the side of her thumb.

'I can't believe as someone would have the bold-faced cheek to kill a body right under the chief constable's nose and then just a little later try to steal his daughter's diamonds.' Alice topped up Kitty's cup with the last of the tea from the small silver pot.

'I know. It sounds incredible, doesn't it,' Kitty said thoughtfully. It was almost as if someone wanted to cause trouble for Sir Montague.

'I expect as you and Captain Bryant will be investigating along with the inspector?' Alice asked. 'What with Sir Montague and Lady Rose being friends of your grandmother's.'

Kitty frowned. 'I'm not sure how much investigating will be done. It's a delicate matter. Scotland Yard may have to be involved, since Sir Montague is of such high standing locally.'

Her friend's eyes brightened. 'Oh, that would fair be exciting. Proper like in the films, that would be.'

Kitty laughed. 'You and your films. I agree though, it would at least take some pressure off poor Inspector Greville.'

Alice grinned at her then finished her cup of tea. 'I'd best get back before I'm missed. You'd better get a move on as well, Miss Kitty, if you want to be about when the inspector comes back.'

'Alice, I'm so glad you came in this morning. I've been worried that I'd upset you about the wedding.' Kitty knew she had to broach the tricky subject of her wedding and Alice's refusal to be her bridesmaid.

'No, miss, I'm not upset. Like I said before, I'm flattered and honoured that you should want me to be in your wedding party, but it wouldn't be right. Lady Lucy should be your matron of honour as she's your cousin and all. It would cause bother for you and for me if I was to be your bridesmaid. But I'll be very happy and pleased to be a guest instead.' Alice's tone was firm as she tidied up the breakfast tray ready to carry it back down-stairs to the kitchen.

'Are you quite certain that I cannot persuade you? Lucy would love to have you stand with her.' Kitty gave it one last shot.

'That's right kind of Lady Lucy to say so, but my mind is made up on the matter.' Alice's cheeks had flushed, and Kitty could see her friend was determined.

'Very well, if you are sure.' Although she was disappointed, Kitty knew that her friend could be as stubborn as a mule once she had set her mind to something.

'Thank you for asking me though.' Alice gathered up the tray.

'You are my dearest friend,' Kitty said and was rewarded by the flush deepening on Alice's face.

'And you, mine, Miss Kitty.' The girl hurried from the room anxious to be back about her work before Mrs Homer, the hotel housekeeper, could discover her slacking.

* * *

Matt was just finishing his own breakfast when a barrage of barking from Bertie let him know that someone was at his front door. He set aside his boiled egg and toast to see who was knocking.

'Inspector Greville, this is an unexpected pleasure. May I offer you some tea?' He stood aside as the inspector entered the hall.

'Thank you, sir, but no. I thought I would call in on my way back to the Dolphin.'

Matt led the way through into the sitting room, while Bertie happily sniffed around the policeman's ankles.

'What can I do for you, Inspector?' Matt invited the policeman to take a seat on one of the black leather and chrome armchairs.

'I've had a long telephone conversation this morning with the brigadier.'

Matt took a seat opposite the inspector. 'I see.'

'He was most concerned to learn of Herr Freiberg's murder and even more concerned when he was informed of the circumstances.' The inspector looked most unhappy. The dark puffy circles under his eyes testament to lack of sleep.

'I take it he made you aware of my involvement in the matter?' Matt phrased the question delicately. He knew that the inspector had signed the Official Secrets Act, as indeed had Kitty following her involvement in several cases lately.

'He did indeed.' Inspector Greville sighed miserably.

'Are you to hand the case over to Scotland Yard? I presume with someone of Sir Montague's standing it might be awkward for someone at your level to investigate,' Matt asked. He had been giving the matter some thought earlier over his boiled egg and wondered if a London man might be dispatched.

'That is still to be decided upon. My instructions for now are that I am to complete all of the preliminary enquiries. I have to interview Sir Montague and all the members of his party and then, based upon my findings, the powers that be will decide if London's involvement is required,' the inspector explained.

'I see. I had heard that they were somewhat short of manpower there at the moment,' Matt said thoughtfully.

'The brigadier has also asked me to request that you be involved in the case.'

Matt nodded. 'Of course. That would I think be sensible, given the nature of the victim and the social standing of the suspects.'

The inspector appeared to relax a little at Matt's ready acquiescence to his request.

'Thank you, sir. I need hardly tell you that I am not looking forward to this interview.'

Bertie heaved a sigh as the inspector spoke and dropped his head to rest on top of the policeman's highly polished brogues.

'I think Bertie sympathises with your position, Inspector, as do I. Let me collect my hat and coat and I'll be happy to accompany you to Dartmouth,' Matt said.

CHAPTER TEN

Kitty's grandmother had arranged for Sir Montague's party to take breakfast slightly later than the other residents of the hotel. This had been agreed even before the events at the party, since she had thought they might enjoy a longer time to sleep after the late night. She had also since arranged matters so that they would continue to have the smaller residents' lounge for their exclusive use.

Accordingly, when Matt arrived, accompanied by Inspector Greville, Kitty was able to take them straight to the lounge where morning coffee was being served.

'Greville, what brings you here so early this morning? Social call, is it?' Sir Montague asked in a jovial tone as he caught sight of the inspector.

Kitty watched discreetly from a corner near the door as Inspector Greville removed his hat and awkwardly shuffled his large feet.

'Not exactly, I'm afraid, sir. Unfortunately, it's a more official matter. If I might speak to you privately for a moment?' the inspector asked in an apologetic tone.

'The policeman's lot, eh, never off the clock,' Sir Montague responded cheerfully and set down his cup to follow the inspector and Matt into the privacy of the nearby housekeeper's room.

Kitty busied herself with small tasks in her corner and waited for the explosion she was certain would erupt from the housekeeper's office. The family appeared unperturbed by the inspector's appearance and Kitty guessed they must be used to Sir Montague being called away on police business.

She noticed that Theodore appeared suitably subdued this morning and could not even meet her gaze. Lady Rose was talking with the baron and Flora, while Serafina and Edward were seated together on one of the other plush covered sofas.

Suddenly Kitty became aware of the distant muffled sounds of shouting. The other occupants of the room exchanged puzzled glances and conversation dwindled.

'Preposterous. The whole thing is preposterous.' Sir Montague came storming back into the lounge trailed by the inspector and Matt.

'My dear, whatever is the matter?' Lady Rose stood to greet her husband.

'One of my own officers has just informed me that the man who served us dinner last night on the paddle steamer has been found murdered.' Sir Montague's complexion had turned a shade of puce.

A gasp ran around the room at this unexpected piece of information.

'Oh, my dear, that's dreadful.' Lady Rose took hold of her husband's arm only for him to shake her off with an impatient air.

'More than that, the inspector here has the temerity to suggest that we are all suspects.' Sir Montague glared at Inspector Greville.

'But that's ridiculous.' Lady Rose turned a bewildered face towards the inspector.

'I'm afraid not, my lady. I have instructions from London that I am to interview all of you,' the inspector replied.

Edward Forbes had also jumped to his feet. 'What? I can't see what any of us could have to do with the man's death. Why would any of us wish to kill a steward? We barely saw the man.'

Serafina nodded in agreement. 'Exactly, it's nonsensical.'

'However strange it may seem, I do need to take statements from all of you,' the inspector's expression and tone was impassive. Kitty was impressed by the inspector's resolve.

'Monty, my dear fellow, surely this cannot be so?' Baron Rochelle joined in the chorus of complaint.

'It seems the inspector has instructions from a source higher than myself, Philippe. Very well, Greville, you had better get on with it. The sooner this ridiculous charade is over the sooner we can get on with our day. Then you, perhaps, can get about your business and catch the real murderer.' Sir Montague scowled.

'Very good, sir. Mrs Treadwell has kindly given her permission to use her salon. If you would care to accompany me first, sir?' Inspector Greville raised his hand and gestured toward the door.

Matt winked at Kitty as he followed Sir Montague and the inspector from the room. 'See what you can find out here and we can exchange information later,' he whispered as he passed her.

'Well, really. How can any of us be suspected of murdering a man we don't know? And it happening on Saffy's birthday too.' Lady Rose resumed her seat on the sofa clearly indignant at the idea of being suspected of murder.

'You would think Father would be able to do something.' Theo kicked at the nap on the rug at his feet in disgust.

'I daresay it will all end up being a waste of our time. They will find the captain did it or some other crew member.' The baron helped himself to the last of the coffee.

Flora gave a delicate little shiver. 'It's a horrid thought

though that a man was killed while we were all dancing and enjoying ourselves.'

Serafina looked at her friend. 'Yes, you're right. I wonder when he was killed? It's quite odd that we are suspects. There must be lots of people going off and on the boat, the riverside was terribly busy last night. I don't recall seeing him after we all went up on deck after finishing our coffee.'

'Was he not in the saloon when you went back for your wrap, Lady Rose?' Flora asked.

Lady Rose looked down her nose at Flora with a cold expression. 'I think he must have been around somewhere. There were still cups on the table, as I recall. I'm not really certain. I collected my shawl from the chair and returned to the deck.'

'I didn't see him when I went to the lavatory.' Theo gave a yawn.

'You were already in your cups by then, you fell up the steps to the deck,' his sister pointed out. 'Do you recall when you last saw him Edward, or you Flora? You both went to collect my flowers for me from downstairs.' Serafina turned to her friend.

'I think he was packing up boxes.' Flora gave a shrug. 'So, he was very much alive then.'

'It is most peculiar.' Baron Rochelle still sounded indignant. 'Who would wish to kill a steward? I do not think he was an Englishman. When he spoke I thought he sounded German.'

'Perhaps he'd upset one of the local men then. Stolen his girlfriend or had an affair with his wife. Aren't most murders a crime of passion?' Serafina said.

'Or carried out for money,' Theo added.

'I doubt robbery would be a motive. Not for a steward.' Lady Rose glanced at her silver fob watch. 'I do hope this does not take long. It's such a lovely day and a walk to the castle before luncheon would be most delightful. It is such a romantic setting.' She glanced meaningfully at her daughter and Edward Forbes.

* * *

Matt accompanied Inspector Greville and Sir Montague to Kitty's grandmother's salon. Mickey, the hotel maintenance and security man, was outside the suite as instructed, to ensure the safety of the Firestone necklace in the hotel safe.

The inspector took a seat at the table in the bay window that overlooked the embankment, while Sir Montague took his place opposite him. Matt seated himself on one of the upright chairs near the door.

'I do apologise for the inconvenience, sir, but I'm sure you would wish that all procedures are properly followed.' Inspector Greville took out his notebook and fountain pen.

Sir Montague harrumphed at this but then conceded, 'I would obviously wish to set a good example to the force by showing that no one was above the due processes of the law.'

'Thank you, sir. May I ask when you last saw Herr Freiberg alive?' the inspector asked.

'Freiberg, eh? German? Austrian? Swiss? I'm not sure. It must have been just before we all finished our drinks in the saloon and went up on deck. Philippe, Baron Rochelle that is, has some confounded gadget, a camera, wanted to take pictures for Serafina. He's very keen on photography.' Sir Montague stared ahead impassively as the inspector made notes.

'So you saw the steward in the saloon just before you all went upstairs?' Inspector Greville asked.

'That's what I just said. He was packing some of the things up ready for collection, I suppose. We had all finished our after-dinner drinks and it was almost time to return to the hotel.' Sir Montague shifted impatiently in his seat.

'Thank you, sir. Did you return below deck at any point

after this? Before disembarking from the steamer?' Inspector Greville raised his head to meet Sir Montague's gaze.

Sir Montague blinked. 'I don't know. I mean I think we all probably did at some point. Rose fetched her wrap. She's always leaving her things lying around. I've lost count of the number of umbrellas she's misplaced. Philippe was messing about with that camera, and I may have gone back to use the lavatory before leaving the boat.'

'Did you encounter Herr Freiberg again when you went back down?' the inspector asked.

'No, not at all. Young Forbes was in the corridor about to go back on deck and Flora was just leaving the saloon but no one else was there.'

'And, I know this may sound odd, but you didn't know Herr Freiberg? Hadn't ever seen him before?' the inspector asked.

Sir Montague's complexion began to redden once more. 'No, certainly not. I wouldn't know the chap if I were to fall over him. How could I possibly know some foreign steward?'

'Thank you, sir, I appreciate this must feel very bizarre.' Inspector Greville looked towards Matt, who gave a small shake of his head to indicate that he had no special questions for Sir Montague.

'Perhaps, sir, you could ask Lady Rose to come up next?' the inspector said as he showed his superior officer to the door.

He closed the door behind Sir Montague.

'Oof, well that was awkward.' Matt gave the inspector a sympathetic smile.

'Indeed. It's not a situation I had ever thought I would encounter in my career.' Inspector Greville gave a wan smile as a tap on the door announced Lady Rose's arrival.

She settled herself at the table opposite the inspector and glanced outside at the sunlight on the river giving an audible sigh. 'It's such a fine day. I do hope this won't take long, Inspector?'

'I'll be as quick as I can, Lady Rose.' The policeman opened his notebook once more. 'May I ask, when did you last see the steward?'

'It was shortly before we disembarked, I suppose. Philippe was taking photographs on the deck, and he was having some kind of difficulty with the flash. I remember feeling chilled and realised that I had left my shawl in the saloon.'

'You returned downstairs?' Inspector Greville scribbled away in his book.

'Yes, I didn't see the man as such, but the box where he was packing away the crockery was there so he must have been about his duties. I picked up my wrap and returned upstairs.' Lady Rose gave a faint shrug.

'You didn't actually see the man? Was anyone else down there at that time?' the inspector asked.

Lady Rose shook her head. 'Well, no, I didn't see him. I don't recall seeing anyone else either but any of the others may have been in the lavatory, I suppose.'

'May I ask how long this was before you departed the boat?' Matt asked and Lady Rose turned her head to look at him as if surprised to find him there.

'About ten minutes or so before we left to return to the hotel,' Lady Rose confirmed.

'And you had never seen the steward before last night?' the inspector asked.

She turned back to face him. 'I don't think so. I mean one can't be sure as I didn't really look at him, but I imagine it to be highly unlikely.'

'Thank you, Lady Rose. Perhaps you could ask Miss Serafina to come up next?' The inspector accompanied her to the door.

'I doubt if Saffy can tell you very much. It was her birthday after all.' Lady Rose gave a faint huff as she departed back to the ground floor.

Serafina seemed to find the whole process mildly amusing. She smiled at the inspector and at Matt as she entered the suite.

'I didn't expect my birthday celebrations to be quite so eventful, Inspector. Do you really think Father killed the steward?' she asked mischievously as she sat down.

Inspector Greville eyed her with a grave expression. 'A man's death is no laughing matter, miss.'

The girl sobered. 'Of course not, Inspector. It just all seems so preposterous, doesn't it? I mean was it definitely murder? The man didn't just have a heart attack or something?'

'No, miss, he was attacked from behind by someone wielding a wrench. It was definitely murder.'

Serafina's eyes widened in shock. 'Gosh, I'm sorry, that is quite awful.'

'Indeed, miss. Perhaps you would be so good as to tell me when you last saw Herr Freiberg alive?'

Serafina's round face crunched in concentration. 'It would have been when he served the coffee after dinner in the saloon, I suppose. He must have returned to the deck to clear the dinner things while we had coffee and liquors because when we went back upstairs everything had been put away.'

Matt leaned forward in his seat. 'We have heard that the baron was taking photographs of the evening and he took pictures of you all just before you left the boat.'

Serafina rolled her eyes. 'Oh yes, he was making the most frightful fuss. We all had to keep posing and smiling. It seemed to go on for ages. He does love that camera.'

'And various members of your party returned downstairs while the pictures were being taken?' Matt asked.

'Well, yes. Mother had left her stole in the saloon, Theo and Daddy went to use the lavatory. Flora and Edward went to collect the flowers they had given me for my birthday, and I think the baron went to collect a piece of his camera equipment.'

'Thank you, Miss Serafina. May I ask if you too returned below deck before disembarking?' Inspector Greville asked.

The crease on Serafina's brow deepened. 'I believe I may have gone to call Theo. The baron wanted him in the photographs, and he was taking an absolute age.'

'You seem uncertain about going down to call your brother?' Matt said.

'Well, it was my birthday and I had rather more champagne than normal but, yes, I remember going down a step or two and calling out to him,' Serafina answered crossly.

'I see. That's been most helpful, thank you. Perhaps you could ask your brother to come up next?' Inspector Greville escorted the girl to the door.

'What a muddle,' Matt said as the door closed behind the chief constable's daughter.

'Indeed. It will be interesting to hear what Master Theodore has to say,' the Inspector said with a sigh.

CHAPTER ELEVEN

Theo definitely appeared rather the worse for wear when he entered the salon. The boy's eyes were bloodshot, and his clothes were crumpled and indicated that he had dressed in haste. Dark circles were under his eyes, and he looked dull and exhausted. Matt almost felt sorry for him, until he recalled that Theo had been hassling Kitty only a few hours previously.

'I don't know what I can possibly have to tell you about this murdered man,' Theo said as he slumped into his chair, his hands in his trouser pockets.

The inspector's bushy eyebrows rose. 'I see, sir. I think, however, that I shall be the judge of that.'

Theo scowled. 'I don't even remember all of last night.'

Matt exchanged a glance with the inspector.

'I suggest you try, sir,' the inspector replied mildly. 'Had you ever met Herr Freiberg before last night?'

'Who? Oh, is that the steward chap? No, I'd never seen him before.' Theo dug his hands deeper into his trouser pockets and affected an air of boredom.

'When did you last see the steward alive?' the inspector asked.

Theo shrugged. 'I'm not sure. It was probably after dinner when we went for coffee. It had gone cool on deck, so we went downstairs while the table was cleared.'

'And afterwards, when you all went back on deck so the baron could take photographs, did you see anything of Herr Freiberg then?' Matt asked.

Matt was certain that Theo was keeping something back. The boy was certainly suffering the after-effects of having imbibed too much champagne the previous evening, but he also thought Theo might be playing on it for some reason.

'No, not that I recall. I'm pretty sure the last time I saw him was when he was serving the coffee.' There was a touch of belligerence now in Theo's tone.

'You returned below deck during the photography session?' Inspector Greville resumed the questioning.

'Yes, it was chilly on deck, and I'd had a lot to drink so I went to use the lavatory. I felt a little ill so I think I was in there for a while.'

'Did you see or hear anyone else while you were below deck?' Inspector Greville asked.

'Only my sister calling for me to hurry up as the baron was waiting.'

'I see. Thank you, please could you ask Baron Rochelle to come up next.' Inspector Greville dismissed Theo.

'All of them deny knowing Gunther and claim they last saw him alive when coffee was served.' Matt rose from his chair and walked about the room to exercise his legs before the baron arrived.

Inspector Greville replaced the cap back on his fountain pen, a dissatisfied expression on his face. 'Yet none of them saw anyone else enter or leave the boat and the man is dead, killed in the room at the end of that same corridor.'

'It doesn't make sense.' Matt resumed his seat as the baron knocked at the door and entered the room.

Baron Rochelle had clearly taken umbrage that he might be suspected of involvement in the crime. His round, florid cheeks were puffed out and his small black eyes sparkled with irritation at being summoned for questioning by the inspector.

'I really must protest, *Monsieur l'inspecteur*, it is unbelievable that a person like myself and my good friend the chief constable should be suspected of the murder of a manservant.' The baron took his seat and pulled out a silver cigarette case.

He selected a tiny black cigarette and lit it with a silver lighter. The inspector placed a large polished onyx ashtray in front of him.

'I'm sure the chief constable has told you that all the formalities must be followed, sir. After all, a man has been killed.' Inspector Greville picked his fountain pen up once more and prepared to write.

'*C'est incroyable*. I do not know what I can possibly tell you that will be useful.' The baron blew a thin stream of pale-blue smoke into the air.

'May I ask, sir, if you had ever met the murdered man, Herr Freiberg, before?' the inspector asked.

The baron tapped some ash from the end of his cigarette into the ashtray. 'No, I don't think so.'

'And when did you last see the steward alive?' Inspector Greville continued.

'I don't know. I think probably after dinner, when coffee was served. We were all together. The others no doubt have told you the same thing.' The baron took another pull on his cigarette.

'You are a keen photographer I understand, sir? You took some pictures of the group on the deck just before you all disembarked?' Inspector Greville looked at the Frenchman.

'*Oui*. I have an excellent camera. I thought Serafina would like some pictures as a memento of her day. A little extra gift for her and her parents.' The baron beamed.

Matt stifled a cough as the pungent aroma of the baron's cigarette reached him.

'That was most generous of you, sir. I'd appreciate it if I could take the films and get them developed,' Inspector Greville said.

The baron's smile expanded further. 'Of course, Inspector.'

'Did you return below deck at any point before disembarking?' The inspector's pen was poised over his notebook.

Baron Rochelle frowned and extinguished the remains of his cigarette in the ashtray. 'No, I don't think I did. Oh yes, wait, yes, I was about to leave the boat when I realised I had left my spare rolls of film on the table down below. I had to turn around and hurry back to get them.'

'And you saw no sign of the steward then?' the inspector asked.

'No, nothing at all,' the baron said. 'There was no one in the room. I collected my film and came back onto the deck ready to leave for the ball with the others.'

Inspector Greville rubbed his free hand across his eyes. 'Thank you, sir. Please could you ask your daughter to come up next.'

'Very well.' Baron Rochelle rose and gave the inspector a small nod of his head in farewell before leaving.

'Just the two to go now, sir,' Matt said. 'Flora Rochelle and Edward Forbes, Serafina's suitor.'

'Yes, the two that were below deck together getting Miss Serafina's flowers.'

He had scarcely finished speaking when Flora Rochelle appeared. She was a very attractive girl. Her short chestnut curls held back with a sunny-yellow hairband trimmed with daisies that matched her yellow and green printed dress.

'Please take a seat, Mademoiselle Rochelle.' Inspector Greville indicated the chair that had recently been vacated by her father.

Miss Rochelle sat down carefully and smoothed her skirt as she crossed her stocking-clad ankles demurely.

'As perhaps by now you are aware, we are trying to establish whether anyone knew Herr Freiberg before the party yesterday evening? Perhaps had seen him somewhere?' Inspector Greville asked.

The girl shook her head. 'No, I'm sorry, Inspector. I really couldn't say that I had ever seen him before.' She adjusted the fine gold bracelet on her wrist.

'When did you last see the steward yesterday evening?' The inspector made a few notes in his book.

The girl shrugged. 'After dinner when we had coffee, I think. I don't recall seeing him after that. When Edward and I went to collect Saffy's flowers he must have been around as I noticed that the table had partly been cleared, but I didn't see him, or anyone else.' Flora smiled apologetically. 'I'm afraid that isn't much help to you.'

'Not at all, Mademoiselle Rochelle. Any information at all is useful in painting a picture of the evening,' the inspector said.

'Mademoiselle Rochelle, may I ask, several members of the party returned below deck at different times. Can you recall at all in what order people went back to the saloon?' Matt asked.

Flora blinked and for the first time since she had entered the room Matt thought her composure had been ruffled.

'Of course. I think perhaps Sir Montague went first, then Lady Rose to collect her wrap. Then Edward and I, then Theo. Or perhaps Theo was already down there, I'm not certain. Saffy went down to call Theo and then Papa went to collect his films just before we got off the boat. At least I think that was the order. I wasn't exactly taking notes.' Her smile revealed a small dimple in her cheek.

'Thank you, Mademoiselle Flora.' Inspector Greville smiled back at her. 'Most helpful and concise.'

Matt's gaze met that of the inspector. He thought that

perhaps the policeman was a little swayed by Flora's obvious charm.

'If you could send Mr Forbes up to us?' Inspector Greville asked, rising from his chair to escort Flora to the door.

'Of course.' The girl flashed them both another enchanting smile and disappeared off downstairs.

'A most charming young woman,' Inspector Greville observed as he retook his seat.

'Indeed, sir.' Matt suppressed a smile, satisfied his suspicions were correct and waited for the arrival of Edward Forbes.

Edward Forbes was smartly and expensively attired in well-cut trousers, navy blazer and a pale-blue silk cravat. He took his place opposite the inspector, crossed his legs and waited for the questioning to commence with a calm air.

'Mr Forbes, I understand from Lady Rose that you are a close personal friend of Miss Serafina Hawkes?' the inspector asked.

The younger man's mouth quirked in a mix of amusement and pride. 'Saffy and I have been walking out together for about four months.'

'How did you meet?' Inspector Greville leaned back in his seat. Matt could only assume that of all the people in the party Edward Forbes was the one they knew the least about.

'We share an interest in art. I met Saffy at an exhibition in Exeter, and we were introduced by a mutual acquaintance. We hit it off and have been seeing one another ever since.' Edward picked a small piece of lint from the sleeve of his blazer and dropped it down onto the Turkish rug.

'I see, thank you, sir. Did you know the victim, Herr Freiberg, at all? Had you ever seen him before last night?' the inspector asked.

Edward laughed. 'No, Inspector, I don't think so. Not unless he had ever served me drinks somewhere before.'

'And when did you last see the steward alive?' the inspector asked.

'I suppose it would be when we were all below deck. He served the coffee and left the saloon. Afterwards when Flora and I went to collect Saffy's flowers, Flora went upstairs and I went to the lavatory. I saw him then walking away towards the rear of the boat.'

A gleam appeared in Inspector Greville's eyes. Matt knew this was the first time any of the party said they had seen the steward after he had served coffee.

'Have you any recollection of what time this may have been?' the inspector asked.

Edward frowned. 'I suppose it would have been shortly after the baron began arranging us into groups on deck for photographs. I'm afraid I didn't look at my watch.'

'So, probably between eight fifteen to eight thirty?' Matt asked. He knew that Kitty had set off to escort the party back to the hotel shortly before eight thirty.

'Yes, I suppose it must have been,' Edward agreed. 'Are you working with the police, Captain Bryant? I hadn't realised.'

'Captain Bryant is assisting with the investigation. An independent pair of eyes to ensure that everything is done correctly until, or if, Scotland Yard take over. I'm sure you will appreciate that everything has to be above board given Sir Montague's position,' Inspector Greville replied smoothly.

Matt was grateful for the inspector's intervention. He didn't wish London's true interest in Herr Freiberg to be hinted at. It was important that they discovered who the man's contacts had been and where he had been receiving his information from.

'Oh, I see. Yes, I seem to recall Sir Montague saying that you were a private investigator.' Edward appeared to accept the explanation.

'Thank you, Mr Forbes. We appreciate your assistance,' the inspector said.

Edward Forbes took his cue. 'Not at all, Inspector. I'm sorry I couldn't be of more help. I'd better get back downstairs. Lady Rose intends us all to walk to the castle and back before luncheon. Fresh air to blow the cobwebs away, I'm sure it will do Saffy good. She won't let on, but I think this has quite upset her, it having been her party and everything.'

He nodded a farewell to Matt after shaking the inspector's hand and took his leave.

The inspector sighed and closed his notebook. 'What a bunch, eh? No one saw anything, no one knows anything, no one heard anything. Like the three wise monkeys.'

'And yet a man is dead and one of them must have killed him. I take it that the captain and the mate have been exonerated from the list of suspects?' Matt asked.

'Yes. The mate left the boat shortly after it docked, and Gunther was alive and serving dinner for a good hour or so after that. The captain didn't go below deck at all. He left all that malarky up to our deceased friend. My constables have found various witnesses attesting to seeing the captain in the wheelhouse during that time and everyone on board agrees that he stayed on deck. That boat was lit up like a Christmas tree and guests were arriving on the riverside all the time for the party.' The inspector's moustache drooped.

There was the sound of crockery rattling outside the door and Kitty appeared along with a laden tea trolley.

'Sir Montague's party are all off to walk to the castle and back before lunch. I thought you might care for some refreshments after interviewing them all.' Kitty wheeled the trolley into the room and the inspector's expression brightened at the sight of the selection of cakes and biscuits that were accompanying the tea.

Matt sprang to his feet to assist her.

'Thank you, Matt darling. Now, shall we compare notes?' Kitty asked brightly once the trolley was in position.

CHAPTER TWELVE

Kitty poured the tea and listened attentively as Matt and the inspector told her the outcomes of the interviews.

'Oh dear, it doesn't sound as if we are much further forward,' she observed as she passed around a plate of jam tarts. She thought it sounded as if the inspector was in an impossible situation. It seemed to her that it would have been far better if Scotland Yard had come and taken charge from the beginning.

She told them of the conversations amongst the family while they had been waiting for their turn to be interviewed. She also told them of Flora and Edward's intense private conversation in the ballroom.

'That all confirms the details they gave us,' Matt remarked.

'They are all still intending to return to Exeter this afternoon. The baron and his daughter are staying with the family for another week, and I believe Mr Forbes has also been invited to extend his stay.' Kitty watched with secret amusement as Inspector Greville finished off the last of the jam tarts.

'Yes, I shall be warning them to remain at Exeter. I imagine that you will not be too sorry to see them depart, Miss Underhay?' the inspector asked.

Kitty sighed. 'Obviously Lady Rose and Grams have been friends for many years, but I think even Grams will be relieved to know they and the Firestone necklace are all safely returned home.'

'That was a very odd business. That necklace disappearing and reappearing like that. Almost like a conjuring trick,' the inspector mused.

'Very. I mean, all the guests were known to the family or were high-ranking police officers and their wives. The staff I had working had all been employed by us for quite some time, so the only explanation must be that a member of the party was playing some kind of prank. However the timing to me seemed to indicate someone who knew the party schedule,' Kitty said. 'Theodore suggested that Serafina had done it herself for attention or to delay a proposal from Mr Forbes.' She still thought this sounded unlikely and had wondered if Theo had been the prankster.

'It's very possible,' the inspector agreed.

'I doubt Lady Rose or Sir Montague would have done such a thing and the baron is hardly of a build to make nipping off and on the stage speedily very likely,' Matt agreed.

'I suppose Theo himself could have been the culprit. He may have suggested it was Serafina to throw us off his scent. If he were jealous of his sister and he had drunk enough he may have thought that sort of jape amusing,' Kitty said.

'Or I suppose Flora or Edward Forbes may have been involved. Perhaps Mademoiselle Rochelle might be envious of her friend or may need money. As indeed this Mr Forbes may not be as well heeled as Sir Montague believes. He is something of a mystery man, Mr Forbes,' the inspector said.

'Then it may not have been taken as a prank after all. Whoever took it may have intended to keep it.' A chill ran along Kitty's spine. Suppose it *had* been stolen? Such a high-profile theft at the Dolphin would be bound to unsettle their guests and generate bad publicity for the hotel.

'I think that has to be considered.' Inspector Greville brushed pastry crumbs from his moustache. 'Thankfully the necklace was found in short time, and you have been very vigilant with your security.'

'Yes, we have tried to take every precaution, but I shall still be glad to know it is gone safely back to Exeter with Sir Montague.' Kitty smiled at the inspector's approval of her arrangements for the safety of the necklace.

'I don't suppose there is any connection between Herr Freiberg's death and the snatching of the Firestone necklace?' Matt mused. 'It seems a pretty awful coincidence the two events occurring so closely together.' He looked at the inspector.

'I can't think of a connection, but I agree it is a queer coincidence and I dislike and distrust such things,' Inspector Greville said.

Kitty agreed with him. Since she had become more involved with Matt's cases, she too had learned to distrust coincidences.

Inspector Greville left shortly afterwards to return to Torquay as he wished to type up his notes and to discuss the case further with his colleagues in London. Matt too departed to return to Churston, fearing that Bertie the dog would have destroyed half the house in his absence.

Kitty went to meet with Cyril to ensure that her grandmother's plans for the Hawkes' family luncheon would all run smoothly on their return.

'Everything is in place as requested,' Cyril assured her. 'Pan fried lemon sole with buttered potatoes and vegetables and a lemon sorbet with fresh raspberries to follow.'

Kitty thanked him and left to look for her grandmother, who

Cyril had informed her was in the small lounge they were using as a private area for Sir Montague's party.

'Kitty darling, I was just putting the finishing touches to the dining table for lunch. I thought it better they dine in here away from the other guests.' Her grandmother stood back to admire the floral centrepiece constructed of pink and white roses with complementary greenery.

'It looks marvellous.' Kitty watched her grandmother as she tweaked the pale pink linen tablecloth and adjusted a folded napkin. 'Cyril said that everything is ready for Sir Montague's return.'

'Mr Lutterworth is indeed a treasure; I can't believe he has only been here two days. I must confess I shall be glad to see Lady Rose and her party depart. Fond though I am of her, this has been quite exhausting, especially after that business with the necklace last night. I have asked Mickey to continue to keep watch even though it has been safely back inside the safe ever since it was returned to Sir Montague.'

'I know how you feel,' Kitty said. The business of the jewels bothered her.

'I really don't know if Rose still has expectations of Mr Forbes. To my mind he does not appear to show any especial fondness for Serafina. Not the kind that would lead to a betrothal at least,' her grandmother mused as she straightened a fish knife.

Kitty knew what her grandmother meant. And what about Serafina's fondness for Mr Forbes? Theo had even claimed that Serafina had no desire to become engaged. She supposed that could be why there seemed so few signs of any great affection between them.

'Do you know much about Mr Forbes?' Kitty asked.

'Not really, darling. I think he met Serafina at some exhibition or other and she invited him to a party at the house. Rose says he is something to do with finance in the city. He has connections locally, I understand, but who his family are, well, of that I'm really not certain. One of these modern self-made young men, I suppose. A stockbroker or something. After all those poor souls who lost so much money a few years ago now I wouldn't have thought it a terribly stable profession myself. Then again, I might be a little old-fashioned.' Her grandmother smiled at her.

Kitty enveloped her in a hug. 'Never, Grams darling.'

Her grandmother laughed and shooed her out of the dining room. 'Everything is ready. Come, we'll make sure they have a good luncheon and then we can wave them off home with light hearts.'

Sir Montague's party arrived back some thirty minutes or so later. Kitty was in her small office just off the lobby when she heard Mary greeting them at reception.

'I hadn't realised it was so far and so steep on the way up,' she heard the baron complaining.

'You should have some nice photographs, Papa, and the exercise must be beneficial for your health,' Flora soothed her father.

'At least it gives one an appetite for luncheon. The view over the river was quite charming,' Edward Forbes joined in the debate.

'Welcome back, may I show you through to the lounge. I believe Mrs Treadwell has personally arranged a private dining area for you all.'

Kitty relaxed back in her chair when she heard Cyril's cultured tones greeting the group. She would have gone out to them herself but guiltily she really didn't feel much like spending a lot more time in their company right now. Especially with the shadow of Herr Freiberg's demise hanging over them.

She stayed in her office for the next hour sorting through the paperwork so that she could ensure that Cyril and Dolly could deal with it later. He already seemed to have a good grasp of how things worked. Her grandmother had promised to come for her just before the party was due to depart so she could bid them farewell.

Sure enough, she had almost completed her tasks when her grandmother appeared in the doorway.

'Kitty dear, the family are off upstairs to ensure their baggage is ready. The cars should be here for them in about ten minutes. I'm going to go with Sir Montague to unlock the safe.'

'I'll come out to the lobby and make sure the luggage is taken care of.' Kitty rose from her seat, ready to supervise the kitchen boy who acted as porter during quiet times.

Her grandmother hurried away up the broad oak staircase to her salon to await the arrival of Sir Montague.

Baron Rochelle and his daughter were first into the lobby with the youthful porter trailing after them, a pile of monogramed leather valises piled on his trolley.

'Are the cars here?' the baron asked as he tried to peer through the plate glass panels of the revolving door.

'I think they should be arriving at any moment,' Kitty assured him.

To her relief she heard the rumble of a motor car and saw the first of Sir Montague's black Rolls Royces had indeed pulled to a halt outside.

'Our porter will assist your chauffeur to load the car,' Kitty said and nodded to the young lad to take the trolley out to the waiting vehicle.

They had no sooner gone outside when Serafina, Theodore and Edward Forbes arrived. Serafina carried a smart burgundy leather beauty box and Edward had a small leather case. Theo had clearly been tasked with transporting his sister's birthday flowers.

'The first car is here. I'll send the boy up to your rooms to collect the rest of your luggage.' Kitty smiled at her guests and collected their keys giving them straight to the boy when he re-entered the lobby.

'Thank you, Kitty. Are Mother and Father down yet?' Serafina asked.

'No, I think your father has gone to collect the Firestone necklace from the safe. I presume Lady Rose will be there too saying her goodbyes to Grams.' Kitty heard the rumble of the second car pulling up as she answered Serafina.

Theodore had positioned himself uncomfortably close to Kitty, so she moved away towards the reception desk.

'Perhaps you would care to take your sisters flowers out to the driver, Theo. It's quite busy in here and I'd hate to step on anyone's feet.' Kitty gave him a dazzling smile to make certain he understood her meaning.

An ugly red flush spread over the boy's cheeks, and he scowled as he pushed past Edward Forbes in his haste to get out to the cars.

'I'm so sorry your birthday was overshadowed by that dreadful incident on the boat,' Kitty turned her attention back to Serafina.

'We shall have to hope they catch whoever was responsible for it soon,' Edward said, glancing at his companion.

'I do hope so, for all our sakes. Poor Daddy is frightfully cross about the whole thing,' Serafina said and slipped her free hand into the crook of Edward's arm.

'Rightfully so. Let's hope this inspector, what was his name – Grenvil? – is good at his job and sorts it out quick smart.' Edward gave Serafina's gloved hand a gentle pat.

'Inspector Greville is considered one of the best detectives in Devon, I believe,' Kitty said. She hoped she was right and that the inspector would manage to solve the case soon.

The lad returned to the lobby with another load of luggage and took it out to the waiting cars.

Serafina looked at the clock on the wall of the reception

area. 'I do wish Daddy would hurry up. At this rate it will be dark by the time we reach home.'

As she spoke Lady Rose appeared on the stairs, followed by Sir Montague and Kitty's grandmother. Lady Rose was dressed for travelling in a pale-green tweed suit and pale-lilac silk blouse, with a neat hat on her handsome head trimmed with a small but jaunty feather.

She carried a box not unlike her daughter's, while Sir Montague held the leather jewel case that Kitty recognised from the previous evening.

Lady Rose bustled towards her daughter. 'Saffy darling, your father wishes to lock the Firestone necklace in your case for travelling. Stupidly I seem to have damaged the lock on my box so I can't secure it.'

Serafina rolled her eyes and detached herself from Edward. 'Honestly, Mother, I told you about forcing the key in that lock.' She brushed past Kitty and Mary at reception to place her own small case down on the desk.

She produced the key from a small pocket inside her jacket and opened the case. Kitty could see that the inside was expensively fitted in shagreen with silver brushes and silver-topped glass bottles. There was just enough room to slide the jeweller's box inside.

'Better let your mother take care of the case, eh, Saffy? We don't want any more mishaps with the necklace,' Sir Montague said in a jovial tone as he approached the desk.

'I doubt I shall see it again for another twenty years once we get home and it goes back into the safe, so it hardly matters who carries it,' Serafina scoffed.

Angry red patches appeared on her father's cheeks.

'Serafina Louise, apologise to your father at once,' Lady Rose commanded.

'Then you had better have a last look at it, young lady. It may have to last you a very long time.' Sir Montague flung open the case revealing the sudden sparkle of diamonds on the burgundy velvet pad.

Kitty heard Mary who was standing next to her gasp. She guessed the receptionist had never seen so many jewels up so closely before.

'Daddy, this is ridiculous, please. I'm sorry. It was thoughtless of me.' Serafina went to close the lid of the box.

As she moved, the expression on Sir Montague's face suddenly changed, and he pulled the necklace from its box and hurried to the window.

'Call the police! This is not the Firestone necklace. We have been robbed!'

CHAPTER THIRTEEN

There was a moment of stunned silence before a babble of voices broke out and Lady Rose and Serafina rushed over to join Sir Montague at the window.

'My dear, whatever do you mean?' Lady Rose peered at the necklace that still sparkled in her husband's hand.

'Look at it, Rose, look at the catch and the links. This is a cleverly made forgery. A fake. If Serafina had not caused me to open the case, we would have been none the wiser. It would have been returned to the vault.' Sir Montague shook the necklace at his wife, the fake jewels sent flashes of light all around the room.

The commotion had attracted the attention of the rest of the party who had been waiting outside the hotel. Theo, Baron Rochelle and Flora all came back into the lobby.

Lady Rose was examining the gold fastening and chain on the necklace. Kitty saw the colour drain from her face as she realised that her husband was correct. The necklace was clearly not the Firestone.

'What is it? What's happening?' the baron asked.

'It seems the Firestone necklace is a fake.' Serafina sat down on a nearby chair. She looked dazed by the discovery.

'That is not possible. The necklace has been under lock and key ever since we arrived.' Flora turned a frightened face towards her friend.

'Except for when it was snatched from around my neck in the ballroom last night,' Serafina said in a small voice.

'Telephone Inspector Greville at Torquay,' Kitty commanded Mary. 'Sir Montague, Lady Rose, perhaps we should all repair to the lounge and wait for the inspector to arrive.' She turned to Mary again. 'Telephone the kitchen for tea after you have called the police, then ask the chauffeurs to remain with the cars and luggage until there are further instructions.'

The girl nodded and picked up the telephone. Kitty's grandmother steered her distraught friend and her husband out of the lobby and along the hall to the small lounge where they had dined earlier.

Edward escorted Serafina, who appeared quite shaken by the unexpected turn of events. Flora, Theodore and Baron Rochelle followed behind all talking animatedly about what must have occurred.

Mr Lutterworth came into the lobby, his usual professional demeanour slightly ruffled.

'Miss Underhay, I heard the commotion. Is it true? The Firestone necklace has been stolen? The one in the case is a forgery?'

'It would seem so. Grams has taken the party into the small lounge and the police are on their way.' She looked at Mary as she spoke and received a confirmation nod. 'It's all quite shocking and unexpected.'

'Is there anything I can do?' Cyril asked.

'Please go and assist Grams. Try and keep everyone calm

until the inspector arrives. I must telephone Matt and tell him what's happened.' Kitty moved behind the desk to take the telephone receiver from Mary.

'Of course.' Cyril bowed his bald head and strode away.

The receptionist left the desk to give Kitty's earlier instructions to the chauffeurs, while Kitty dialled Matt's number on the black Bakelite telephone.

Much to her relief he answered on the second ring.

'Matt, something awful has happened.' Kitty hurriedly told him what had happened.

'Is the inspector on his way?' Matt asked.

'Yes, but I don't know quite what he can do. How can the necklace have been stolen? It was locked away and under guard, apart from when it was taken in the ballroom. Was that when it was exchanged for a fake?' To have a fake version of the Firestone necklace readily available to make such a substitution argued a great deal of planning, Kitty thought.

'I'll just make sure Bertie is all right and I'll come right down. Don't worry, darling.' Matt rang off.

It was all very well for Matt to say not to worry, Kitty thought, but what else could she do. If the necklace had been stolen and substituted during the twenty minutes or so it had been missing during Saffy's party, then someone had gone to a great deal of trouble.

They would have had to have known exactly what the necklace looked like to get such a good replica made ahead of time. After all, Sir Montague had not noticed it was a fake when it had been locked inside her grandmother's safe.

They would also have to have some knowledge of when the necklace would be given to Serafina so that they would know when to take it. In fact, the more she thought about it surely there must have been more than one person involved. How else would the lights have gone out at just that time?

The fuses had all been carefully checked the following day and there had been no problems. The lights at the Dolphin were very reliable so unless someone had tampered with them why else would they have failed?

Someone also had to have known exactly when the best moment would be to plunge the ballroom into darkness to swap the necklaces over.

First a murder on the paddle steamer and now this. The events didn't seem to have any obvious connection so far as Kitty could see, except that the only people who knew the full programme for Serafina's birthday were the members of Sir Montague's party.

Cyril reappeared at the side of the reception desk. 'I've taken the liberty of supplying the party with brandy, Kitty. Lady Rose in particular seemed in need of a restorative. Your grandmother has asked that you come and attend until the police arrive.'

'Of course, would you watch out for the inspector and for Matt and send them in to us as soon as they get here?' Kitty gave her new manager a wan smile and made her way to the lounge.

Her grandmother was seated beside her friend and was busily engaged in encouraging her to take restorative sips of brandy. Sir Montague appeared to be venting his energy by marching up and down the room, his colour building with almost every step.

Edward, Serafina and Flora were huddled together, and Saffy looked as if she had been crying. Theo was sprawled out in one of the armchairs, his hands thrust deep in his trouser pockets, while the baron had taken out a pince-nez and was examining the fake necklace.

'It is a remarkable thing, but the stones they seem exact to the original as far as I can recall.' Baron Rochelle peered at the necklace.

'You've seen the original before, sir?' Kitty asked as she

moved closer to where the baron was seated at the table beside the window.

'*Mais oui*. Not for some time obviously, but a few years ago. I took some photographs for the family for the insurance company.' The stones sparkled against the aristocrat's pudgy fingers.

'May I see?' Kitty asked.

The baron shrugged and dropped the necklace into her hand. The forgery was certainly very well done. She guessed the stones must be glass or rock crystal polished up to look like diamonds. They looked very convincing. The settings around the stones were also well made, even if they were paste of some kind. Kitty would never have realised the whole piece was costume jewellery.

She turned her attention to the catch on the necklace since it was this that seemed to have alerted Sir Montague. At first, she could see nothing obvious unless one looked really closely. Then she could see that the fastening wasn't quite right, and the safety chain appeared to be clumsily fixed. The metal was also duller than she would have expected since that part of the necklace should have been made of gold.

'This seems to have been skilfully done,' Kitty observed. It was clear to her that whoever had made the forgery must either have had access to the original or to very good drawings or photographs.

'If a fire were lit, I should be tempted to fling it in the flames.' Sir Montague snatched the necklace from her hands and glowered at the offending piece.

Serafina gave a hollow laugh. 'I knew that wretched necklace would be trouble. I never wanted it in the first place.' She scowled at her father.

'Well, now your legacy will be equal in value to mine,' Theo muttered.

'Children, please!' Lady Rose had her fingertips pressed to

her temples. 'Do you not realise the enormity of this, and you two are indulging in petty squabbles?'

'I presume the necklace is insured?' Edward Forbes asked.

'Oh God, the insurers. I must inform them at once.' Sir Montague turned to Kitty's grandmother.

'Of course, I'll take you upstairs to my salon. It will be more private there,' Kitty's grandmother suggested.

Sir Montague slipped the fake necklace inside his jacket pocket and followed the older woman from the room.

'If you had not angered your father this would never have occurred.' Lady Rose glared at her daughter.

'I hardly think that this is my fault, Mother. I was almost strangled last night at my party by whoever stole the necklace. Surely, it's better to discover this substitution now rather than a few years down the line when the necklace is next taken out of the vault?' Serafina said.

Lady Rose fished in her white leather handbag for a handkerchief and dabbed at her eyes. 'I had hoped you would wear the necklace at your wedding, along with Granny's tiara. Now everything is spoiled.'

'Honestly, Mother. I really would have absolutely no desire to wear the Firestone necklace real or fake if I were to marry. Or, even for that matter Granny's tiara, which is quite the ugliest thing.' Serafina's tone was sharp.

Lady Rose gave a doleful sniff. 'No, I suppose not, but a mother has dreams for her children.'

Kitty was feeling quite uncomfortable at having witnessed this exchange. The baron and Flora, however, seemed to be unmoved by the melodrama. Edward appeared to be pretending not to have heard any of the argument. Kitty could only assume it was something they were used to witnessing.

Theo sat himself up on the sofa. 'The whole thing is ridiculous, if you ask me. The necklace is insured so Father will no doubt get oodles of money to pay for Saffy's mythical nuptials.'

'Theodore!' Lady Rose glared at her son.

Theo's words sparked an idea in Kitty's mind, and she wondered if Sir Montague himself might have engineered the theft. Perhaps he wanted or needed the money more than the Firestone necklace.

After all, the necklace wasn't technically his. It was in trust to be passed on down the female line of the family. What good was a diamond necklace too precious for everyday wear that spent all its time in a bank vault?

The door to the lounge reopened and Sir Montague entered with Kitty's grandmother. He flung himself down on the sofa and rubbed his hand across his face.

'Have you spoken to the insurers?' Lady Rose asked. Her anxiety evident on her face.

'Yes. They'll need to speak to the police and there'll be a load of bally forms to fill out.' Sir Montague scowled at his wife.

'At least they will pay though, won't they?' Lady Rose persisted.

'I imagine so. It doesn't get the wretched necklace back though. No doubt it's been broken into pieces by now and the stones dispersed.' Sir Montague looked at his daughter. 'This will certainly be a birthday to remember, for all the wrong reasons.'

Colour mounted in the girl's cheeks and Kitty felt a little sorry for her. She was about to suggest that she return to the lobby to see if the police were on their way when Inspector Greville himself entered the room. Matt was just behind him.

Matt winked at Kitty before crossing around the room to sit on the chair beside her. She was reassured by his calm demeanour after all the drama she had just witnessed.

'About time too, Greville! There has been a serious crime committed here. The Firestone necklace has been stolen and replaced by this worthless fake.' Sir Montague pulled the necklace back out of his pocket with the air of a conjuror producing a rabbit from a top hat. 'There, now what do you make of that?' the chief constable demanded.

'My apologies for the delay, sir, but there is also a murder investigation in progress, and we are some small distance from Torquay.' The inspector's expression was unreadable.

'The necklace must have been taken last night when the lights went out and someone snatched it from Serafina's neck,' Lady Rose said.

'May I, sir?' The inspector picked up the fake necklace from where Sir Montague had dropped it on the polished rosewood table beside him.

He examined it carefully, even producing a small magnifying glass from his pocket to look more closely.

'I agree, sir, it seems to be a very well-made forgery.'

'We know that already, you idiot,' Sir Montague spluttered and Kitty saw little bits of spittle fly from the corners of his mouth.

The inspector appeared unmoved by Sir Montague's wrath. 'I mean, sir, that this was not the work of a moment. This substitution has clearly been planned for quite some time. May I ask, sir, when the necklace was recovered during the ball was there anything then that aroused your suspicions?'

'Of course not, man. I was relieved to have it back. I had a quick look for any obvious signs of damage, returned it to its case and locked it in the safe.' He looked at Kitty's grandmother for confirmation.

She nodded her head. 'That is exactly what happened, Inspector. We had no reason to suspect that someone may have made a substitution. It was also very late in the evening.'

'Of course. What caused you to examine it now, sir?' The inspector looked at Sir Montague.

Kitty saw colour flame into Serafina's pale cheeks.

'My daughter made a comment about the necklace, so I opened the box.' Sir Montague shifted uncomfortably.

Inspector Greville looked at Serafina. 'Otherwise, I take it the deception would not have been noticed for some time?'

'No, Inspector. There would have been no reason to take it from its case,' Saffy agreed.

Kitty could tell from Serafina's expression that she wished she had not caused her father to open the box.

CHAPTER FOURTEEN

'Well?' Sir Montague demanded. 'We have been robbed of a priceless heirloom, Greville. What do you intend to do about it?'

The inspector placed the forgery back down on the table. 'I think the first thing to determine, sir, with all due respect, is when the robbery actually took place.'

Matt noticed the vein in Sir Montague's temple had started to throb. 'You know dashed well when it was stolen. Last night when the lights went out someone snatched the Firestone necklace from around my daughter's neck then left this... this piece of tat in its place.'

'I take it then, sir, you are absolutely confident that the necklace Miss Hawkes wore at the ball was the original Firestone necklace? Did you examine it at the time when you put it around your daughter's neck? Or have it out of the case beforehand?' Inspector Greville asked.

Sir Montague looked as if he were about to explode. 'Of course I didn't examine it. I took the box from the safe, carried it downstairs, opened it and then placed it around Serafina's neck.

We were on stage in front of everyone. You were there.' He glared at the inspector.

'Actually, sir, I'm afraid I missed that event. The small matter of Herr Freiberg's murder. So, you can't be certain that the necklace Miss Hawkes had snatched was the original Fire-stone necklace?'

'Well, no,' Sir Montague sounded a little uncertain, 'but dash it all, man, it must have been. When else could it have been taken?' he demanded, glowering at the inspector.

'The necklace was returned though, sir. Perhaps whoever took it discovered they had stolen a forgery,' the policeman remarked, his tone still mild.

'You are suggesting that the necklace we brought with us was the fake?' Lady Rose asked. Matt could see she was horrified by this idea.

'I think we have to consider the possibility, my lady. Who had access to the necklace before you came to the Dolphin?' Inspector Greville asked.

'No one. At least, I arranged for it to be collected from the bank vault by a very reputable jeweller in Exeter. They cleaned it and checked all the catches and returned it to me just before we came away. Surely they will be able to verify it was the genuine article that they had in their care.' Sir Montague looked at his wife, who nodded in agreement.

'Indeed, Inspector, Monty wanted to ensure the necklace was at its best as it hadn't been worn for quite some time. It arrived from the jewellers and went into the house safe for a few hours, then Monty fetched it out and we travelled here,' Lady Rose said.

'I rather think that the last time it was worn may have been at your wedding anniversary ball a few years ago, my dear.' Kitty's grandmother looked at her friend.

'Yes, I think you're right. Until it went to the jewellers it had only been out of the bank a couple of times since I inherited it when I was twenty-one.' Lady Rose frowned in recollection. 'Philippe photographed it for the insurers, and I rather think it may have been assayed too.'

Inspector Greville had taken out his notebook and was busy writing. 'How long was the necklace with the jewellers?'

'A few days. I think they had it on the Tuesday and returned it to us yesterday morning.' Sir Montague appeared to have calmed down a little.

'And the name of the company, sir?' the inspector asked.

Lady Rose gave the name of a very reputable jewellers in Exeter.

'Thank you, my lady. I shall, of course, ask them to verify who had access to the necklace while it was with them.' The inspector stowed his notebook back inside his pocket. 'I shall also be making enquiries to ascertain if anyone has ordered a copy of the Firestone necklace. Clearly it has been professionally made in great detail. If we can discover who made the copy, we may get a lead on the thief.'

Matt could see that this would make sense. It could be that it could have been copied while the necklace was at the jewellers. It seemed to him that there were a few windows of opportunity for the necklace to have been substituted.

'So, what happens now, Inspector?' Lady Rose demanded. 'Are we to stay here or return home?' She looked to her husband and Inspector Greville for an answer.

'I think you may as well return home to Exeter, my lady. The investigation into Herr Freiberg's death is continuing and now, of course, we shall also be investigating the theft of the necklace too. I think you said Baron and Mademoiselle Rochelle and Mr Forbes were staying with you as your guests?'

Lady Rose nodded. 'Yes, for the foreseeable future.' She bit her lip as she looked at Mr Forbes. Matt knew that she had hoped he was to be her future son-in-law. How welcome he would continue to be in her household if a proposal was not forthcoming Matt wasn't certain.

'*Eh bien*, my daughter and I are at your disposal, *Monsieur l'inspecteur*. I have those rolls of film you requested.' The baron reached into his pockets and handed over three canisters of film. Matt assumed that they must be the photographs that the baron had taken on board the paddle steamer at Serafina's birthday dinner.

'Thank you, sir. We shall return the photographs once they have been developed and examined.' Inspector Greville tucked them away inside his own pockets.

'Of course, I'm also at your disposal, Inspector. Lady Rose and Sir Montague have most graciously extended their hospitality to me for a little longer.' Edward Forbes looked at Serafina.

'Thank you, sir. I must also request that you all stay at Exeter until the case has been resolved.' Inspector Greville looked at the people assembled before him.

'I expect all of this to be cleared up quickly, Greville, and with as little fuss and palaver as possible. I shall be keeping a close eye on the matter.' Sir Montague prepared to take his leave, along with his family.

'Naturally, sir.' The inspector stood aside as the Hawkes family departed the room, Kitty's grandmother accompanied them, while Kitty remained in the lounge with Matt and the inspector.

'The forgery was obviously made well ahead of time and whoever did it must have known about Serafina's birthday and Sir Montague's plans to present her with the necklace,' Kitty said.

'Absolutely. I shall get on to Inspector Pinch at Exeter. The jeweller's used by Sir Montague must be our starting point,' the inspector said.

'Are you any further forward with the murder case, sir?' Matt asked.

Inspector Greville frowned. 'It has to be one of the chief constable's party. I can see no other solution, but the question is who?'

'And why?' Kitty added. 'If we could work out why Herr Freiberg had to be killed that night, then we could discover his killer. I wonder if there is a connection with the stolen necklace? It seems to me that someone in that party also knows about that too.'

'At least for now Sir Montague and Lady Rose are out of your way, Kitty old thing.' Matt gave his fiancée a warm smile.

'We shall have to hope that there are no negative repercussions for the hotel from this birthday weekend,' Kitty remarked with feeling.

As she spoke, the sound of a female voice could be heard in the corridor outside the lounge.

'Inspector Greville!' Mrs Craven entered the room followed by an apologetic-looking Mr Lutterworth.

'I'm so sorry for the interruption, Kitty. This lady insisted that the inspector would see her.' Cyril's usual calm seemed a trifle ruffled.

'Well, of course he will see me. Thank you, Mr Lutterworth.' Mrs Craven turned and gave the hapless hotel manager her most regal dismissive glare.

'Thank you, Cyril. Mrs Craven, what can we do for you?' Kitty addressed her grandmother's friend as Mr Lutterworth took the opportunity to make good his escape.

'I was about to set off for Torquay to the police station when I thought I should call to see dear Lady Rose and Sir Montague before they left. I was horrified when I heard about the Firestone necklace. To do such a thing, stealing from the chief constable himself.'

Matt looked at Kitty as Mrs Craven paused for breath.

'How did you hear about the necklace?' Matt asked.

Mrs Craven fixed him with a glance. 'The chauffeurs were talking, of course, outside the hotel. Smoking while waiting for the family to come out to the cars. Idling away their time. If *I* employed them there would be none of that nonsense.'

'You wished to see me, Mrs Craven?' Inspector Greville asked.

'Yes, indeed. Of course now that it seems the necklace is in fact a fake I don't know if what I have to say is actually of any use to anyone.' Mrs Craven adjusted her cream linen jacket in a self-important manner.

'Perhaps I might be the judge of that, Mrs Craven.'

Matt wondered how the inspector managed to keep his patience.

'It suddenly occurred to me that I may have seen something important at the ball. Of course, it never occurred to me at the time, but as I was having luncheon with my friend, Joan Ponsonby-Bell, I told her, and she said that I ought to come and tell you. I was in two minds as the jewels seemed to have been recovered but it was bothering me. Now one doesn't know quite what to think,' Mrs Craven continued.

'What do you wish to tell me?' Inspector Greville asked.

'Well, just before the lights went out at the party, I noticed the baron's daughter, Flora, leave the room. I thought it most odd, she knew the cake was about to be cut and as Serafina's dearest friend one would have thought she would have been at the front of the stage. It was the big birthday moment after all with a toast and everything. She didn't come back until after the lights came back on and she looked quite flustered, as if she had been hurrying. Now, I know the fuse for the lights is down by the maintenance office. I remember from when you had that problem with the Christmas tree that one year, Kitty. Do you remember?' She looked at Kitty. 'It struck me that she could have been in cahoots with whoever took the necklace. I mean why else would she leave just at that moment?'

'I see. Well, thank you for that information, Mrs Craven,' the inspector said.

'French, you see,' Mrs Craven continued as if that explained everything. 'I know her father is a baron but from what Lady Rose has told me in the past, his title is pretty much all he has left. That and a rather run-down chateau in the Dordogne. I think he is hoping his daughter might marry well. She is a pretty little thing. If I were Serafina I should not be letting her spend too much time alone with Mr Forbes.'

'Mrs C, you are a marvel,' Matt cut Mrs Craven off before anymore salacious speculation could pass her lips.

The older woman preened under his praise. 'You know how I pride myself on my observational skills.'

'Absolutely. I'm sure the inspector is most grateful to you,' Matt said as he took Mrs Craven's arm in his and started to lead her from the room.

'Oh yes, indeed, most grateful,' Inspector Greville agreed as Matt skilfully removed Mrs Craven from the lounge.

'An interesting observation,' the inspector remarked when Matt returned to the room minus Mrs Craven.

'Very. She could be in league with her father if he were the one who had a copy of the Firestone necklace made at some point. After all he had taken photographs of it for the insurers a couple of years ago. They may have thought enough time had elapsed to attempt the theft if Baron Rochelle is indeed in financial difficulties.' Inspector Greville stroked his moustache thoughtfully.

'Of course it could all be Mrs Craven putting two and two together and coming up with five. Except there was that conversation I saw between Flora and Edward.' Kitty raised her eyebrows.

'True, but still worth knowing all the same. Of course that

could have been an innocent chat those two were having. I wish we could get a lead like that on Gunther's murder, however tenuous. His death had to be connected in some way to his espionage activities, surely. The trouble is that apart from that signal I saw from the *Sigrid* there is nothing at all to go on.' Matt took his seat back beside Kitty.

'I understand that the brigadier thought there might have been some kind of connection with the Naval College?' Inspector Greville said.

'That was his initial thought, but I haven't yet been able to dig anything up. Sorry, sir, not much use to your investigation, I'm afraid,' Matt said.

'Not to worry. If we lift enough stones, I'm certain something will scuttle into the light,' the inspector remarked.

'I presume the brigadier must have some inkling about who in the college would be in a position to hold information useful to a potentially unfriendly nation?' Kitty asked.

Matt shrugged. 'I'm rather afraid he is slightly hampered by the services liking to take care of problems themselves.'

'You mean the navy deals with naval affairs and the army should not interfere?' Inspector Greville asked.

'Something like that, I'm afraid. Oh, I believe there is cooperation at least at a higher level but I'm sure you know how it is, sir.' Matt knew the brigadier had been slightly frustrated at not being able to get a man inside the college whom he felt he could trust.

Certain information had been planted and the source of the leak could only be from a small group within the college, but how the information was being passed on was a mystery. Gunther had represented a real opportunity to finally uncover the complete trail but with his murder that chance had been scuppered.

Matt could only assume that someone had realised they were in jeopardy and had moved to eliminate the weak link,

Gunther, before they could be caught. However, if the murderer was one of the chief constable's party, then how were they linked to the dead man? Or to the college?

'Miss Underhay, may I trouble you once more for the use of your telephone? I think an early call to my colleagues in Exeter will set the ball rolling.' Inspector Greville looked at Kitty.

'Of course, Inspector. You know the way to the office,' Kitty replied.

Her pretty face was troubled as the inspector left the room to make his call. 'This is all becoming very complicated, Matt. Do you think the Firestone was ever at the Dolphin? Or do you think Sir Montague had only the fake one in his possession and didn't know it?'

Matt met her gaze. 'Or even worse he did know it. I know it's very unlikely, but we have to consider the possibility that Sir Montague staged the disappearance of the Firestone himself.'

Kitty stared at him. 'I had thought the same thing. He was next to Serafina when the necklace was snatched after all. But he is the chief constable.'

'We both know of people in high positions who have not been as honest and trustworthy as we thought they were. It is unlikely, but we need to still bear it in mind as a possibility.' Matt slipped his arm around her shoulders and gave her a quick hug. 'You look so shocked, darling. I'm sorry.'

'No, you're right, of course. It's just that Lady Rose has been Grams' friend for such a long time.' Kitty shook her head, making her blonde curls bob about her face. 'I must confess, I'm glad the whole party are gone back to Exeter. For one horrid moment I thought the luggage would have to be unloaded from the cars.'

'My poor darling, this whole affair has been a trial for you and your grandmother.' Matt tugged her to her feet. 'Let's go and see if the inspector has made his telephone calls and then, if you like, we'll go for a walk by the river and get a little air, perhaps we may find a new perspective.'

Kitty smiled at her fiancé and they walked back to the lobby to discover the inspector was just leaving the office behind the reception desk.

'Thank you, Miss Underhay. I've spoken to my colleagues in Exeter, and they have dispatched a man to visit the jewellers.' Inspector Greville paused and lowered his voice before continuing. 'While I was talking to Inspector Pinch, he informed me that Esther Hammett has been sighted in the city in the last few days. He has men watching out for her but he felt I should forewarn you.'

Matt saw the colour drain from Kitty's face at the inspector's words. Esther Hammett's brother had been responsible for the death of Kitty's mother many years before. Kitty had worked hard to prove he was responsible for her mother's murder and the man had been killed attempting to escape from justice just a few months earlier.

Esther blamed Kitty for her brother's demise and had vowed to avenge him. Only a few weeks ago the headless and decaying corpse of a rat had been left as a warning on Kitty's desk.

'Thank you, Inspector. I've been expecting her to reappear. She's like a bad smell that you can't quite get rid of.' Kitty's chin tilted defiantly upwards. 'I'll be extra vigilant but please don't let my grandmother know about this, she'll only worry.'

Matt had known that Esther would resurface. He could only hope that the woman would do something, cross a line somewhere that would actually get her arrested before she could do anything that might harm Kitty.

She had come very close once before to murdering his fiancée by cutting the cable to the brakes on Kitty's car, sending her crashing off the road into a field. If Matt had not found her when he had that night, then he was sure that Kitty would not have survived. He had lost his first wife and child in the war, and he had no intention of losing Kitty.

'Please take care, Miss Underhay, you know how dangerous the Hammett family can be,' the inspector warned. He raised his hat in farewell and stepped outside into the sunshine.

'Well, that was somewhat unexpected.' Kitty straightened her shoulders. 'I think I need that walk more than ever now.'

CHAPTER FIFTEEN

After a refreshing walk with Matt, followed by supper with her grandmother, Kitty decided on an early night. The excitement of recent events had all felt rather too much. Then the news that Esther had returned to Exeter had shaken her but it had not been unsurprising.

She could only hope that her grandmother didn't hear anything of it. Otherwise, Kitty could see herself being banished to her great-aunt Livvy's home in Scotland until either the wedding or the perceived danger from Esther had receded.

To her surprise she slept well and woke early the following day determined to make a good start on catching up on all the tasks she had pushed to one side while dealing with Serafina's birthday ball.

After rising, she made herself a cup of tea in the hotel kitchen and took it into her office behind the front desk. Mary, her receptionist, had not yet arrived for work and Bill, the night porter, nodded good morning to her as she unlocked her office door.

'Lovely day today, Miss Kitty.'

'Yes, it does look rather splendid out there,' Kitty agreed.

She had noticed the rosy glow over the mouth of the estuary as the sun made its appearance.

'Just to let you know, miss, there's been an odd-looking fellow a-hanging about the last half hour or so. I don't much care for the look of him.' Bill inclined his head towards the street.

'Oh?' Coming so quickly on top of the inspector's warning about Esther, Kitty couldn't help feeling slightly alarmed.

'I'll hang about myself for a bit after Miss Mary comes in just to be on the safe side,' Bill assured her.

Kitty blew out a breath to steady herself and tried not to show any alarm. 'Thank you, Bill. Let me know if there are any problems.'

She took her tea into her office and started to set up her work for the morning. It took a few moments and half of her cup of tea before she could concentrate properly on the tasks at hand. After a while, however, she heard Bill greeting Mary and assumed that all must now be well.

She had accomplished quite a lot of her chores by the time Dolly arrived looking fresh-faced and pretty in a pale-green cotton-print frock.

'Good morning, Miss Kitty. I've just seen Bill go off home, he's late a-going today,' Dolly remarked as she hung her straw hat on the bentwood coat stand.

The girl had scarcely had time to take her seat when Kitty heard the raised sound of a male voice in the lobby and the sound of the brass bell being 'dinged' on the reception desk.

'Whatever is a-going on out there?' Dolly rose from her seat.

'I'll go.' Kitty was swifter than her assistant and reached the door first.

A young man of a similar age to Kitty was leaning against the countertop. His charcoal-grey suit looked as if it had seen better days and the white collar of his shirt appeared dingy and frayed.

Mary was eyeing him with an icy glare. 'Please stop ringing the bell, sir. You have my full attention. How may I assist you?'

Kitty watched for a moment knowing that the man probably couldn't see her as the door to her office was partly obscured by a small noticeboard that advertised the hotel's evening entertainment.

'I'm here to see Mr Lutterworth,' the man announced.

'I see, and may I ask if he is expecting you?' Mary asked.

The man gave a short laugh. 'I doubt it very much. Just get him down here.' The man dinged the bell once more and Kitty saw her receptionist's hand twitch as if she longed to smack his fingers away from the bell.

'I'm afraid I will need a name, sir,' Mary said.

'Just get Lutterworth down here.' The man leaned further forward over the reception desk and Kitty stepped out of her office into the lobby.

'We shall do no such thing unless you provide a name and state your business,' Kitty said.

The man took his attention from Mary to stare at Kitty. 'Now you listen up, blondie, be a good girl and fetch the hotel manager.'

Mary's eyes rounded at the temerity of the man's words.

'I am the hotel owner and I suggest that you leave immediately before my assistant telephones the police. Whatever your business with Mr Lutterworth, I suggest you conduct it elsewhere.' Kitty drew herself up to her full five foot two inches.

A sneer passed across the man's face. 'All right, blondie, keep your hair on, just tell him that Henry called to see him.'

Much to Kitty's relief the man removed himself from the counter and, after a salacious wink in Mary's direction, sauntered out of the lobby and away up the street.

'Oh my word, Miss Kitty, what a horrible man. How do you think he knows our Mr Lutterworth?' Mary asked.

'I don't know but it is quite concerning. I expect Cyril will be down here shortly. Please send him in to see me when he arrives.' Kitty turned to return to her office, almost tripping over Dolly who had crept out behind her to see what was going on.

'That was quite a scene. 'Tis a good thing as the guests were all in breakfast.' Dolly shook her head in dismay.

Kitty had been having the same thought. She hoped that would be the last appearance of 'Henry', or anyone else like him asking for their new manager.

Mr Lutterworth arrived shortly afterwards looking as dapper as ever in his neatly pressed suit and fresh pink rosebud in his buttonhole.

His face was grave as he entered Kitty's office. 'My dear Miss Underhay, Mary has just informed me of the visitor that called earlier.'

'I presume you know the young man in question? This Henry?' Kitty asked.

Mr Lutterworth sighed and bowed his head in acknowledgement. 'Unfortunately, I do. You will recall that I mentioned my late sister's child? My nephew, and that I said I feared he had not turned out well?'

'I presume Henry is this nephew?' Kitty said.

Mr Lutterworth nodded, looking quite distressed by the admission. 'I can only apologise, Miss Underhay. I shall have strong words with that young man to ensure that this doesn't happen again.'

'I take it that you were not anticipating such a visit?' Kitty asked. She could see that the older man was clearly perturbed by news of Henry's appearance at the hotel.

'No, Miss Underhay, I wasn't. However, I must be honest with you and say that it shouldn't have surprised me that he has called or that he behaved in such an obnoxious manner. His father was a very similar character and led my poor sister quite a dance.'

Dolly raised her eyebrows at this and caught Kitty's gaze.

'Do you know why he may have called?' Kitty asked.

A faint dismissive snort escaped from Mr Lutterworth. 'The only reason Henry has ever called on me is to try and extract money. Up until my poor sister's death I sent money regularly to assist her. I knew that he probably took most of it from her, but I did what I could to ensure she had a roof over her head and food to eat. I asked her many times to come to London and she could lodge with me, but she refused to leave her son.'

'Oh dear,' Dolly murmured sympathetically.

'Indeed, Miss Miller. Up until the day she died, Maude persisted in believing that young wastrel would come good. She believed all his excuses about why he was let go from so many jobs, why people thought ill of him and that it wasn't his fault. He was misunderstood. As you have seen for yourselves, he is boorish and deeply unpleasant and that is with the, I think, somewhat generous version of events that Mary has relayed to me.'

'I'm so sorry, Mr Lutterworth. You can't choose your family though, can you? You'm stuck with them,' Dolly remarked.

'One cannot escape the relationship, that's true, Miss Miller, but one can choose how it is acknowledged. When I moved here I had hoped to learn he had reformed. It seems that is not the case and I think it best to put paid to any financial expectations Henry may have sooner rather than later, or I fear he may try to become something of a nuisance.' Mr Lutterworth's mouth set in a grim line.

'If you need some time to deal with the matter, please feel free to go and find him. I agree with you that it is best dealt with quickly,' Kitty said.

'Thank you, Miss Underhay. I am most obliged. I daresay he has headed back to Paignton and whichever public house is likely to open its doors at an early hour.' Mr Lutterworth's tone was bleak. 'I shall be back as swiftly as possible, and I assure you he will not be returning here again in a hurry.'

He strode out of the office leaving Dolly and Kitty to their work.

'Bless me, Miss Kitty. 'Tis all happening around here just lately,' Dolly remarked as she flexed her fingers ready to start her typing.

Kitty agreed with her young assistant. It seemed that even their new hotel manager had secrets.

* * *

Matt was having an interesting morning of a different kind. It had started with a telephone call from London in the middle of breakfast.

'Matthew, I'm calling to find out the latest on Freiberg's murder. Greville's not at his desk yet. Something about a valuable stolen necklace, so the sergeant chappie said.' Matt moved the black Bakelite telephone receiver a little further away from his ear.

Brigadier Remmington-Blythe had a tendency to shout into the telephone as if under the impression that the normal volume of his voice would not be sufficient to travel along the wires.

Matt provided the brigadier with a succinct explanation of both the happenings in the murder enquiry and also the mystery of the stolen necklace. 'We can see no connection between the two incidents, but it is troubling.'

'Hmm, I did some digging on Sir Montague Hawkes and the fella is as clean as a whistle. Nothing shady in his past, so far as I can ascertain. Lady Rose is one of Miss Underhay's grandmother's friends, I believe. Known each other since their younger years, again, nothing there. No money troubles or stories of drinking or gaming.'

Matt tried to imagine Sir Montague or Lady Rose in a gambling den and failed. He was not surprised that the brigadier hadn't discovered anything untoward with either of them.

'Yes, sir, Mrs Treadwell, Lady Rose and Mrs Craven are good friends.'

'Mrs Craven? Oh good heavens, yes, the former mayoress of Dartmouth. Encountered her before in some of the other cases, haven't you?' The brigadier guffawed down the phone and Matt winced as his employer's laugh devolved into a momentary hacking cough.

'Yes, sir, Mrs C is a force to be reckoned with. She was on the train when Travers was killed a few weeks ago.' The murder in the first-class carriage had been another case that the brigadier had involved him in. That case had led to him inheriting Bertie.

'Hmm, now this Baron Rochelle on the other hand, I asked for reports on the entire group by the way, and this one is a very dodgy blighter. Nothing definite, but a shady character. French, of course, and poor as the proverbial church mouse. Moves around taking extended stays with whichever wealthy friends he and his daughter can leech off. Some questionable financial shenanigans.'

'Apparently he saved Sir Montague's life some years back, hence the friendship,' Matt said.

'Hmm, did he now? Well, the baron has severe money problems and his debtors are growing more pressing. There's a rumour circulating that he may have to declare bankruptcy. He's been trying to get his daughter a wealthy suitor, splashing out on gowns and such, taking her to various soirées, but to no avail. What's she like?' the brigadier asked.

'Pretty and knows it. I don't think a wealthy marriage is a solution she is particularly keen on from what I've seen.' Matt couldn't say that the baron's daughter was particularly flirtatious from his brief observations. She had seemed aware of her attractiveness but that was all.

'Then there's that Forbes chap.' The brigadier's tone changed slightly.

'Miss Serafina's beau. No one seems to know too much about him. Not sure if he is a local man or from London. He dresses well and has an expensive watch and taste in footwear. Lady Rose said he was a broker or banker?' Matt said.

'He has an office in the city and on the surface seems to keep the right company. There's nothing certain but I don't know how much is window dressing, and how much is substance. No one seems to know much about his family or where his money has come from.' The brigadier sounded thoughtful.

'I take it that Sir Montague's children are in the clear? Miss Serafina and Master Theodore?' Matt asked.

He knew the brigadier would have been thorough in his checks of all members of the party.

'Miss Serafina is reputed to be something of a bluestocking. She attends a lot of gallery openings and exhibits. She applied for a fine arts course, but her father has consistently refused to allow her to attend any kind of education. Something that has not sat well with the young lady. She has expressed her opinions forcibly and publicly on the matter on several occasions.'

Matt could see that might be why Theo had thought his sister didn't wish for a proposal from Mr Forbes. Her parents were clearly keen to see her married, and presumably Sir Montague felt this would put a stop to any ambitions of studying.

'You say this has not gone down well with Serafina, sir?'

The brigadier chuckled. 'No, not at all, the young lady seems to have found various classes and opportunities to enhance her education without her father's knowledge or permission.'

'And young Theodore?' Matt asked. He wasn't terribly fond of the youth given the boy's clumsy attempt to flirt with Kitty.

'Ah, the usual strivings of a young man attempting to make a mark on the world. He has a place at Cambridge and is reported to be quite bright, but is somewhat gullible and easily led. Some gambling and drinking, mixing with a bit of an odd crowd.' The brigadier sounded thoughtful again. 'He has already spent a good deal of his allowance in a very short space of time. He owed quite a sum at one time, but that has all been cleared in the last few weeks.'

'Thank you, sir. It sounds as if there are possibilities with all of them, both for the murder and for the theft of the necklace. If we could just find the link back to the Naval College then that would help enormously with a possible motive for Freiberg's murder. It could help us determine if there is any kind of link to the Hawkes' party. I have it on authority from the harbour master that the *Sigrid* is to sail on the morning tide tomorrow.' Matt had made discreet enquiries amongst his connections.

'The sooner she is gone the better. I can't see how anyone on board would have had a motive for murdering Gunther. He was the postman, so to speak, as far as we are aware. With him gone they will have to find a new fellow to deliver the goods. Do you know if she is due back again?' the brigadier asked.

'She returns again in about three weeks I believe, sir. It's a regular run for her.' Matt tried not to let his frustrations show in his tone.

It aggravated him that the ship and her crew was to sail unimpeded. Who knew what secrets they might be carrying with them.

'Right ho, pass this info onto Greville, it may prove helpful to the inquiry. I expect your young lady is involved with the investigation?' the brigadier asked.

'Of course, sir.' Matt suspected that the brigadier knew full well that Kitty was bound to be involved even if the incidents had not taken place right on her doorstep so to speak.

'Jolly good show. Keep me informed of any progress.' The brigadier rang off leaving Matt with plenty to consider.

Certainly, the information about the baron tied in with Mrs Craven's story. Then there was the mysterious Edward Forbes. It also seemed the baron's daughter and even Theo could not be discounted as suspects. Most interesting right now though was the question of how Theo had cleared his debts?

CHAPTER SIXTEEN

Kitty listened attentively as Matt passed on the brigadier's information while they ate an informal supper. She had driven her small red car to Matt's house, and they were dining together accompanied by Bertie the dog.

In return she told him of Mr Lutterworth's unwelcome visitor. Bertie lay hopefully at her feet under the table as they tucked into the toad-in-the-hole and mashed potatoes that Matt's housekeeper had provided for their meal.

'That does sound interesting but where do we go from here?' Kitty asked as she snuck a piece of sausage under the table to the dog. 'With the investigation into Gunther's death, I mean? Sir Montague and his family are all back in Exeter and the *Sigrid* sails first thing.'

Matt rested his fork down on his plate and poured some more beer into his glass. 'I'm not sure. I wish we had some way of getting into the Naval College. It seems to me that if we could somehow find the link to how information could possibly get from the college to someone like Gunther it would help us enormously.'

Kitty frowned. 'Maybe, but we can't escape the fact that

Gunther must have been killed by someone in Sir Montague's party. Why was he killed? And why that evening? Surely whoever did it must have realised that they would be suspected? It was such a daring thing to do. I mean with the chief constable right there.'

'Sir Montague's party were only staying overnight and returning to Exeter the next day, so there was a limited window of time from that point of view.' Matt sipped his drink.

'So, the supposition is that whoever killed him couldn't afford to be seen here outside that time or who had no other way to get back here? Or is there something else entirely that we are missing?' Kitty's frown deepened as she thought about Matt's reply.

'Or did Gunther say or do something during that evening on the boat that meant he had to die that night?' Matt set his glass down and resumed eating his meal.

'Perhaps then we need to try and find out what went on earlier during the dinner party? Before the boat returned to dock?' Kitty said. 'What about the other crewman who was with Gunther on the boat, he may have witnessed something? Some kind of interaction? Or even the captain? The inspector has asked them about the end of the evening but not much about when they first boarded the boat.'

Matt appeared to consider her questions as he finished his meal. 'I suppose it's worth a shot. All of the Hawkes' party denied knowing Gunther. They said they hadn't met him before, but one of them killed him and you don't tend to go around murdering complete strangers at random for no reason.'

'Especially when you are with the chief constable and attending a party as his guest.' Kitty raised her own glass of ale and chinked it against Matt's. 'I think we may have found a lead.'

There was a muffled woof of agreement from beneath the table at the mention of a lead.

'The business of the necklace is a puzzle too. I wonder if Inspector Pinch uncovered anything when his men went to interview the jeweller in Exeter?' Kitty said as she stacked their empty dinner plates ready to take them to the kitchen.

'It would be interesting to know. However I don't suppose the jewellers will admit to any kind of negligence while the necklace was in their care,' Matt said.

'It simply must have been the genuine article that they retrieved from the bank vault for cleaning and repair. They would have noticed a forgery straight away and raised the alarm with Sir Montague,' Kitty called over her shoulder as she carried the crockery away.

She returned in a couple of minutes bearing two dishes containing apple pie and another dish with clotted cream.

'That's true. So, if the real necklace was received by them, either the substitution took place there or afterwards when Sir Montague took it from the vault and came here.' Matt's brow creased in concentration.

Kitty sighed as she helped herself to a large dollop of cream. 'Unfortunately, Sir Montague doesn't appear to have much information on the matter. From what he told the inspector he barely gave the necklace a glance after he collected it before he placed it around Serafina's neck.'

Matt dug into his slice of pie with his spoon. 'That necklace seems to have spent all of its time in various safes and vaults. I think Serafina may have had a point when she said she didn't think it was much of a gift.'

'From what the brigadier told you this morning I suspect money would have been much more welcome so she would have been free to do what she wished,' Kitty said, savouring the rich goodness of the crusted top of the cream. She couldn't help feeling rather sorry for Serafina. It was no wonder the girl always appeared to have a chip on her shoulder.

Since their engagement these cosy informal suppers at

Matt's home had become one of the highlights of her week. It gave her and Matt the opportunity to relax together in private. She hoped this would be a good pointer to what their married life would be like.

'Theodore seemed rather sour about Serafina receiving the necklace,' Matt observed.

'I asked Grams about it and she said there is no matching heirloom to be handed down on the male side, but he will inherit Priory Hall, that's the family home, and there is quite a large sum of money his grandfather left in trust for him for when he is twenty-five.' Kitty placed her spoon down in the empty bowl with a small sigh of regret.

Matt's housekeeper was a very good plain cook and the supper she had left for them had been delicious.

'That money is still seven years away and from what the brigadier said Master Theo is quite good at spending his allowance.' Matt smiled at Kitty.

'I believe that is not an uncommon situation when young people leave home for the first time and have to learn how to manage things for themselves. Theo seems quite impressionable. I wonder how he managed to clear his debts? I doubt his father would have bailed him out,' Kitty said.

'Perhaps Lady Rose may have helped him without Sir Montague knowing,' Matt suggested.

'I suppose that's possible.' Kitty thought Matt might have a point.

'I keep thinking about how the theft of the necklace was managed. When the lights failed, Sir Montague was next to Serafina. The compère had stepped away. Mrs C said Flora had left the room.' Matt looked at Kitty.

'Lady Rose was at the side of the stage with Grams. Edward had been nearby too, I think. He was certainly near Flora earlier. I don't recall where Theo was or the baron.' Kitty started to clear the dishes.

'Darling, I'll take those in and make us some coffee.' Matt took them from her. 'Shall we go and sit out in the garden for a while? It's still a fine evening.'

Kitty agreed and followed Bertie out through the open French windows to take a seat on the wooden bench beneath the apple tree. Matt's garden afforded a view over the fields with a distant glimpse of the sea, sparkling like silver in the late evening sun.

Kitty draped her dark-blue cardigan around her shoulders and leaned back contentedly to listen to the bees humming amongst the last of the blowsy pink summer roses. The problem of the Firestone necklace and Gunther's murder seemed very far away.

Matt appeared a little later carrying a small round metal tray with a chrome coffee pot and a couple of cups, with a jug of cream. He set it down on the rustic wooden table in front of the bench.

'I hope Mr Lutterworth settles in all right, Kitty.' He poured coffee into a cup and handed it over to her so she could help herself to cream.

'Me too. Our wedding is getting closer now. Going for the first meeting with the dressmaker made it all seem much more real somehow. I really want to be certain that the Dolphin will be in good hands so Grams doesn't have to worry.'

Matt helped himself to coffee and sat beside her, his weight making the bench creak as he stretched out his long legs. Bertie roused his head and sniffed the air in anticipation of the biscuit he knew that Matt had carried outside for him in his jacket pocket.

'I'm sure it will be fine, old thing. This issue with the nephew will settle down. Cyril seems a very capable man. The Porteboys Club seemed to be very well run under his stewardship.'

Kitty smiled at her fiancé. 'I do hope so. Grams is still not as well as I would like her to be. She puts a brave face on things but, honestly, I'm a little worried about her. She needs to be taking it easy. This business with the Hawkes family hasn't helped.'

Matt slipped his arm around her shoulders, and she snuggled against him as they gazed out at the sun setting over the sea. The silver water turning pink and gold with the reflection from the sky. Bertie lay contentedly at their feet crunching on his biscuit.

'It's all very new at the moment remember. Mr Lutterworth has barely had a chance to unpack his trunk. I'm sure your grandmother will start to feel better now all the stress of Serafina's party is over. I know she and Lady Rose are great friends, but it has been a lot of work even without the necklace incident.'

Kitty knew he was probably right, but she couldn't help worrying. Her grandmother had done so much for her. She had raised Kitty alone ever since Kitty's mother had vanished in 1916. Now she deserved to have time to travel, relax and enjoy herself with her friends.

Matt took her hand in his, gently touching her emerald and diamond engagement ring which was an heirloom from Matt's family. 'Darling, promise me that you'll take extra care while Esther Hammett is back in Exeter.'

Kitty swallowed, the familiar shiver of fear making itself known along her spine. 'You know that I will. She has tried and failed before to harm me. I doubt if she will be tempted to try repeating any of those methods.' She only hoped Esther wouldn't try any more drastic measures to be revenged on her.

The shadowy figure of Esther and her late brother haunted her. The Hammett family had managed in the past to infiltrate the police and were responsible for crimes not just locally but also in the capital. She wished she knew how Esther managed to keep evading arrest and prison.

'Even so, be careful where you park the car and check underneath it for any sign of leaks before you get in. You know I could not bear it if anything were to happen to you.' His gaze locked with hers.

'I promise I shall take great care.' Kitty gave his fingers a gentle squeeze of reassurance.

She was determined to take every precaution she could against Esther Hammett. Matt waved her off home an hour or so later having arranged to meet her the following day to interview the other crew member of the paddle steamer.

Kitty had just opened her eyes the following morning when there was a tap on her door and Alice arrived bearing the morning tea tray.

'Morning, Miss Kitty. The weather has turned today, proper miserable it is out there,' the maid announced morosely as she deposited the tray on Kitty's bedside table, before whisking the curtains open to let in the pallid morning light.

Kitty sat up and straightened her bed covers while Alice poured them both a cup of tea, before perching herself on the edge of Kitty's bed.

'I heard all about the kerfuffle yesterday with that there necklace, miss. They say as it weren't the real diamonds after all?' The girl's eyes were wide as she peered over the brim of her cup.

'No, it seems someone made a copy of the Firestone necklace and substituted it for the real thing. Sir Montague only noticed at the last minute as they were about to leave.' Kitty assumed either Mary or Dolly had told Alice all about the events of yesterday.

'That must have taken some planning,' Alice said in a thoughtful tone. 'Not exactly something done on the fly.'

'I agree. Inspector Pinch is making some enquiries at the

jewellers in Exeter. They had the necklace for cleaning just before Sir Montague came away.' Kitty stirred her tea and settled back against her pillows.

'I don't suppose he'll find much out. In the film I saw the other week the gang made impressions of the jewels in clay and then had some dodgy place make up the fake. It would only take a few minutes to get the impressions. The innocent people were none the wiser. At least that was what I saw in the cinema when I went with Robert Potter.'

Kitty knew her friend was very fond of the movies. 'I expect you're right, Alice. I suppose the Firestone necklace is long gone. The centre stone was very valuable. The other thing the inspector told me was that Esther Hammett is back in Exeter.'

Alarm spread across her friend's face. 'Then you keep well away from there, Miss Kitty.'

'I shall, Alice, have no fear of that.' Kitty gave a small shudder.

Her friend looked relieved at the reassurance. 'Have they caught whoever killed that German man yet, miss?' Alice asked as she topped up Kitty's teacup with the last of the tea from the small chrome pot.

'No, not yet. It's a most peculiar affair. Matt and I intend to talk to the crew of the paddle steamer again today. There must be something that we've missed that will shed light on it,' Kitty said.

'Well, the captain has a good reputation in the town. He attends the Methodist Hall and he doesn't touch the drink, which as you know for a sailor is an uncommon thing. Everyone reckons him to be a very honest bloke,' Alice said before she finished her tea.

'There was another crewman on the night of Serafina's party. He left the boat when it moored. I think he worked in the engine room,' Kitty said. She knew Alice's family knew virtually everyone in the small riverside town.

The murder would have been the talk of the place so she guessed her friend would know who she meant.

'That'll be Herbert Moody. He's worked on the river ever since he were a lad. Lives by himself since his mother died. He's in one of the cottages up near where Mickey lives.' Alice collected up Kitty's empty cup and placed it back on the tray with her own.

'I reckon as you'll find him down on the water if he's working on the paddle boat. Keeps himself to himself he does. Not a great talker mind, so I don't know if he'll tell you much,' Alice warned as she prepared to return to her duties.

'Thank you, Alice. At least we can try,' Kitty thanked her friend.

Alice had certainly given her something to think about. The captain's reputation was clearly good so no wonder the inspector had found him to be a reliable witness. Perhaps this Mr Moody might have some information for them.

Kitty dressed with care in a heather-coloured tweed two-piece suit and pale-green blouse. The weather had definitely turned cooler overnight. A reminder that autumn would soon be upon them.

She joined her grandmother for breakfast in her private apartment.

'Good morning, Kitty darling.'

'Morning, Grams.' Kitty took her seat after kissing her grandmother's cheek and helped herself to toast and marmalade.

She thought her grandmother looked tired and pale in the grey light coming through the large, leaded bay window.

'I heard that Mr Lutterworth had an unwanted visitor yesterday?'

Kitty paused in her toast buttering. 'Yes, the disreputable nephew, Henry, showed up. Cyril went off to deal with him. He has assured me that we won't have any further problems with him.'

Mrs Treadwell's elegantly arched brows rose. 'I do hope so. Mr Lutterworth has seemed most capable so far, especially with all the difficulties over Serafina's party. I would hate this nephew to cause problems.'

'He is working with Dolly today. I thought it would be good to give him some space to settle in without feeling as if I am constantly checking on him.' Kitty took a bite of her toast and chewed it thoughtfully.

'Very wise, my dear. I have a luncheon date with Millicent, followed by a visit to a friend in Torquay this afternoon and then I am dining out. I shan't return until late evening,' Kitty's grandmother announced.

Kitty was relieved her grandmother had made some plans. 'That sounds nice.' She was sure that the break from running the hotel would do her good. She had been worried that her grandmother might find it difficult to step away from overseeing the management of the Dolphin.

'And what are your plans for the day, my dear? I hope you are going to rest after all the effort you made to try and ensure Serafina's celebrations ran smoothly.' Her grandmother took the top off her boiled egg with a silver teaspoon.

'I think Matt and I are going to potter around town. He's bringing Bertie down later,' Kitty dissembled slightly, knowing how her grandmother felt about her involvement in Matt's cases.

'It's such a shame the weather appears to have broken. Still, I don't suppose the dog will mind too much.' Her grandmother gave her a benign smile.

Matt duly arrived shortly after breakfast, having taken the local bus down to Kingswear before crossing the river as a foot passenger. Bertie rushed straight up to Kitty and immediately gave himself a good shake, sending small droplets of water all over the lobby.

'Sorry, Kitty,' Matt apologised as he carefully held his wet, black umbrella over the doormat at the entrance.

Kitty laughed. 'It's quite all right. I hadn't realised it was raining so much.'

'It's just a shower. It had almost stopped by the time I got here. We just got a little damp when we came off the ferry. It is supposed to improve later.' Matt glanced over his shoulder at the dull, grey street beyond the revolving door.

'I'll get my hat.' Kitty stepped into her office to collect her outdoor things, leaving Matt to talk to Mary at reception for a moment.

She took her things from the stand as quietly as she could not wishing to disturb Dolly or Mr Lutterworth, who appeared to be working on the book work for the hotel. They barely seemed to notice her presence and she slipped back out into the lobby satisfied that all seemed to be well with her new employee.

'Alice has given me the name of the man we need to see and where we are likely to find him,' Kitty told Matt as she buttoned up her jacket.

'Is that Mr Moody?' Matt asked. 'I checked with Inspector Greville to obtain his name.'

'That's the one.' Kitty hoped it wouldn't rain too heavily while they were talking to Mr Moody. Matt's umbrella might not provide much protection if the wind gusted in from the estuary.

She tugged on her gloves and stepped out next to Matt as they left the Dolphin. Bertie trotted on ahead of them, his nose to the ground and his plumed tail waving like a flag. The captain had been given permission to resume his business. The wet weather, however, meant that the *Kingswear Castle* had not embarked on a day trip to Dittisham and was moored in its usual space.

The wooden gangplank was in place, but the gate was closed, preventing entry onto the boat. Kitty peered through the faint drizzle at the wheelhouse.

'I think the captain is on board.'

Matt raised his hand to wave at the figure and a moment later the captain walked out to greet them.

'Good morning. Miss Underhay, isn't it, from the Dolphin? How can I help you?' The man nodded to Kitty. She had made some of the arrangements with him for Serafina's party and no doubt he recalled her from the other night.

'This is Captain Bryant. I'm sure you'll remember that we were both here with Inspector Greville when Herr Freiberg was murdered. May we come aboard for a moment?' Kitty asked.

'Aye, I recollect you well enough, Captain Bryant. Terrible business that murder.' The captain unlatched the gate and allowed them onto the boat. 'Come down to the saloon out the weather.' He led the way down the steps to the room they had visited previously.

Kitty was quite glad to be out of the drizzle. Bertie sighed and flopped down at Matt's feet as they took a seat at the captain's invitation.

'How can I be of assistance, Miss Underhay?' the man asked.

'We wondered if you might spare us a few moments just to check on a few things. You and Mr Moody, if he is free?' Kitty asked.

'I am assisting the police in the investigation.' Matt produced his business card from the silver holder that he kept inside the breast pocket of his jacket.

The man glanced at the card and tucked it away inside the

top pocket of his navy woollen jacket. 'Aye, as I said I remember you, sir. What is it that you want to ask?'

'I believe Herr Freiberg had worked for you before the evening of the party?' Matt said.

'Yes, he had. I told the inspector that. Gunther worked for quite a few of the boats hereabouts. He was a good worker. Always on time and didn't go slacking off like some as you gets.' The captain scratched the side of his grizzled head.

'When the chief constable's party boarded the boat did you notice if any of the members of the party seemed to know Gunther at all? Recognise him in any way?' Kitty asked.

'I were in the wheelhouse when they come aboard. Gunther greeted them and let them settle to their places before we made ready to cast off.' The captain frowned.

'Did you see him speak to any of them or they to him?' Kitty asked.

'I wouldn't like to say for certain, Miss Underhay, but I think as he exchanged words with the young lad and the well-dressed young man. It were probably only to answer a question though, miss. Nothing that would have stood out like. Oh, and the older Frenchman, he were taking a picture.' The captain seemed pleased at his recall of this particular event.

'Thank you, Captain. Is Mr Moody on board?' Kitty asked.

'Aye, miss, he's in the engine room.' A shadow passed over the man's face at the mention of the area where Gunther had been killed.

'Would you mind asking him if he could spare us a minute?' Matt asked.

'Aye.' The captain got to his feet and left the saloon, returning a moment later with a middle-aged man dressed in navy coveralls that appeared to be liberally spread with grease.

'This is Mr Moody. He were just doing some maintenance on the engine.' The captain ducked back out of the room, leaving them with the crewman.

'I won't sit if it's all the same to you, sir, miss. On account of the oil. I don't want to mark the seats.' The man had a soft local burr to his voice as he stood rather awkwardly in front of them.

'Of course, Mr Moody. This won't take very long. We're terribly grateful to you for sparing us the time to answer a few questions,' Kitty said.

'On the night Herr Freiberg was killed you were looking after the engine?' Matt asked.

'That's right, sir. The captain was doing the steering and overseeing everything while Gunther did the fancy work, serving the drinks and dinner and all. I saw as the engine were stoked and running smooth and did the casting off and on.' The words came out in a bit of a rush and Kitty noticed that the man was constantly fiddling with the side seam of his overalls.

'You didn't have much to do with the party then?' Kitty asked.

'No, miss. My job is more looking after the engine, we'm coal-fired see,' the man replied.

'And you left the boat that night once she was tied back up at her mooring?' Matt verified.

'Aye, sir. My part were done then.' Mr Moody shuffled his feet as if eager for the questions to be over.

Bertie let out another sigh and flopped onto his side as if tired of the whole proceedings.

'Did you see Herr Freiberg talk to any of the passengers as if they had met before at any time?' Kitty asked.

The crewman looked confused. 'I don't rightly know, miss. He brought them on board. I were on the bank then waiting to cast off once they were all settled in like. The Frenchman he took a photograph I think, and Gunther spoke with a couple of the men.'

This seemed to tie in with what the captain had witnessed. The man was looking as if he wished to be dismissed when Kitty had a thought.

'Mr Moody, did it surprise you that Gunther was killed in the engine room?' she asked.

Matt glanced at her.

'Aye, miss. It did. I mean he had no business to go in there and usually 'tis kept locked once we've docked and everything has been shut down like.'

'Could he have had a reason to go in there? The electrical power or anything?' Kitty suggested. She had no idea of what might be in the engine room beyond the engine, but wanted to hear Mr Moody's thoughts.

'No, miss. If'n there were a problem then the captain would see to it. Gunther were just the steward. He had all the things for the party set up in the fore saloon. He had no call to have fetched a key to go in the engine room.' The crewman looked shocked by Kitty's suggestion.

'Where was the key usually kept?' Matt asked.

'Captain has the master key and I usually gets it from out the little cupboard there, sir. Near the door to the room.' Mr Moody turned to Matt.

'So, anyone could have taken the key and unlocked it? I assume that you locked it when you left?' Matt asked.

'Of course, sir. This ship is my baby. Takes a lot of care to make sure as she runs nice and smooth. Not many paddle steamers hereabouts so I takes pride in her.' Mr Moody raised his chin to meet Matt's gaze.

It was clear the man took care over his work. It sounded as if Gunther or one of the guests had opened the door to the engine room. Had Gunther been lured there to meet his murderer? Or had he gone there to make an assignation? Perhaps to deliver or receive something?

'Where was Gunther when you left the boat?' Kitty asked.

The man shrugged. 'He were on deck opening champagne or something like for the party. They had finished their first course and was on the second. I just raised my hand to him and went home.'

'And you didn't see or hear anything untoward during the evening?' Kitty asked one last question.

'Can't hear much of anything when they wheels is turning and you'm downstairs, miss. I did think as how I saw one of the young ladies in the corridor speaking to him when I looked out the door one time. I expects as she were asking for the ladies' room.' Mr Moody glanced between Matt and Kitty as if seeking reassurance from them that this must be a good guess.

'I expect so. Which young lady was it?' Kitty asked. She expected to hear it was Flora for some reason.

'The one having the birthday,' Mr Moody said.

This wasn't the answer she had anticipated, and she wondered if the encounter had been for the reason Mr Moody had put forward.

'Thank you, Mr Moody. No doubt we are keeping you from your work. That's been most helpful.' Matt thanked the man and the crewman escaped back to his beloved engine room.

The drizzle had stopped by the time they emerged onto the deck of the boat. Matt furled his umbrella as Kitty took Bertie's lead.

'It seems to be brightening up a little.' She could see the cloud had lifted over the estuary and patches of blue sky had appeared.

They waved farewell to the captain and stepped ashore.

'Now what?' Kitty asked as they strolled along the damp embankment. Bertie, happy to be back on dry land, trotted ahead on his lead.

CHAPTER SEVENTEEN

'Miss Underhay, Captain Bryant!'

They halted and turned around to see who could be hailing them.

'Inspector Greville.' Kitty was surprised to see the policeman coming towards them.

'This was a stroke of luck seeing you both.' The inspector raised his hat to Kitty as Bertie investigated his ankles.

'Oh?' Kitty said as she tugged Bertie away from the policeman's bootlaces.

'I've just come from Herr Freiberg's lodging house.' Inspector Greville lowered his voice and glanced around to ensure they could not be overheard.

'Perhaps we should go and get some tea out of this wind, and you can tell us all about it, sir,' Matt suggested as a gust threatened to tear Kitty's favourite hat from her head.

The inspector agreed to the suggestion, and they hurried to the café on the Butterwalk. Kitty hoped Bertie would behave himself while they were inside. Once they had been seated and their order taken, Kitty drew off her cotton gloves and looked expectantly at the inspector.

'I've been talking to Herr Freiberg's landlady. I took the liberty of taking along some of the baron's photographs from the party. The photography studio in Torquay has developed the films for us. The photographer gave up his whole day yesterday to develop them. I thought it worth seeing if she recognised any of the people,' Inspector Greville said.

'Oh, good thinking, Inspector. And did she?' Kitty was impressed at the inspector's initiative.

She was forced to curb her impatience while the waitress delivered their pot of tea and a plate of sponge fingers.

'She said that Herr Freiberg didn't usually have visitors to the house. However, she identified Edward Forbes. She said she'd seen him talking to Gunther the day before the party. Out in the street she said, near the house. She was on her way to her sister's when she saw them together.' The inspector loaded his cake plate up with sponge.

'That's very interesting.' Matt glared at Bertie who had developed a sudden interest in the inspector's plate.

'She also said that Mr Forbes was accompanied by a young lady.' The inspector leaned back in his seat and munched happily on his cake.

'Serafina or Flora?' Kitty asked.

'Mademoiselle Rochelle. She picked her out on the photographs as well.' The inspector brushed cake crumbs from the front of his coat onto the floor where Bertie pounced hopefully.

Matt gave the inspector the information they had gleaned from Mr Moody.

'It sounds as if he intended to meet someone and didn't wish to be seen. I can see no other reason for his being in the engine room. He was wearing his steward's clothes and the engine room is a mucky place,' Inspector Greville mused.

'Or he was expecting to be paid?' Kitty suggested. 'Someone had to be rewarding him for passing on information, surely?'

She could see what the inspector meant about the engine room. She had taken great care herself the night of the murder not to get soot on her dress.

'It seems to me as if Mr Forbes and Mademoiselle Rochelle have some explaining to do. They both denied knowing Herr Freiberg when I interviewed them. I intend to go to Exeter this afternoon to talk to them both again.' The inspector sipped his tea.

The mention of Exeter reminded Kitty about the necklace. 'Did Inspector Pinch learn anything from the jeweller, sir?' Kitty asked.

'The shop manager confirmed he had accompanied Sir Montague to the bank where the Firestone jewels were collected from the vault and signed into their custody. The necklace was with them for three days. During that time, it was cleaned, and a small repair made on the setting of the main stone. After which time Sir Montague collected it and presumably that was when he set off for Dartmouth, on the day of Serafina's birthday.' Inspector Greville looked mournfully at the now empty cake plate.

'I presume he has looked into the members of staff at the jewellers? They are all above board?' Kitty asked.

'So far as we know. The staff who handled the necklace have all worked there for quite some time. Such a prestigious and valuable piece was handled only by senior staff. The very nature of their business means that they are most security conscious,' the inspector confirmed.

'It sounds as if the copy of the necklace can't have been made then.' Matt leaned back in his chair.

'I doubt if the forgery could have been made locally. It would have been too risky and I'm not sure the expertise would have been there. No, for my money the most likely place is Birmingham. The inspector has made enquiries with the police force there.'

Kitty could see why the inspector would think this might be likely. Birmingham had a reputation for its excellence in jewellery manufacture. 'I suppose it might also be where the original necklace could get taken to be broken up and disposed of?' she suggested.

'Indeed, Miss Underhay, either there or London. The piece is quite well known for the quality of the stones it contained. The name Firestone referred to the central stone as it refracted and reflected light in a very particular way.' Inspector Greville dabbed at the corners of his mouth with the cream linen napkin from the table.

'I wonder if Sir Montague will gift Serafina the money from the insurers? After all, the necklace was technically hers at the time it was stolen,' Kitty said thoughtfully. Somehow, she thought that was unlikely. Serafina's father did not seem to wish his daughter to have any independence.

The inspector looked at his now empty teacup and sighed. 'I had better get off to Exeter.'

'I don't suppose I could accompany you, sir?' Matt asked. 'Only, the brigadier is very keen to try to discover who the source of the leaked secrets might be. Gunther was his main lead on the matter as you know. It could be that this Forbes chap or Mademoiselle Rochelle may have pertinent information.'

'Of course,' the inspector agreed quite readily.

Kitty suppressed a sigh of her own. She could see that she was about to be sidelined and no doubt expected to take care of Bertie too.

'I think it may be better, Kitty, if you steer clear of Exeter for now while Esther Hammett is back in the city.' Matt's expression was grave.

Although it irked her, Kitty could see the sense in this. It was better to lie low and hope that Esther would forget her ridiculous vendetta.

'Very well, but only if you promise to tell me everything when you return,' she agreed. 'And I suppose I am to look after Bertie?'

The dog lifted his head at the mention of his name and dribbled onto the toe of her black patent shoe.

'Would you mind terribly, old thing?' Matt asked.

'I suppose not,' she agreed. She did mind really, and Matt probably knew it. Not the looking after Bertie part. She was very fond of Matt's dog; it was more that she would far rather have accompanied them to Exeter to hear what Flora and Edward had to say for themselves.

* * *

Matt paid the bill at the tea room and left Kitty to finish her tea, while he accompanied the inspector to where the policeman had parked his motor car. The weather had lifted, and the drizzle had ceased. Over the river a weak and watery sun was attempting to break through the clouds.

'I expect Miss Underhay would have liked to accompany us?' Inspector Greville observed as he started the engine.

'Of course, you know Kitty,' Matt agreed as he cracked open the passenger side window to allow a flow of air into the car.

'It's all a bit tricky with it being the chief constable's party that is involved with Freiberg's murder.' The inspector glanced across at Matt as the car started the climb up the hill out of town past the Naval College. Matt glanced at the ornate wrought-iron gates as they passed by.

'I know, sir. Kitty understands your position. It concerns me too that Esther Hammett is back in the city.' He knew she did understand the inspector's difficulties with involving non-police personnel in investigations. He himself was only there because of pressure from the brigadier on the powers that be.

'Inspector Pinch is keeping an eye on Esther Hammett. Are

you feeling the heat?' Inspector Greville asked, nodding towards the partly opened window.

Matt immediately felt the shadows of his past at the man's innocent enquiry. 'Sorry, sir, is it too cold? I have some problems with being in an enclosed space. A hang-up from the war. I can close it if you prefer?' He placed his hand on the winder.

'No, it's quite all right. These police vehicles can be a bit awkward when it comes to regulating the temperature.' The inspector changed gear as they reached a more level part of the road and the car picked up speed.

Matt was grateful the inspector didn't press for more details, but guessed the man understood how Matt's service may have affected him.

'Do you think Forbes might be our murderer, sir?' Matt asked.

'It looks more likely given the evidence from the landlady and it's clear too that Mademoiselle Rochelle knows more than she's been letting on.' The inspector took the turn towards Exeter.

'Do you think she may be involved with the disappearance of the necklace too?' Mrs Craven had certainly believed that Flora had been behaving suspiciously that night at the ball.

'Her father photographed the necklace some years previously. Both of them would have had information at their disposal to get a copy made at any time in the intervening years. They could just have waited for the right moment to make a bid to take it,' the inspector replied.

'As a kind of insurance policy you mean, sir?' Matt could see the logic in the inspector's reasoning. Everything they had heard about the baron's finances would indicate that he might be desperate enough to try such an audacious theft.

'Exactly, Captain Bryant.' The inspector navigated his way through the narrow lanes at the outskirts of the city. 'The chief constable's house is along here. It has grounds extending to the river. Quite an old place, I believe.'

Matt looked around him curiously. They were in a rural setting with a few cottages scattered along the edge of the roadside but still not far away from the city centre judging by the signposts he had noticed. The breeze from earlier seemed to have dropped and the sun had come out.

The inspector turned the police car from the road onto what appeared to be a private driveway, past a small thatch-roofed gatehouse. A moment later the chief constable's home came into view. A large grey stone building set behind an immaculately manicured emerald-green lawn, with gravelled parking to the side next to a tennis court.

In the distance gaps in a row of trees afforded glimpses of the river sparkling in the sunlight behind the house.

The inspector pulled the car to a halt and looked in the rear-view mirror to adjust his tie.

'Let us hope Mr Forbes and Mademoiselle Rochelle are at home. I wouldn't mind a word with young Theodore too, about those debts he suddenly managed to pay off,' the inspector remarked grimly as he clambered out of the car.

Matt followed him and they crunched their way over the gravel to the imposing black-painted front door. The inspector pressed the highly polished brass bell push and they waited on the stone step.

A uniformed maid opened the door.

'Inspector Greville and Captain Bryant to see Mr Forbes and Mademoiselle Rochelle. Are they at home?' the inspector enquired.

'I believe so, sir. If you would care to follow me, I'll go and see if they are receiving.' The girl led the way inside a large square hall with several doors leading from it.

In the distance Matt heard the sound of someone playing the piano. They waited inside the hall while the girl went off to locate Edward and Flora. Inspector Greville looked around the room at the wood panelled walls and fine oil paintings of various family members.

'Nice place,' Matt murmured.

'Very,' the inspector agreed.

The sound of the piano stopped and a moment later the maid returned. 'Please to follow me, sirs. Miss Flora is in the music room.'

Matt wondered if she were the mystery pianist. They followed the girl along a wide corridor and to a spacious room with views of the rear gardens. A small grand piano stood at one end of the room and the walls were lined with books suggesting the room doubled as a library.

Flora was dressed in a dark-green shantung silk dress with a pink orchid print and was seated on the piano bench.

'Gentlemen to see you, miss.' The maid bobbed a curtsey and left.

'Inspector Greville and Captain Bryant, this is a surprise. How may I help you?' Flora asked.

Matt took a seat on one of the overstuffed brown leather club chairs and waited for the inspector to commence his questions. He wondered where Edward Forbes was.

'Mademoiselle Rochelle, you are aware that I am investigating both the murder of Herr Freiberg and also the theft of the Firestone necklace?' The inspector continued to stand next to the finely carved marble fireplace.

Matt thought he saw a flicker of alarm cross Flora's face.

'Of course, Inspector.' She rose from the piano bench and crossed the room to take a seat on the sofa opposite Matt, before reaching for a tortoiseshell cigarette box from the coffee table.

She opened the box, selected a cigarette, and proffered the box to Matt and the inspector. When they both refused, she took a small jade cigarette holder from the pocket of her dress and slotted her cigarette into it.

Matt took out his silver lighter and leaned forward to offer her a light.

'*Merci.*' Flora inhaled, then blew out a small pungent cloud of cigarette smoke.

The act of choosing her cigarette seemed to have restored Flora's sense of composure as she crossed her slender silk-stocking clad legs and surveyed them both through the haze of smoke.

'Mademoiselle Rochelle, when I interviewed you following the murder of Herr Freiberg you stated that you had not met the man before.' Inspector Greville directed his gaze at Flora. 'This was untrue.'

Colour crept into her cheeks and Flora blew out another small plume of smoke. 'Yes.'

'You are aware that lying to a police officer in the course of a murder enquiry is a very serious matter?' Inspector Greville's tone was stern.

Flora gave a faint gallic shrug of her silk-clad shoulders. 'My apologies, Inspector. It slipped my memory.'

Matt could tell that Flora was lying through her back teeth. She had deliberately lied to the inspector and now she was speaking as if that were of no consequence.

'Then, perhaps, mademoiselle, you will permit me to refresh your memory,' Inspector Greville said. 'You accompanied Mr Forbes to Dartmouth the day before Miss Serafina's birthday party where you were both witnessed having a conversation with Herr Freiberg.'

A faint tinge of colour crept into Flora's cheeks. 'Edward knew Herr Freiberg. I had not met him before that day. So, I did not really know him. It was a brief meeting, and I personally did not speak to the man.'

'So, you are claiming that Mr Forbes knew Herr Freiberg and you were merely accompanying him to this meeting?' the inspector asked. 'Is that correct?'

'That is what I said.' Flora extinguished her cigarette in a large crystal glass ashtray and returned her cigarette holder to her pocket as if bored with the conversation.

'And what was this meeting about?' Matt asked.

Flora gave another small shrug. 'They conversed in German. I don't speak German, only French and English so I'm not certain. I know that the man who was killed seemed annoyed about something.'

'Why did you lie when the inspector asked if you knew the man? You could have mentioned this meeting then.' Matt leaned back on the sofa and narrowed his gaze at the French girl.

'I did not think it important. I did not know the man; I only saw him briefly for a few moments. It was a matter of an instant really, and it would have looked bad for me if I had said anything to you.' Flora clasped her hands together and rested them on her lap.

'You knew that Edward had also not mentioned this meeting. Why was that?' The inspector resumed the questioning.

Flora swallowed. 'I don't know. Edward had told me he wished to arrange a surprise for Saffy for her birthday. He asked me to accompany him so I said I would go with him to Dartmouth. I assumed this man was something to do with the surprise. When he was on the boat, to me this confirmed this.'

'What was this surprise that Edward was supposed to be arranging? And how did he know Herr Freiberg?' the inspector asked.

Matt noticed that Flora's fingers were clasped tightly together as if to prevent her hands from shaking.

'I do not know. We were expecting a proposal for Saffy's birthday, so I had thought it to be to do with that. I didn't ask him how he knew the man. Later when you told us the man was dead, I panicked. I thought you would not believe me that I had no part in his murder.' Flora's voice rose as she spoke, betraying her anxiety.

The door opened as she finished speaking and Serafina appeared.

'Flora darling, whatever is the matter? Inspector?' The girl looked first at the policeman and then at Matt as she rushed to comfort her friend.

'Mademoiselle Rochelle is assisting us with our investigations, Miss Hawkes,' the inspector explained.

Flora had produced a lace-edged white handkerchief and was making a great show of dabbing at the corners of her carefully made-up eyes.

'You can't bully her, you know. My father will have something to say about this.' Serafina placed her arm protectively around her friend's shoulders.

'I assure you that no one is bullying your friend, Miss Hawkes.' The inspector looked to Matt for confirmation.

'That's correct, Serafina. Flora had omitted a few things in her first interviews and was just clearing up some of those omissions,' Matt explained.

'I don't understand.' Serafina's puzzlement showed in her dark-brown eyes. 'What omissions?'

'Flora knew Herr Freiberg, the man that was killed. She and Mr Forbes had met with him in Dartmouth the day before your birthday. Something neither of them mentioned when the inspector questioned them about the murder,' Matt said.

'It was a mistake. I did not think it important. It could have had nothing to do with this man's death.' Flora clutched at her friend's hand. 'Saffy, you must help me.'

'Perhaps you should speak to Edward, Inspector. I'm sure he will be able to clear the matter up,' Serafina said.

'Your maid went to find him a while ago and has not returned. Is he in the house?' Inspector Greville asked.

CHAPTER EIGHTEEN

Flora looked blank while Serafina seemed confused. 'He was here earlier this morning, but he may have gone into the city. He often has business meetings there.' She stood and crossed the room to the servant's bell, a discreet brass button set in the wall near the fireplace.

A few seconds later a maid appeared, a different girl from the one who had let them into the house.

'You rang, miss?'

'The inspector wishes to speak to Mr Forbes, is he in the house?' Serafina asked.

'I dunno, miss. There was a telephone call for him earlier and he was here then. I'll go and see if his car is gone.' The maid bobbed out of the room and Serafina resumed her seat beside her friend.

'Mr Forbes didn't say he was going anywhere in particular today?' the inspector asked.

Serafina shook her head. 'No, but he does have his business to consider, Inspector, so he may well have gone into the city for that reason.'

The maid returned. 'His motor car is gone from the garage,

miss. The gardener thinks he went off with Master Theo just after the inspector arrived.'

Matt exchanged a glance with Inspector Greville. It sounded to him as if Edward might be anxious to avoid speaking to the police.

'I see, thank you. I don't suppose they mentioned to anyone where they were going?' Serafina asked.

'No, miss. The gardener just heard the engine and happened to look up as they went past him,' the girl replied.

'Very well. Let us know immediately if they return.' Serafina dismissed the servant. 'I'm sorry, Inspector, it seems you have just missed him.'

The inspector did not appear pleased by this news. Matt wondered where Edward had gone and why Theo had accompanied him. Was Edward avoiding the police or was it something to do with the telephone call he had received just before their arrival?

'Just one or two more questions, Mademoiselle Rochelle, Miss Hawkes. I wonder, you mentioned that you thought Edward Forbes was planning a surprise or a proposal on the night of Miss Hawkes' birthday. Did anything of this nature occur in the end?' the inspector asked.

Serafina looked discomfited by the question.

'That is a rather personal question, Inspector, but, yes, Mr Forbes in fact proposed to me that evening and no, I did not accept.'

Matt blinked at this revelation. He hadn't considered this possibility. He had been sure that Lady Rose's machinations regarding her daughter's marriageability had come to nothing. He hadn't anticipated that Serafina may have refused Edward Forbes' marriage proposal.

'I see. May I ask when this occurred, Miss Hawkes?'

Serafina's cheeks had turned red. 'On board the paddle steamer. We left the party together just before dinner to look at the view down the river towards the estuary. He asked me to marry him and I refused. I saw no reason to share this information with anyone. Well, except Flora, of course. I had to tell someone.' She reached for her friend's hand.

'Your parents were unaware of this?' Matt asked.

'Of course. Mother would have killed me. She had made it patently obvious that she expected Edward to ask and I to accept.'

'How did Mr Forbes take the rejection?' the inspector asked.

Serafina shrugged and looked at her friend as if seeking support to carry on. 'He was all right about it. At least he seemed to be. He said he understood and hoped we could continue as we were and that perhaps in time my feelings towards him might change from friendship to love.'

'May I clarify from your refusal of the proposal, Miss Hawkes, that you do not have strong feelings towards Mr Forbes?' Inspector Greville appeared to be choosing his words with care.

'Not that it is anything to do with the police but, no, I do not have strong feelings for Edward. He is a friend. I enjoy his company but as for marrying him, no.' Serafina's voice wobbled.

'Were you surprised by the proposal?' Matt asked.

Serafina frowned. 'Yes, and no. I knew that my parents were keen on the idea, but I hadn't thought that Edward would go along with it. He knew how things were between us. At least I thought he knew.'

'And Mr Forbes is not resentful of your refusal?' Inspector Greville asked.

'No, he said he was prepared to wait for me, and everything has continued as before,' Serafina said.

'It was a very eventful night for you,' Matt said. 'Your birthday dinner, a proposal of marriage, a man is murdered and then the theft and recovery of the Firestone necklace.'

Serafina exchanged a look with Flora. The colour in her cheeks receded leaving her looking quite pale.

'Perhaps you could tell us again what happened when the lights in the ballroom went out?' Matt suggested.

'I was with my father on the stage. The necklace had been presented to me a few moments before and I had accompanied him to show the jewels off to the guests at the party. Then the compère signalled for us to return to the stage. The lights were dropped down, except for one near the stage and the cake was carried in with the candles all ablaze. Everyone sang and I blew out the candles. At that instant the remaining light went out and the other lights did not come back on.' Serafina sucked in a breath.

'I stood there for a moment wondering what to do. I could hear people talking about the lights. Then someone brushed up close to me and I felt a sharp pain around my throat. I screamed and tried to catch hold of whoever was there, but it was so dark it was impossible. My father was shouting for help next to me. Then a few seconds later the lights came back up and the necklace was gone.'

'Thank you, Miss Hawkes. Would you agree with this account, Mademoiselle Rochelle?' the inspector asked Flora.

Flora licked her lips with the tip of her tongue as if her mouth had suddenly dried.

'Of course.'

'I see. You agree with Miss Hawkes' description of events even though you yourself were not in the room when the necklace was taken?' Inspector Greville asked.

'I... well, I may have stepped out for a few seconds, but I came back as soon as I heard the commotion,' Flora said.

'You left the room right at the moment your dearest friend was being presented with her birthday cake? A moment that coincided with the room being plunged into darkness and a valuable necklace taken? And returned just after the lights were restored?' Inspector Greville asked.

Flora sat up straighter in her seat. 'Are you accusing me of something, Inspector?'

'Not at all, mademoiselle. I was simply clarifying the facts,' the policeman remarked blandly.

At that moment the door opened, and Sir Montague appeared.

'I saw the car outside, Greville. Do you have news on the necklace yet?'

'Inspector Pinch is working on it, sir,' the inspector replied gravely.

'Well, what are you doing wasting time here then, man? Get out there and find out what happened. The force is going to be a laughing stock if this gets out. Not to mention my own reputation,' Sir Montague grumbled.

'There is also the matter of the murder, sir. It would appear from our investigations so far that no one else boarded the paddle steamer during the period of time that Herr Freiberg was murdered,' Matt said.

Sir Montague seemed to notice his presence in the room for the first time. 'What do you mean? No one else boarded? Impossible! What are you trying to say, Bryant?'

'It appears inescapable that it has to be a member of your party, sir, that was responsible for Gunther Freiberg's death,' Matt said.

'Nonsense, absolute nonsense. Of course someone else must have been responsible. For heaven's sake, man, they could have come onto the ship and hidden away before we even got there,' Sir Montague blustered.

Matt shook his head. 'We have investigated that possibility, sir. The captain had checked the ship all over just before your party was welcomed aboard. There was no one else present.'

'Greville! Do you concur with this nonsense?' Sir Montague turned his fury back onto the inspector.

'Captain Bryant is correct, sir. We have since learned that various members of your party have been less than honest when we first interviewed them after the murder.'

Matt saw both Serafina and Flora's eyes widen at the inspector's words.

'We would like to speak to Edward Forbes again, and your son, Theodore,' the inspector continued.

'Theo? What's Theo go to do with all of this?' Sir Montague asked.

'It's merely a matter of clarifying a few things, sir,' the inspector said. 'It would be better if we spoke to both gentlemen sooner rather than later, but it appears we just missed them when we arrived.'

'Humph, I think you'll find my son has nothing to hide.' Sir Montague drew himself up to his full height to stare down at the inspector.

'Of course, sir. I'd appreciate if you could inform me immediately when either gentleman returns to the house. I have to make a full report to Scotland Yard later today and I'd like to ensure that I have included all the relevant information.' Inspector Greville looked at Matt.

Matt rose from his seat guessing the inspector intended to leave.

'Thank you, Miss Hawkes, Mademoiselle Rochelle, for your assistance. I may need to return to speak to you both again at some point,' the inspector warned as he tipped his hat to both girls.

'Good day, sir.' Matt nodded to Sir Montague and bid farewell to the girls, before following the inspector out of the room and along the corridor to the front door.

He wondered what Kitty would make of all this new information. Her insight into the story of Serafina's reasons for refusing Edward's proposal would be very instructive. It seemed clear to him at least that neither of the girls had been entirely frank during the interview. There was still something they were both keeping back. Were they protecting someone? Theo? Edward? Or in Flora's case, the baron? Could Flora and Edward have conspired together to steal the necklace? Or was there something else between them?

* * *

Kitty took her time finishing her cup of tea before she and Bertie departed from the tea room. The weather was clearing rapidly now with the sky developing into a soft hazy blue, which denoted the promise of a fine afternoon. The breeze had dropped, and the air was warmer.

The space where the *Sigrid* had lain at anchor was empty and Kitty wondered when she was due to call into the port again. Further along the river she noticed the ship used by the college to train the naval cadets.

She was familiar with groups of cadets under the instruction of the officers coming down to train and do various exercises both on the larger boat and a couple of smaller ones which were at their disposal.

She stood for a moment with Bertie at her side lost in thought as she looked out across the river towards the small village of Kingswear on the opposite bank. Suppose this had somehow been where Gunther managed to collect his information? It could have been left by one of the officers for him to pick up under the cover of darkness at a later point.

She frowned. Even if this was the case, why then had the man been murdered? And by someone in the chief constable's party? Had someone realised that Matt had been watching Gunther? Perhaps that same person had then panicked when Matt had also been there for Serafina's party.

Officers came down into the town all the time, as did the young sailors when they had leave. Information could have been passed then in one of the many pubs or hostelries in the town. Surely that was a more likely scenario.

It all felt vaguely unsatisfactory. She wished she could have accompanied Matt and the inspector to Exeter. It would be very interesting to learn what they had managed to discover.

Why did Edward Forbes and Flora seem to have been connected to Gunther? Was one of them the paymaster or another espionage agent taking the information on further? But what would they have gained from this? Theo was the only one who had had a mysterious windfall recently. She couldn't see that Sir Montague would have paid Theo's debts, at least he wouldn't have done so without creating an enormous ruckus. So where had that money come from?

A gust of cool air suddenly blew again along the river and Kitty shivered despite the breakthrough of the sun. She called Bertie away from his investigation of a tussock of grass and decided to walk back along the embankment and down towards Warfleet Creek. It was more sheltered there and she could think as she walked.

The stroll might help clear her head and it would give the energetic Bertie some much-needed exercise. More people were around now that the drizzle had lifted, and she greeted quite a few acquaintances as she walked along past the Customs House towards the cottages at the tail end of the town.

She passed Mickey, her security and maintenance man's cottage, and the steep upwards flight of worn stone steps leading to the cottages above where she assumed Mr Moody resided.

Deciding against going up to the castle or St Petrox Church, she instead took the lower road towards the creek itself and the water's edge. Bertie forged ahead of her, his tail wagging with delight at the prospect of probably getting a paddle at the shore of the creek.

The creek was surprisingly quiet, and the tide was clearly on its way out. Kitty ambled down to the side of the shore. She perched herself on a boulder in the sunshine while Bertie amused himself exploring the pebbles at the water margin.

Her chosen seat was shielded from the casual passers-by thanks to a scrubby group of bushes at the side of her protecting her from the breeze. Kitty sat enjoying the feel of the early autumnal sun on her face and listened to the sounds of the birds and the gentle lapping of the water at the shore.

She was about to move on and make her way back to the Dolphin for lunch when she heard the sound of a motor car halting on the road above. This was followed by footsteps crunching on the scree near to where she was seated.

Something made her gently tug Bertie's lead so that he ambled back towards her and flopped at her feet, a questioning look in his big brown eyes. Kitty could hear the murmur of male voices and peeked out around the bush expecting to see a boat owner or a local fisherman.

Instead, she was surprised to see Edward Forbes with Theo Hawkes standing on the foreshore. She wasn't close enough to hear what they were saying but she could tell from their body language that the debate was quite heated. Snatches of the row floated towards her.

'I refuse...' Theo said.

'You know the consequences... Your sister...' Edward barely raised his voice.

Theo gesticulated with his hands at Edward who in turn had his own hands in his trouser pockets as if unmoved by the younger man's argument. Kitty shrank back closer to the bushes and hoped that neither man would move further towards the water where they would inevitably catch sight of her.

She stroked the top of Bertie's head and hoped the dog would remain quiet and calm at her feet. It really was all quite awkward. After a few minutes, Theo turned away and strode off leaving Edward standing on the strand.

Kitty waited, expecting Edward to either follow or for the sound of the motor car to start up, signifying that perhaps Theo had driven away leaving Edward behind. She wished he would move on so that she and Bertie could make good their escape without being seen.

Edward, however, showed no sign of leaving. He took out his silver cigarette case and lit up as he surveyed the river in front of him. Kitty wondered what could have brought him there. It was a quiet, out of the way spot, perfect for an assignation perhaps. The idea sent a shiver down her spine.

She continued to wait, hoping that he wouldn't walk in her direction or move closer to the water. She was pressed right back into the bushes now. The biggest concern was Bertie. Concealing herself was one thing, hiding Matt's dog quite another.

If the inspector hadn't told her that Edward had met with Gunther, then perhaps she wouldn't have been so worried. Now though, she was certain that whatever he was doing at Warfleet, he was up to no good. It seemed too, that Theo Hawkes was also somehow involved.

CHAPTER NINETEEN

Forbes finished his cigarette, then threw the smouldering end down on the stones before grinding it out with the polished toe of his shoe. Kitty held her breath as he then glanced at his wrist-watch. Perhaps he was about to move on.

Theo must have walked away as she hadn't heard the sound of a car engine when he had left. Edward must have been the driver. She wondered where Theo had gone and if he would come back. It seemed from what she had witnessed that the two men hadn't parted on good terms.

She risked a quick peep to see if Edward had started back up towards the road. To her dismay he continued to stand on the foreshore. He had to be waiting for someone or he would have gone by now. Bertie sighed and flopped onto his side, clearly tired of whatever game Kitty was playing.

Another minute passed before Kitty heard the sound of more footsteps crunching on the shingle. Another quick glance showed her a male figure in a nondescript grey suit and hat approaching Edward. From her position she couldn't see the stranger's face. He didn't seem familiar in any way.

She strained to try and hear any of the conversation.

'You're late.' Edward's voice carried on the light breeze.

The stranger's reply was inaudible. Kitty watched as the man looked around and then withdrew a brown envelope from the inside of his jacket and passed it to Edward. Forbes opened the end and took a quick look inside.

He tucked it inside his own jacket and gave the stranger a quick nod. 'Payment will follow.'

The other man seemed uncertain and in no hurry to leave. Kitty ducked back when she saw the stranger glancing around again as if concerned that someone might witness the exchange.

She waited for a moment and risked another quick look. The stranger seemed to be arguing with Edward who was clearly having none of it.

'I said payment will be made as our usual arrangement.' Edward's voice carried towards her.

The stranger turned and left. Kitty blew out a relieved breath as she heard the sound of his boots receding from the shingle. Now all she had to do was wait for Edward to leave and she and Bertie could get away. Surely he would go now the rendezvous had been made.

Once she was back at the Dolphin she could try and telephone Sir Montague's house to speak to either Matt or the inspector and tell them what she had just witnessed. It seemed obvious that Edward must be the one who had been Gunther's contact. Why else would he be having clandestine meetings here of all places? The exchange of the package must confirm it.

What was less clear though was why Theo had accompanied him? When they had argued they had mentioned Serafina, what was her part in all of this? Were both brother and sister involved in something shady, and could one of them have murdered Gunther?

She heard the sound of footsteps on the stones once more and relaxed when she saw there was no sign of Edward. He must have made his way back up to the road. Surely the car engine would start up in a moment and she and Bertie could leave.

Bertie roused himself and gave a shake when Kitty moved his lead ready to slip away from her hiding place as soon as she was certain it was safe. She was about to stand up so that she could take a better look up towards the road when the sudden weight of a heavy male hand on her shoulder sent a cold rush of fear through her body.

'I would advise you not to scream or to try to run away.' Edward's voice sounded close to her ear. His breath warm against her cheek.

Kitty gave a muffled squeak. All capacity to speak let alone scream appeared to have left her.

'Now, Miss Underhay, you will please accompany me to my motor car.' Edward's grip tightened on her shoulder making her wince in pain.

Bertie let out a low growl as Kitty stumbled under the pressure Forbes was exerting, before beginning to bark and snap at Edward's ankles.

'Get away from me, you mangey mutt.' Edward attempted to kick out at the spaniel.

'Don't you hurt my dog.' Kitty aimed a kick of her own at Edward's shin.

Her actions triggered a torrent of curses from her captor, and he plunged his hand into the pocket of his jacket and pulled out a revolver.

'I suggest that you walk nice and quietly with me to the car or the dog pays.' He dug the nose of the gun into Kitty's side.

Forced to comply, Kitty released Bertie's leash and hoped that for once in the dog's life he would actually do as she told him.

'Run, Bertie. Go find Matt. Go, run. Good boy, find Matt.' She did her best to shoo the confused little dog away.

After Bertie had given her a long puzzled look, he finally

trotted off in the direction of town, trailing his lead behind him. Edward let out another curse as the dog sprinted away out of sight. Kitty gave a sigh of relief that at least Matt's dog was hopefully safe.

'Now, Miss Underhay, move quickly. I have been here far too long as it is.' Edward prodded her hard again with the gun and forced her to accompany him to the road where his gleaming dark-green sports car stood waiting.

Kitty could only hope that someone would see Bertie and take him to the Dolphin, where the alarm would be raised. He was quite well known in the town so to see him loose without her or Matt must surely cause concern.

'What are you doing?' Kitty asked as Edward opened the door to his car and shoved her inside.

'I presume that you witnessed my meeting since you were hiding in the bushes?' He pushed her hard to force her across into the passenger seat, before climbing into the driver side and putting the key in the ignition.

Kitty automatically reached for the passenger door release hoping she might be able to escape while he juggled starting the car with keeping the gun trained on her.

'Don't get any smart ideas, Miss Underhay. I have been warned about you already.' Edward raised his hand with the gun and cuffed her on her temple sending a shower of sparks mixed with blinding pain across her head.

Stunned and hurt she gasped for breath and slumped against the seat, raising her hands to her head in protection in case any further blows were to follow. Edward started the car and the powerful motor roared into life.

Kitty opted to remain curled into a ball on the passenger seat, afraid to lift her head in case Edward might hit her again. At least in this position she could attempt to recover her senses and look for an opportunity to escape his clutches.

She wondered where he was heading. And how was Theo

involved? Had the boy been aware that Edward was a traitor? Did Serafina know or suspect something? Was that why the girl had been reluctant to accept a proposal?

Kitty's head was buzzing from the blow she had received, and her ears were still ringing. From the way Edward was changing gear and the higher pitch of the engine note she surmised that he had taken the road out of Dartmouth leading up the steep hill past the Naval College.

Was he headed for Totnes or Exeter she wondered? Why had he taken her with him? He could have simply killed her down on the shore. The idea sent another rush of fear coursing through her body. She had to keep calm and try to work out a way to escape.

The car was flying along now. A quick peep showed her that the hedges and fields were whizzing past the car. Unless they passed through one of the small towns or villages and he was forced to slow down she couldn't see that she would be able to shout for help or try to get away.

She risked a quick glance at Edward and saw his jaw was set and his mouth fixed in a grim line. A movement of her head sent another wave of stars flashing across her vision and a small whimper escaped her.

Edward glanced at her. 'You will keep very quiet and very still if you know what is good for you.'

'What are you doing? Where are you taking me?' Her voice sounded croaky, and she hated the way it made her sound weak and helpless.

'You have no need to worry, Miss Underhay. You will not be accompanying me all the way,' Edward leered.

Kitty swallowed at the ominous threat in his words. 'Why don't you just let me out here? You would be miles away before I could raise any sort of alarm,' she suggested.

'Oh no, my dear Miss Underhay. You are going to be my insurance to ensure that I can get away when I want without any hindrance.' The corners of his mouth tilted upwards in a faint unpleasant smile. 'It's the very least you can do after complicating my plans today.'

'I don't understand.' Kitty attempted to raise her head to try to see if she recognised where they were or gain a clue to the direction. They seemed to be taking steep narrow country lanes with high banks on either side of the car. The movement made her feel nauseous, however, and she was forced to close her eyes again before she saw anything useful.

'Don't worry your pretty head about it.' Edward pressed his foot down harder on the accelerator and the car picked up speed once again.

* * *

After it became clear that Edward Forbes and Theodore Hawkes were not likely to return very soon the inspector took Matt back into Exeter. Inspector Greville went to see his colleague, Inspector Pinch, at the police station, while Matt decided his time would be better spent returning to Dartmouth via train.

He disembarked at Kingswear and crossed the river on the passenger ferry since the rail line had never been extended over the estuary, even though somewhat bizarrely a station had been built some time earlier in Dartmouth in expectation of the event.

Kitty would be fascinated by the results of the investigation so far and he couldn't wait to collect Bertie and tell her all about it. Therefore, Matt was somewhat unsettled on his arrival at the Dolphin to be greeted by Dolly and Mr Lutterworth who had Bertie in their care.

'Oh, Captain Bryant, sir. We have Bertie here. Did he run off from you or Miss Kitty on his walk?' Dolly said as his dog rushed to greet him, tail wagging in delight.

'Kitty said she was taking him for a walk. I was in Exeter with Inspector Greville. Has he come back alone?' Matt bent to fuss his dog. A sick feeling was building in the pit of his stomach. Bertie might have some behaviour problems, but he would never run off from Kitty.

'Yes, sir. The dog returned alone almost an hour ago. Pawing at the door of the hotel he was. Mary heard the scratching noise and fetched him inside. We went out to look for Miss Kitty or yourself but there was no sign of either of you,' Dolly said.

Mr Lutterworth's narrow face looked extremely concerned. 'We naturally expected Kitty or yourself to return quite quickly. As time ticked by and neither of you appeared we began to worry.'

'Kitty had him. Something must have happened as he is still attached to his leash.' Matt realised the dog's lead was still fastened to his collar. Kitty had obviously not had Bertie running freely so something must have happened to make her release him.

'Perhaps he was tied up somewhere and come loose,' Dolly suggested. ''Tis likely then as Miss Kitty might be searching for him.'

Matt swallowed. Dolly's reasoning was sound but since he knew that Esther Hammett was back in the area, he could take nothing for granted until he knew Kitty was safe. 'It's possible, Dolly, but usually Bertie won't leave Kitty's side unless she sends him off. She's been doing a lot of training with him since we got him.'

Dolly nodded. 'Do you think as we should go looking for her, sir?'

'I was about to suggest exactly that, sir. It's been well over an hour now and I would have thought Miss Kitty would have come back to see if the dog had returned home by now.' Mr Lutterworth's gaze met Matt's.

'Miss Kitty usually walks up towards the castle,' Mary suggested.

'She might have twisted her ankle or something if she went into the woods. The rain from the morning could have made the ground proper slippy.' Dolly was already reaching for her coat from the stand inside the office.

'A good point, Miss Miller,' Mr Lutterworth agreed.

'I'll go and see if our Alice will come and search as well, and Mickey.' Dolly finished shrugging into her coat and darted off along the corridor towards the kitchens.

'Shall I accompany you too, Captain Bryant. I am not as familiar with the area as Miss Miller and the others, but you may have need of my assistance if Miss Underhay has injured herself,' Cyril suggested as he collected his hat from the stand.

'Thank you. I appreciate it.' Matt hoped the explanation would turn out to be something as simple as a turned ankle in the woods near the castle.

'If Miss Kitty returns before any of you, sir, I'll tell her where you've gone looking,' Mary said.

Dolly returned to the lobby accompanied by her sister, Alice, Mickey and the young kitchen boy.

'Right, I think we should split up. Perhaps Alice, you and Dolly might head towards St Petrox and the tea room at the castle. Ask along the way if anyone has seen Kitty. Mickey, if you and the lad would take the woods above the castle. Myself and Mr Lutterworth will go along the bottom near Warfleet Creek in case she has gone along near the shore.' Matt directed as he collected Bertie's leash.

The others nodded their agreement and they hurried out of the hotel together. Matt could see the worry on Alice's face. She and Kitty had undergone many dangers together and he could see the girl was frightened by this strange turn of events.

They parted company where the road divided, with the girls and Mickey heading upwards. Matt and Mr Lutterworth took the turn leading down towards the creek. Bertie trotted happily ahead of them, his nose down and tail in the air as if on the trail of something.

The two men walked together down onto the shore looking for any kind of sign that Kitty may have passed that way.

'There are paw marks here in the sand.' Mr Lutterworth showed Matt the marks that were rapidly being swallowed up by the turning tide.

Matt compared them to the marks Bertie was currently making. 'They look the same as Bertie's but it is by no means definite. He could have come here after he got loose. Look around, Cyril, see if there are any more signs that Kitty may have been here.'

Mr Lutterworth continued to look at the softer patches of ground between the stones for any footprints. Matt walked closer to the water's edge and followed along the shoreline towards a large clump of scrubby bushes that grew near the water.

As he drew closer, he could see there were footmarks in the soft ground in front of a large grey stone boulder.

'Mr Lutterworth,' he called to the hotel manager who promptly came to join him.

'A lady's shoe, small size and more paw marks.' Cyril's face was grave. 'It suggests that Miss Underhay may have been here.'

Matt pointed to some other marks at the side of the boulder. 'And not alone.'

CHAPTER TWENTY

When Kitty next opened her eyes, it was to complete blackness. She was no longer in the car. Wherever she was now was hard and smelt of damp and stale air. Her whole body ached, and she had cramp in her arms and legs. Tentatively she tried to stretch out in the confined space and discovered her hands and feet had been bound with some kind of rope.

She lay still for a moment and listened, hoping for some kind of clue about where she might be. Everything was quiet and at first, she didn't think she could hear anything. Then she heard a faint noise that she recognised. Water, lapping against wood.

She wriggled carefully to try and bring herself up into a sitting position so she could better assess her situation. Forbes had evidently dumped her somewhere after tying her up. He hadn't covered her mouth so she could only assume there must not be anyone nearby should she attempt to call for help. She decided against testing the theory, and alerting Edward to her being awake.

The surface beneath her felt moist and seemed to be made of timber. Was she in a boat of some sort? The floor seemed to move when she moved. Her head ached and her stomach was still rolling in faint waves of nausea from the blow to the head she had received earlier in the day.

After some considerable effort she finally managed to sit. Her hands were bound behind her back and her feet seemed to be tied together. Somewhere along the way she seemed to have lost one of her shoes and her feet were cold.

Kitty shivered and tried to think. The air didn't smell of salt so she had to assume that she must be on a river boat of some kind. Had they travelled back towards the Dart? Where was Forbes? Why had he left her here? At least he hadn't yet killed her, so she supposed that was something to be grateful for.

She attempted to stretch herself upwards, straightening her spine to ease her shoulders and bumped her head on something hard and wooden. She must be in the hold of some kind of vessel. Her movements made whatever was holding her sway gently and her stomach rolled once more.

Kitty took a few deep breaths to try and calm the rising tide of panic at her situation.

'Think, Kitty, think,' she muttered to herself. She wriggled her feet and realised that the rope binding her ankles together was not as tight as she had first thought. Using her stockinged foot, she pushed at the heel of her remaining shoe until she was able to ease it free.

With both her feet now shoeless she concentrated on working her feet back and forth until she could feel the rope holding her legs together start to loosen. After quite a few minutes she managed to slide her one leg free of its binding and stretch her leg out more.

At least now her legs were free she could move them to relieve the awful cramping pains in her calves. She quickly found that the space holding her was quite confined and she had little room in front of her. Her tweed skirt was soaked and smelt like river water.

Kitty wished she knew what time it was and how long she had been unconscious for. It could be night now outside for all she knew, the space in which she was being held was so dark. If Bertie had gone back to the Dolphin there would be people searching for her, but Edward had taken her miles away in his car so they would be looking in vain.

A tear rolled down her cheek and she sniffed hard as she tried to stop the sense of panic from overwhelming her. Her legs were free, now she had to try and work on her hands. Edward had taken more care it seemed when he had bound her wrists and the ropes felt tighter.

She shuffled around carefully in the darkness trying to feel about her for anything at all that might be in the space that could possibly help her. The movements made the boat holding her rock quite perilously and she was forced to halt a few times afraid she might capsize into the water.

The hull of the boat was of rough wood and at first all she encountered was the feel of old tar and splinters. She had just begun to despair of finding anything when she cut her finger on what seemed to be a jagged fragment of metal.

Hoping she hadn't done herself too much damage she manoeuvred her way so that she could rub the ropes holding her hands together against the metal in an attempt to saw through her bonds.

There were many false starts and she acquired quite a few more scratches before she finally started to feel the rope slacken. At last, she felt the rope give and she was able to get her one hand free.

Kitty slumped forward in relief as she stretched her fingers and massaged her wrists to try and get the feeling back in her hands. At least she was no longer tied up. Now she had to try and work out how to get out of her prison.

* * *

'If she was here, where would she go next?' Matt looked at Mr Lutterworth.

'Perhaps the others may have had more luck, sir. She could have gone up the hill towards the castle,' Cyril suggested.

Matt nodded. He didn't like this at all. There had definitely been a set of male footprints next to the boulder and he doubted that Kitty intended to meet anyone. He called Bertie back and he and Cyril left the creek and walked up to the road.

A patch of oil on the road above the shingle beach caught Matt's attention. A motor car had clearly been stood on that spot recently and long enough for it to lose a small amount of engine oil. Did it belong to whoever had met with Kitty down by the water? Or was he putting two and two together and coming up with five.

'No one has seen Bertie or Miss Kitty up near the castle or tea rooms, sir,' Dolly panted, having sprinted down the hill to meet them.

Alice followed behind close on her sister's heels. 'We asked at several places and looked all around the church and the castle. There's no sign of her, sir. Mickey and the boy are still searching but no one saw them go into the woods.'

''Tis like she's vanished into thin air. Do you think as she might have gone off in her motor?' Dolly suggested.

'It would be unlikely given that Bertie was loose, but I suppose we should check,' Matt agreed.

They left Dolly to meet Mickey and the lad to tell them they were going back to the hotel via the shed where Kitty kept her car.

The shed was still padlocked and one of the women who lived nearby said that she hadn't seen anyone there all day.

'I think I need to inform Inspector Greville,' Matt said.

Alice nodded in agreement. 'You don't think as that Esther Hammett is behind this, sir? Miss Kitty told me as she was back in Exeter and after that funny business the other week with that rat, well...'

'I hope not, Alice.' Matt wished he could be certain there was some innocent explanation for Kitty's disappearance but the news that Esther was in Exeter again made him fear the worst for her safety.

Mary was waiting anxiously for their return. 'No sign of Miss Kitty yet,' she reported.

'Has Mrs Treadwell returned home yet?' Cyril asked.

Mary shook her head. 'No, sir, she was going out for the day, and I don't think she intended to return until later this evening. She said as she was dining out.'

Matt exchanged a glance with Cyril. At least Kitty's grandmother was unaware of their concerns. He could only hope that Kitty would be safely back at the Dolphin before her grandmother came home.

He left Mr Lutterworth and Alice to tell Mary where they had been and entered Kitty's office to telephone Inspector Greville.

He tried the number for Exeter Police Station first hoping that Inspector Greville might still be there.

'I'm sorry, Captain Bryant, Inspector Greville has returned to Torquay. Did you wish to speak to Inspector Pinch?' the constable that had answered the telephone asked.

Matt was about to refuse but changed his mind. If Esther were behind Kitty's disappearance, then Inspector Pinch might have some idea where she might be.

The inspector came on the line and Matt explained his concerns re Kitty's disappearance as succinctly as possible.

'I see, sir. I think you can be assured as Esther Hammett is not directly involved if there has been any kind of foul play. We have that lady under lock and key at the moment and she has been with us since lunchtime.'

Matt released the breath he had been holding. 'I understand. Is she likely to remain under arrest, sir?' It seemed that whatever had befallen Kitty at least it was not Esther that was responsible.

'Unfortunately, her solicitor has negotiated her release and she is about to leave the station, but we are expecting her to return to London by this evening.' The inspector sounded regretful.

'Thank you, sir. I had better try Torquay.'

'Good luck, sir. I do hope Miss Underhay is all right.' The inspector rang off and Matt immediately redialled. Normally he would have asked Inspector Pinch for details about Esther's arrest, but his mind was consumed with fear about what could possibly have happened to his fiancée.

'Captain Bryant, how may I help you?' Inspector Greville came on the line.

'It's Kitty, sir. She's missing.' Matt repeated the information he had just given to Inspector Pinch.

'You say the dog came back to the hotel alone?' the inspector asked.

Matt knew the inspector knew Bertie well and would be well aware of just how odd that would be.

'Yes, sir.' He described discovering Kitty's footprints at the creek. 'I know Bertie can be disobedient, but he would never leave Kitty unless she sent him away for some reason. It's as if she's simply vanished.'

'I'll come over right away.' The inspector rang off. Matt leaned back in Kitty's office chair and ran his hand through his hair in a despairing gesture. Bertie sat at his feet and released a small whine.

If Esther was not behind Kitty's disappearance, then who was? His only conclusion was that it must be connected in some way with their current case. Dartmouth was a safe place, a small town. Kitty was well known locally. No one else would wish her any harm. Had she stumbled on something or someone that had placed her in danger in some way?

There was a light tap on the office door.

'Did you speak to the inspector, sir?' Alice asked. He could see tears forming in her eyes and he knew the girl was desperately worried for her friend.

Matt nodded. 'Yes. He's coming here now.'

The maid bit her lip. 'I feel awful, sir. I keep thinking about what could have become of her. That there dog never leaves her if she has him on her own.' Alice looked at Bertie, who promptly wagged his tail.

'I know. Inspector Pinch has, however, assured me that Esther Hammett is in custody and whatever has become of Kitty this afternoon, at least Esther is for once not responsible,' Matt attempted to reassure the young maid.

'I'm not sure if that makes me feel better or worse,' Alice said. 'If it's not that Esther then where is Miss Kitty? Who else could have took her? For somebody has, sir, I'm certain of it.'

Any further speculation on Kitty's whereabouts was broken up by the sounds of a scuffle and shouting outside the front of the hotel. Matt immediately jumped from his chair and rushed into the lobby where he was greeted by a somewhat dishevelled Mr Lutterworth holding a younger man firmly by his earlobe.

Under the younger man's arm was a cream leather handbag, which Matt immediately recognised as Kitty's.

''Ere let go of me. I haven't done nothing wrong.' The man aimed a kick at Mr Lutterworth's ankles and the older man skipped smartly backwards to avoid the blow from landing.

Mickey arrived in the lobby with the young kitchen boy and promptly blocked the man's exit into the street. Once satisfied his captive could not escape Mr Lutterworth released the man's ear.

'Perhaps you could tell us why you are in possession of my

fiancée's handbag?' Matt asked, glaring at the scruffy-looking man.

'I come here to return it, didn't I? I thought there might be some money, you know, for finding it like and then Uncle Cyril here pounced on me and dragged me in 'ere afore I could explain things.' The youth scowled at Mr Lutterworth who was occupied with straightening his cuffs and tie after the altercation.

'Where did you find it?' Matt demanded as he held out his hand to take Kitty's bag.

The youth immediately looked shifty. 'It depends if there's a reward or something?'

Matt took the bag, opened it and looked inside. He knew Kitty carried very little in her bags. A handkerchief, her lipstick, her purse and comb and usually a small paper twist of hard-boiled sweets.

The contents appeared intact. He took out Kitty's worn brown leather purse and looked inside. The change she kept was there, a few pennies and shillings but the note section was empty. Matt knew Kitty always carried a few notes with her.

'It seems you may have already claimed a reward since the notes are missing.' He dropped the purse back inside the handbag. 'Now, I suggest you tell us where you found Kitty's bag and when.' He took a step towards the man who automatically attempted to back away from him.

Mickey took a pace forward to trap the youth so he couldn't get away from Matt.

'You'd best tell the captain here all as you know,' Mickey said.

The man's gaze skittered from side to side as if seeking an escape route as he licked his lips in a nervous gesture.

'I would ask you to bear in mind, Captain Bryant, that my nephew has always had a somewhat tenuous relationship with the truth.' Mr Lutterworth straightened the rosebud on his lapel and glared at the younger man.

'That ain't fair. I found that there bag just lying on the sand with nobody beside it. It was next to a big rock down by the creek at Warfleet,' Mr Lutterworth's nephew burst out angrily.

'We have just returned from Warfleet Creek and there was no sign of Kitty's bag then. There were, however, men's footprints next to the rock and prints left by a lady's shoe.' Matt looked at the man's feet.

Mr Lutterworth's nephew's feet were shod in a pair of very down at heel worn black boots. Matt could see that they would not have been capable of leaving the clearly defined outlines he had noticed to the side of the rock. Whoever had left those prints had been wearing much newer shoes and in good condition.

Mr Lutterworth looked disdainfully at his nephew. 'I'm sure he probably collected the bag earlier and, judging from the smell of beer on his person, has spent Miss Kitty's money in a local hostelry before deciding to try his luck with a reward.'

Matt thought Mr Lutterworth was probably correct in his assumption. He had noticed the stale odour of ale and sweat emanating from the man in front of him.

'Now look 'ere, I come here in good faith as an honest citizen to return this property to the lady what has her name inside the bag.' The younger man huffed and straightened his collar. 'Get the lady 'ere and she can decide for herself if I've done right.'

'Miss Kitty is missing. Her dog come back without her and now you've turned up with her handbag.' Alice folded her arms.

Her stern gaze seemed to cause the man to wilt. 'Listen, miss, I don't know nothing about no disappearance. I just found that bag not long after lunchtime. There weren't anybody about at all. Dropped in the bushes by the rock it was.'

'Perhaps Inspector Greville will be able to decide if you

know anything when he gets here,' Alice retorted with a sniff. 'Taking Miss Kitty's money and spending it in a pub before coming here with some cock and bull tale.'

Dolly had come to stand next to her sister and the two Miller girls stared Mr Lutterworth's nephew down, causing him to start to sweat.

'I'm telling the truth. There weren't nobody there. I'd been mooching about looking for a bit of work and there weren't nothing happening, so I thinks to myself I'd try where the fishing boats lie in Warfleet Creek.'

'A likely story. You've never done a day's honest work in your life. You were probably hoping to steal something,' Mr Lutterworth muttered.

'Like I was saying, I was going along the road when this flashy green sporting motor almost run me down. Had to jump out the way I did. Then when I got to the beach there weren't nobody about. So, I sits on that rock and sees the handbag just lying there in the bush.' The younger man raised his arm and wiped his nose on the cuff of his jacket. 'And that's the God's honest truth, that is.'

Matt frowned. He had noticed the patch of oil on the road surface himself earlier. It could be that whoever had been driving that car might hold a clue to Kitty's disappearance.

'What kind of car was it?' he asked.

The man shrugged. 'A dark-green Singer sports car. One of them with the fancy wheels.'

An expensive motor car and quite distinctive. When the inspector arrived, he might be able to discover who owned such a vehicle locally. 'Did you see who was driving the car?' Matt asked.

'The roof was up, and I was too busy diving for my life to be able to see anything much. It was a man in a dark suit. Light-coloured hair he had, I think.' Mr Lutterworth's nephew seemed to relax a little now the focus of the accusations appeared to be shifting onto the owner of the car.

'Did you see if there was anyone else in the car with him?' Matt could only hope that perhaps Kitty had been accompanying the mystery driver for some reason.

'I think there might have been, but it come by so fast, and I was on my back in the ditch at the side of the road,' the man grumbled. 'Anyway, that's it. That's all I know, so if there might be a bit of a thank you, I'll get on my way.'

'I don't think you are going anywhere just yet, my lad.' The revolving door to the lobby moved and Inspector Greville entered the crowded room.

CHAPTER TWENTY-ONE

Mr Lutterworth's nephew appeared to crumple once more at the sight of the inspector.

'Perhaps we should move this conversation from the lobby to one of the resident's lounges. Guests may arrive at any moment,' Mr Lutterworth suggested.

Mickey immediately took hold of the hotel manager's nephew's arm and, with Mr Lutterworth's aid, escorted him forcibly along the corridor to the room the Hawkes family had used during their stay. Alice, Dolly and Matt followed with the inspector. Mary caught hold of the kitchen lad and sent him back to his duties, much to his chagrin.

'Now, since I only heard the end of this conversation, perhaps, Captain Bryant, you might fill me in on everything that has been said so far.' The inspector took a seat in one of the armchairs and took out his notepad and pen.

Mr Lutterworth's nephew was pushed down into the armchair opposite the inspector. Dolly and Alice perched anxiously on the edge of the sofa, with Alice holding on tightly to Kitty's handbag.

Matt paced up and down the room as he recounted everything that had happened to the inspector. Bertie lay quietly at Dolly's feet, his big brown eyes fixed on Kitty's bag.

'A green Singer sports car? You are certain of that?' The inspector looked at Mr Lutterworth's nephew.

Matt could tell by the inspector's reaction that there was something about the car that was familiar.

'Yes, I told you. Driving like a mad man he was, almost killed me. If I hadn't dived in the ditch, I would have been toast.' The man tried to shake off Mickey's restraining hand from his shoulder. 'I come here in good faith, I did. Now I'm being manhandled and treated like a blooming criminal.'

The inspector's moustache twitched but he refrained from rising to the man's complaints. He asked several more questions and Cyril's nephew stuck to his story.

''Ere, so if I'm not getting no reward money for that there bag, can I go now?' The man attempted to rise from his seat. Mickey immediately pushed him back down into his chair.

'I think you've already rewarded yourself enough with Miss Kitty's purse,' Mr Lutterworth said.

His nephew scowled at Mickey and his uncle. 'What's a bloke to do when his own flesh and blood won't help him out when he's down on his luck?'

No one answered him. Dolly and Alice continued to glare disapprovingly, while Mickey looked as if he would like to murder him.

'I think as there is nothing further to be gained from your evidence you may as well leave. Think yourself lucky that you are not being charged with theft since money is missing from Miss Underhay's purse,' the inspector said to him. 'I suggest you stay well away from this establishment. My constable should be in the foyer by now. Perhaps Mr Lutterworth you might see your nephew off the premises and give his address to my man?'

'Of course, sir.' Mr Lutterworth looked at his nephew who

was still attempting to shrug off Mickey's hand from his shoulder.

'I'll come with you, Mr Lutterworth, see him out,' Mickey said and released his captive so that he was free to stand up.

The two older men escorted the younger one from the room, closing the door behind them.

'That car, sir, you seemed to recognise the description?' Matt turned immediately to the inspector.

The policeman set down his notebook and stroked his moustache thoughtfully. 'Mr Edward Forbes' motor car is a green Singer sports car. It is quite an unusual vehicle. I have alerts placed throughout the county and on the London Road. I arranged it with Inspector Pinch after our friend seemed to wish to avoid our questions this morning.'

Dolly and Alice exchanged worried glances.

'Mr Forbes? Is that the gentleman who's courting Miss Hawkes?' Dolly asked.

Matt knew the girls would be familiar with the names since they had both been involved with various aspects of Sir Montague's party.

'Yes. We believe he may have known the German man who was murdered on the paddle steamer.' Matt felt sick at the thought.

What had Kitty stumbled into? For he was certain now that she must have uncovered something to cause her to vanish and leave Bertie to find his own way back to the hotel. It seemed increasingly likely that Forbes may have taken her in his car, but where was Theo? The boy had been seen leaving with Forbes.

'The force already has men looking out for Forbes and his car. He surely can't get very far,' the inspector said.

Matt's nausea grew. 'Do we know if he has any property locally, anywhere he may have taken Kitty?'

Alice started in her seat. 'I think he does, sir.'

The inspector and Matt turned to face the maid. 'I only

knows, sir, from when I was doing his room. I was straightening it up and he were being a bit fresh like. You know chatting me up like. I weren't saying much as I have a young man already.' She looked at Matt, colour showing in her pale cheeks.

'Of course, Alice, we know that you would not be interested,' Matt assured her.

'Go on,' Dolly urged.

'Well, he asked if I was local, and I said as all my family was from Dartmouth, and he said as how he had had some family at Blackawton, although his mother's family was from Dartmoor. His great-uncle had left him a couple of properties there just outside the village near Millcombe. A house and an old farm he said with a pond. I said as that were nice. He said not really as it were a bit of a wreck.' Alice looked at Matt. 'He sounded a bit sneering about it. I finished my job quick like and come out then. I don't know if that might be helpful or not.'

'Well done, Alice. It might give us something to go on. It sounds like the kind of place he might use to try and lie low for a while.' Matt smiled at the maid. At least this information might give them a clue if Edward Forbes were responsible for abducting Kitty. It was at least a glimmer of hope.

The inspector jumped up. 'I'll make some telephone calls to the constable in that area and see if we can locate the properties.' He hurried from the room.

'Do you think that this bloke, this Mr Forbes has got her, sir?' Dolly asked. The girl looked as if she was about to cry, and her older sister placed a protective arm around her slim shoulders.

'It's possible, Dolly. I'm not sure why though, unless he feels that he might be able to use her as some kind of bargaining chip. If he is the man responsible for murdering Herr Freiberg then he faces other very serious charges besides murder,' Matt said.

He could see no other reason for Forbes taking Kitty, if indeed he was responsible for her disappearance.

Inspector Greville reappeared in the doorway. 'A constable is going to take a discreet look around near the old farm. He knew where we meant. Apparently, it's quite isolated on a narrow road outside Millcombe. The story locally is that it belonged to an elderly man who died suddenly last year.'

'Do we know, sir, if Theodore Hawkes has reappeared yet? He was last seen leaving with Forbes,' Matt said. It had struck him that Forbes might not be acting alone, and the young lad had made no secret of his attraction towards Kitty.

'He has not yet returned to the family home.' Inspector Greville frowned. 'I just spoke to Sir Montague. Naturally he is concerned that his son is missing given recent circumstances.'

Matt frowned. 'Do you know, sir, if the other family members are all still at the house?' He was certain that Serafina and Flora had been concealing more information when he and the inspector had interviewed them. He felt that Flora's explanation of her trip to Dartmouth with Edward Forbes the day before the party had been particularly thin.

'Excuse me, Inspector, you are wanted urgently on the telephone. A gentleman from the Naval College wishes to speak to you.' Mr Lutterworth had reappeared at the door to the lounge before the policeman could answer Matt's question.

The inspector immediately rose and followed the hotel manager back to the reception area. Matt could only assume the call must be important since Cyril had said it was urgent and whoever it was must have tried the police station in Torquay first, before being informed of the inspector's presence at the Dolphin.

This could be the link they had been hoping for that would allow them to discover how naval secrets were being passed to potentially unfriendly nations. It was strange though that they had asked for the inspector and had not contacted the naval chain of command back to the admiralty. Unless perhaps the corruption extended further than the brigadier had feared.

The inspector returned to the room. 'I think we need to leave immediately for the Naval College, Captain Bryant.'

Matt looked at the Miller sisters.

'We'll take care of Bertie, sir, until you comes back. If there is any news of Miss Kitty we can leave messages for you at the college.' Alice seemed to read his mind.

'Thank you, both, I'm much obliged. Hopefully we may get news of Kitty soon.'

He followed the inspector out into the corridor and hoped he was correct. Despite this apparent breakthrough in the case of Herr Freiberg's murder he couldn't stop worrying and wondering where Kitty might be and if she was safe. If anything happened to her, he wouldn't wait for the culprit to face the noose. He would take care of them himself.

'What news from the college, sir?' Matt asked as they hurried out onto the street and headed towards the inspector's motor car.

'Guess who has arrived at the Naval College?' Inspector Greville's moustache perked up as he unlocked his car.

Matt's heart leapt in the hope that Kitty might be there and safe.

'Master Theodore Hawkes has arrived and is with an old friend of his. The two boys are apparently singing like the proverbial canaries to one of the trusted officers.' The inspector started the engine as Matt's spirits dipped as rapidly as they had risen.

'How did Theo gain access to the college?' Matt asked. He knew there was security at the gate and rightly so. Civilians were not usually permitted on the grounds without a great deal of form filling.

'The friend is a cadet, and it is apparently his weekend for leave. He stumbled across Theo in a hostelry in the town. That is as much as could be said on the telephone for security reasons.' The inspector drove his car up the hill leading out of the town and took the turn to the wrought-iron gate leading into the college grounds.

The college was a large imposing building commanding a fine view of the estuary below. It could be clearly seen from Kingswear on the opposite bank of the river and dominated the townscape. In addition to the main building there were extensive grounds surrounding the college and a training ship was moored on the River Dart below.

The inspector halted for the uniformed guard at the gate and gave their names to the sailor on duty.

The man looked at the inspector's details and Matt's calling card before making a short telephone call to the main college to speak to the officer who was expecting them.

'Thank you, sir. You may proceed.' The sailor stepped back and lifted the wooden painted barrier so the inspector could drive to the main building where they followed the signs to the designated visitor space.

'This should prove enlightening,' Matt murmured to the inspector as another uniformed sailor approached them to lead them inside the building.

Normally he would have been delighted to have gained such access and the promise of cracking a case. Instead, all he could think of was his fiancée's safety. He could only hope that perhaps Theo might have some information on the matter. After all he had left Sir Montague's home in Forbes' company earlier that day. He might have some idea of where Kitty might be.

Their escort led them at a smart pace. Not through the main entrance as Matt had expected, but around the rear of the building and in through a small side door. Matt could only assume that whoever they were meeting did not wish to draw too much attention to their visit.

* * *

Once she had restored some feeling back to her fingers, Kitty reached up into the narrow space over her head to try and probe whatever was above her. There had to be a hatch of some kind. How else would Forbes have managed to place her into the space? Had he been acting alone or had Theo reappeared to help him? She felt sick at the thought.

Kitty peered upwards looking for any gleam of light showing in the surface of the wooden ceiling that might indicate where the opening might be. The lack of space and the darkness hampered her every move and if she moved too vigorously the floor beneath her rocked, sending the pool of stagnant cold water splashing against her.

Cautiously, she poked and prodded, listening out all the while for any sound that might indicate that she was not alone. Her stomach growled and her lips were dry and cracked. Her cup of tea with Matt and Inspector Greville earlier in the day now seemed a distant memory.

She could hear nothing except the faint splashing of the water against the hull of the boat from time to time and the muffled sound of birdsong. She crawled forward and tried a different part of the roof. This time she was sure she could feel the edge of a trapdoor.

Kitty carefully positioned herself, so she was in the centre of what felt like the hatch and pushed upwards desperately hoping that Forbes hadn't bothered to secure the door. The door was heavy, but to her relief it moved, and a slither of light entered the hull.

It was tempting to simply push it wide open and clamber out, but she had no idea if Edward Forbes was still in the vicinity. Instead, she lifted the door a little higher until she could peep out and see where she was being held.

The trapdoor appeared to open straight onto the deck of a small boat moored inside some kind of ramshackle wooden boathouse. She was relieved to see that it was still daylight. She looked around and as far as she could determine she was alone.

She pushed the door open and pulled herself cautiously out onto the deck. Once outside the hull she paused to take stock of her situation. There was no sign of her missing shoe and she'd abandoned the other to its fate in the hull. Her wristwatch had stopped working, the glass covering the dial was cracked and broken.

The boat where Forbes had imprisoned her was in much the same state as the boathouse, ramshackle and had seen better days. It was moored to a wooden post at the foot of a small flight of three worn stone steps in a shallow silted up pond. Nettles and brambles grew out of the mud of the bank, and it was clear that few people ever came that way.

Kitty surveyed the area, her heart sinking as she realised her plight. She did not have her shoes or her hat and handbag. She had no real idea of the time except that the shadows inside the boathouse were quite long so it must be approaching dusk.

Her stockings were ruined, and she had dried blood on her arms, hands and legs. She reasoned that Edward could not have carried her far, so they had to be near a road of some sort. She edged her way carefully to the edge of the boat and lowered her legs over the side. The tweed material of her skirt was moist, and her silk blouse clung damply to her back under her jacket.

She manoeuvred herself as closely as she could to the stone step and slid off the boat. There were small sharp stones on the step, and she winced as she landed heavily on the wet gravel. There was still no sign of anyone near the boat. She picked her way up the steps trying to avoid the worst of the nettles and brambles. Once at the top she saw she was on a narrow rotting wooden deck that led to the entrance of the boathouse.

As quickly as she could in her stockinged feet, she made her way along to the door to the boathouse. It was half open, sagging on its hinges. It looked as if it was incapable of closing properly. Weeds were pressing in on the opening and the deck gave way to a narrow rabbit's path that led out through the long grass into a field.

Kitty had little choice but to take it and hope that it might lead her somewhere so that she could get help. The path led upwards through a field towards a drystone wall and some scrubby yellow furze bushes at the top of the field. She was clearly at the bottom of a valley, all around her were hills. How long had they been travelling? The backwater must feed into a river at some point. The Dart? Or the Teign, perhaps?

Her feet were scratched and bleeding by the time she reached the wooden five bar gate in the wall. On the other side of the gate was a cart track with grass growing in clumps along its centre. A small puddle of fresh motor oil on the gravel surface told her a car had been parked there recently.

Probably Edward's she thought, when he had left her tied up in the hull of the boat. She climbed up the gate to perch on the top, hoping the added height might allow her to see where she was and if there was any sign of a farm or house where she might go for help.

Further along the lane, over the tops of the trees she thought she could see a chimney. She would have to be careful, for all she knew it could belong to Edward, or friends of his. He had to know this area well. The boat in the boathouse wasn't something someone would stumble across by accident.

She clambered down the gate and limped along the lane towards where she thought she had seen the chimney. If there was someone there, they might have a telephone and she could at least let Matt know she was safe.

Kitty kept a sharp watch as she rounded the corner leading to what she discovered was a small farmhouse. Built of local grey-brown stone it was clear that it had not been occupied for a long time. The stables on the opposite side of the yard were empty and weeds were growing between the flags before the front door.

Her heart sank as she took in her surroundings.

'Oh, Kitty, what have you got yourself into this time?' she whispered aloud as she looked around the deserted yard.

CHAPTER TWENTY-TWO

Matt and the inspector's sailor escort led them along a narrow service corridor halting outside a plain wooden door where he knocked sharply. On being bidden to enter, he opened the door, saluted whoever was inside and stepped smartly aside for Matt and Inspector Greville to enter the room.

'Captain Bryant and Inspector Greville, sir.' Their escort was dismissed with a nod of his head by the uniformed officer seated at the desk.

'Inspector, Captain, I'm glad you were able to join us. I'm Lieutenant Faulkner.'

'Sir,' Inspector Greville greeted the lieutenant and shook his hand. Matt followed suit. On the other side of the room sitting somewhat stiffly to attention was a young fresh-faced youth in civilian dress. Sitting just as awkwardly beside him Matt recognised the familiar figure of Theodore Hawkes.

'Please take a seat, gentlemen.' The lieutenant indicated a couple of vacant plain wooden chairs near the small oak desk.

Matt took a place on one of the chairs next to the inspector. Lieutenant Faulkner had a pile of papers in front of him and a black leather briefcase.

'I apologise for the somewhat clandestine nature of this meeting. I am given to understand from the preliminary enquiries that I have made that both of you are covered under the Official Secrets Act?' The officer surveyed them both from beneath the brim of his cap with a steely air.

'Yes, sir, we are,' Matt answered.

The lieutenant nodded. 'Then you will appreciate that this is a highly confidential matter concerning the security of the nation.' It was a statement rather than a question.

'Yes, sir. I have been engaged for some time as a freelance agent by my former employer at Whitehall.' Matt met the officer's gaze and handed over one of his business cards. He had no desire to mention Brigadier Remmington-Blythe by name until he was certain that Lieutenant Faulkner was not one of the officers under suspicion.

'I see. Inspector, I am given to understand that you and Captain Bryant are investigating the recent murder of a German national, Herr Gunther Freiberg, aboard the paddle steamer *Kingswear Castle*?'

Matt noticed Theo shift awkwardly in his seat at the mention of Gunther's name.

'Yes, sir, that is correct.' Inspector Greville, like Matt, appeared to be waiting for the officer to reveal his hand.

Lieutenant Faulkner leaned forward in his chair and steepled his hands together on the desk as he considered Matt and the inspector. He appeared to be weighing up how much he could say and if they could indeed be trusted.

Matt prickled with impatience. Theodore might hold the key to Kitty's disappearance and this delay could be dangerous. He decided to push the interview on.

'Herr Freiberg was a person of interest in an ongoing investigation at the highest levels concerning the leak of various documents and pieces of information which could be useful to an enemy.' Matt waited to see the naval officer's reaction.

The lieutenant leaned back in his seat. 'And you believe that one of the sources supplying this man with information was based here at the college?'

Matt met the officer's gaze. 'Yes, sir, that's correct.'

'I asked your escort to bring you into the college via a circuitous route for a reason. The navy takes any hint of disloyalty to our King very seriously indeed. A breach of security should we find ourselves ever again engaged in warfare with another nation could result in the catastrophic loss of countless lives. I presume, Captain Bryant, as a veteran yourself you are very aware of this.'

Lieutenant Faulkner paused for a moment to glance in the direction of Theo who had his head bowed and appeared to be studying his shoes. His companion's cheeks glowed a brighter shade of pink.

'The navy has been aware that there might be someone here at the college in a high position who could not be trusted. I was tasked in confidence with determining who that person might be. As a service we like to take care of our own problems.' He looked directly at Matt.

It was clear that the old service rivalries were still prevalent.

'I had made some headway in the matter. These two gentlemen approached me this afternoon unaware of my brief. I believe that Billings there felt that as I was not regularly based here and therefore less likely to be involved with any kind of treachery, he could therefore safely bring certain information to my attention.' The naval officer looked at the young cadet seated next to Theodore.

'Theodore Hawkes was seen leaving the home of the chief constable this morning in the company of Mr Edward Forbes, a person of interest in the murder of Herr Freiberg.' Inspector Greville also turned his attention towards a miserable-looking Theo.

'Since then, my fiancée, Miss Kitty Underhay, has vanished

and may have been taken by Mr Forbes. I have reason to think she may be in grave danger if that is the case,' Matt added. His concern for Kitty's welfare adding to the need to drag information from the lieutenant and the youths that were seated near to him.

Theo raised his head at the mention of Kitty's name and a look of blind panic passed across his pale features. 'Kitty is missing?'

His outburst earned a glare from Lieutenant Faulkner. 'Silence, please, Mr Hawkes. You may have your say in a moment.'

It was obvious from the officer's demeanour that he didn't care for Theo.

'Perhaps, sir, you could tell us what you have learned so that we can pool our information. Not only is our country's security at risk, Miss Underhay may also be in a great deal of personal danger,' Inspector Greville said.

'Billings, tell the inspector and Captain Bryant the events of this afternoon.' The officer looked to the young naval cadet.

'Sir.' Billings sat up even straighter in his chair and looked directly ahead, avoiding any kind of eye contact with Theodore, who had slumped down once more on his seat.

'I have a day pass, sir, and had left the college this morning in the company of some of my fellows. We wound up at lunchtime in the Ship. A hostelry near the ferry stop.' The lad paused as if uncertain if the inspector and Matt knew where he meant.

'We know the Ship Inn. Please continue,' Matt said. He knew the Ship well, it was one of the oldest pubs in Dartmouth and of a similar age to the Dolphin.

'We'd been in there a while when Theo came in. He and I were old friends from our youth. We were at school together.' Billings risked a very swift glance sideways at Theo. 'I saw him across the bar and thought he looked unwell. I went over to him as I was surprised to see him there. When I approached him, he asked if I was still at the Naval College. He didn't seem to want anyone to hear him speak to me. He kept looking around as if he thought someone might be following him.' Billings round, clear face crinkled into a frown.

Matt struggled to suppress the urge to get up from his seat and shake the boy in an effort to get the information from him more speedily.

'Continue,' Lieutenant Faulkner ordered.

'I took my ale and ordered one for Theo and we went to the back of the bar out of direct sight. Theo told me he was afraid that someone might be after him. He said he'd become embroiled in something that could risk his life.' Billings licked his lips and continued with his tale. 'He asked if there was an officer at the college that I felt I could trust. He said he had to speak to them. He said it was important that no one found out. I could see he was in deadly earnest, and he told me that one man had been killed already. I knew Lieutenant Faulkner might be prepared to listen, so I took a chance and returned to the college.'

'Billings was fortunate to catch me in the grounds. I arranged for him to bring Hawkes there into the college. When I heard Hawkes' story, I contacted London and was advised that you, Inspector Greville and Captain Bryant, were the people I needed to speak with,' the naval officer said.

'Well then, Theo, you had better tell us everything that you know about Edward Forbes and the murder of Herr Freiberg,' Inspector Greville turned to Theo.

'It all started off all right. You have to believe me on that. I had no idea what I might be getting into. By the time I found out it was too late.' Theo looked miserably at them. 'I swear on my mother's life I didn't know.'

'Forbes may have taken Kitty. Do you know his plans? For heaven's sake, spit it out, what do you know?' Matt demanded, anxious to cut through Theo's pleas of innocence and apologies for whatever it was he'd done.

Inspector Greville placed a restraining hand on Matt's arm to keep him from standing.

'Hurry up, man, it's getting late, and we need to find Forbes and Miss Underhay.' The Inspector echoed Matt's thoughts.

'Serafina brought Forbes to the house shortly before I was due to leave for Cambridge. She met him at some art thing; Saffy is frightfully keen on the arts. He seemed like a decent fellow, you know, wealthy, dressed well and Saffy was terribly keen on him. He made a good impression on Mother and Father too. He soon had them eating out of his hand. Flora as well.' Theo squirmed in his seat. 'Well, a fellow likes to enjoy himself and Father can be somewhat miserly with my allowance. I ran into one or two problems. You know shortage of funds, so I'd borrowed money from well, dangerous sources.' He paused once more and sighed.

'Edward bumped into me in Cambridge. He said he was there on business. We went for drinks, and I confided in him. I was desperate, they weren't the sort of fellows that one could not repay. He offered to loan me a few pounds to tide me over. He said we were virtually family now so what could be the harm?'

'He now had a financial hold over you?' Matt asked. He guessed that the meeting in Cambridge had probably been engineered. In fact, he would place money on it that Serafina's so-called chance encounter with Forbes at the art exhibition where they had first met had probably also not been by chance.

Theo nodded. 'He loaned me more money. I owe him quite a packet now. I can't afford to pay it back, not just yet. He started putting a bit of pressure on and then he suggested that I could help him with a few things to reduce the debt. I was in deep by now and what's more I found out by chance that Saffy was in the same boat.'

'Your sister owes Forbes money too?' Inspector Greville asked.

Theo nodded. 'She doesn't get much from Father. A bit of a dress allowance, that's all and she wants to study. Father has forbidden it, so she has been secretly buying textbooks and taking classes. Father found out somehow and stopped her money altogether, so Edward offered to lend her some.'

'And what were these small jobs that Forbes suggested that you might do for him?' Matt asked.

Theo shrugged. 'At first it was just taking some packages to various places. I never asked what was in them or why they couldn't be delivered by post. I knew that the less I knew about the contents the better it would be. Then he encouraged me to find out some information for him. He told me what to look for. I used to sneak into Father's office and read the papers he kept in the drawer of his desk. I knew where the key was kept so it was easy enough to access them.'

'These were papers relating to arrests and upcoming trials?' Inspector Greville asked, his moustache quivering in suppressed indignation.

Theo gave another shamefaced nod. 'I know that some of what I told him was used to help get various people released from custody and could have been used in their trials to get them off.'

'Do you know what tasks he persuaded your sister to aid him with?' Inspector Greville asked.

'I've never spoken to her about it. I assumed it must be something. Forbes never gave anyone anything without there being strings attached. I suppose that was why he was so confident that she would accept his marriage proposal. Mother and Father were keen and well, Saffy is a good egg but in the looks stakes, well, she struggles rather. If he and Saffy married, with Father's position he would be pretty much untouchable,' Theo said.

Matt could see now how Forbes had been working. 'But then your sister refused him.'

Theo shifted awkwardly, squirming in his seat. 'Yes, Edward wasn't pleased. He said he had to meet someone in Dartmouth today and needed my help. He said he was certain Saffy would come around and change her mind. He seemed pretty confident.' Theo paused and frowned. 'I think he said that Flora might persuade her. I don't know, it could be that he has something on her too. It wouldn't surprise me.'

The inspector exchanged a glance with Matt. 'Do you know who he was meeting and where?'

'At a creek below the castle in Dartmouth. I didn't know until we got there that it was someone from the college. He said it was to receive an important document. I told him that I'd had enough and couldn't help him anymore. He threatened me and said I had no choice, that I should think of Saffy. We argued and I walked away. I was frightened he might come after me or try something. He's ruthless, he must have been the one who killed the German chap on the boat. I know he had met him before as Flora let something slip when we boarded. I don't think anyone else heard but as the steward handed her on board, I thought she said something like 'oh, it's you,' and I know Edward had taken her into Dartmouth the day before the party. He'd said he was arranging a surprise for Saffy. I didn't think anything of it until after the ball, when we found out there had been a murder.' Theo looked at his friend.

'I wandered round the town in a bit of a daze. I didn't know what to do. I thought that if he was meeting someone from the college then this bloke's death had to be tied into whatever was going on. I had thought before it might be cocaine smuggling or something, but then I realised it could be something even worse.'

The youth sat straighter in his seat and raised his chin. 'I may have been foolish and done a lot of wrong things, but I am not a traitor. I ended up at the Ship Inn and saw Billings. I had to confide in someone, or I thought I might go mad. Forbes has to be stopped somehow and now you say you think he has Kitty?'

'Did you see any sign of her when you were at Warfleet Creek?' Matt asked.

Theo shook his head once more. 'There was no one around at all. That must have been why Forbes chose it as a rendezvous. I was surprised he let me leave unharmed. I've been looking over my shoulder ever since.' He gave an involuntary shudder.

'Kitty must have stumbled onto the meeting. She must have been walking Bertie along the creek.' Matt looked at the inspector. 'Theo, was Forbes' car parked in the lane?'

'Yes. I left on foot while I assume he stayed to meet whoever was coming from the college. I just wanted to get as far away from him as possible.'

'Do you know the name of the person he was meeting?' This time it was the lieutenant who asked the question.

'No, sir.' Colour flamed into Theo's cheeks. 'I'm sorry.'

'Where on earth is Kitty? Where can he have taken her?' Matt looked at Inspector Greville. 'If Forbes does have her, then I fear the worst.'

CHAPTER TWENTY-THREE

Kitty hobbled into the yard acutely aware of her sore feet. She made her way to the front step of the farmhouse and sank down onto the worn stone. In the dust nearby she noticed what looked like tyre tracks. Thin and narrow as if someone on a bicycle had been there recently.

Perhaps the farm was not so deserted after all if someone had ridden up there. It could mean that there might be more cottages or labourers' dwellings nearby. She looked at her painful feet and sighed. If she had her shoes this would be so much easier. As it was, walking through the countryside in her bare feet was not going to get her very far, especially if any buildings were at a distance.

Her mouth was dry, and she licked her lips trying to moisten them. Surely there had to be something here that she could use to help her. Forbes obviously knew this area, if he came back and found her gone then he would probably guess that she might make for this farm. The sooner she could move on from here the safer she would be.

Kitty hauled herself to her feet and looked around. There seemed to be a small stone well near the side of the derelict cowshed, so she made her way across. The winding mechanism seemed to still be intact, and she lowered the wooden bucket down into the well until she heard a distant splash.

To her relief, the water seemed to be cold and clear when she raised the bucket back up. She took a long draught of water and splashed some on her face and wrists, soothing the marks from the ropes and washing away some of the dust.

Suitably refreshed, she decided to see if there was anything inside the sheds that could possibly be of any use to her. It was too much to hope for that she might find an old bicycle or something, but anything at all might come in handy should Forbes return and catch her.

The first semi open door she tried showed her the stalls of what seemed to be an empty milking parlour. A few heaps of mouldering hay still remained in the wooden feed troughs and a rusted metal pail stood on the flags. Spider's webs covered the small leaded pane window and Kitty shuddered.

The next door along had almost fallen away completely from its hinges. The top half leaning out drunkenly away from the rotten frame. Kitty wrinkled her nose at the smell of old horse and cow manure and peered cautiously inside. This one too was empty, except for a pile of old hessian feed sacks in the corner and a dusty shelf holding some corroded metal tins.

She made her way into the shed and hoped the sacks were not home to vermin. If she could get them, she might at least be able to fashion something to protect her feet. Kitty reached for the sacks and gave them a quick tug sending woodlice running in all directions.

Her toes curled as she dodged the scurrying insects, and she dragged the sacks out into the fading daylight. She gave them a good shake to remove any remaining wildlife and looked at her bounty. Two of the sacks were damp and rotten but the top two were smaller and dry.

She folded the dry sacks and unclipped the tattered remains

of her ruined stockings, thankful for once that they were not her really sheer ones, but instead were of a thicker material. Then she used the stockings to bind the folded sacks to her feet. At least they would offer her soles some protection as she walked, even if they did keep slipping about.

'Not the most fashionable footwear, Kitty,' she muttered as she stood up and tested them out. At least they might stop the worst of the stones from digging into her soles.

A tear slipped down her cheek as she thought of her afternoon choosing her wedding gown. It seemed like a hundred years away and here she was modelling hessian-sacking shoes. She gave a determined sniff and dashed the tear from her cheek. There was no time to feel sorry for herself. She had to get out of there before the light faded and try to find some help.

She made her way back out through the farm gate after checking there was nothing else likely to be useful in the remaining farm buildings. The farm itself seemed to be locked up tight and she couldn't see inside through the grime on the windows.

The farm seemed to be at the end of the track so she had little choice except to venture back the way she had come and keep going hoping that sooner or later she would reach a better road or more cottages.

The road was still uncomfortable beneath her feet and her makeshift footwear kept slipping so she had to stop and make adjustments as she plodded along up the hill. The sun was lower in the sky now and the air had turned cooler. Swifts swooped ahead of her in the lane, darting across to catch the small gnats and other insects that appeared at dusk.

The fields on either side of the stone walls seemed to be mainly used for cattle and there was no sign of any habitation. She listened out as she walked in case Forbes' car should suddenly appear. At least there were plenty of bushes and a narrow drainage ditch should she be suddenly forced to fling herself into hiding.

The thought had no sooner crossed her mind when she heard the unmistakable sound of a car approaching. She hid behind the drystone wall at the entrance to a field and peeped out to see who it might be.

Any hope that it might be someone who could assist her died when she recognised the sleek dark-green nose of Forbes' car. Her pulse speeded up and she ducked back behind the wall under a scrubby hawthorn bush and waited. She knew he would inevitably go to the boathouse, where he would find her gone.

Sooner or later, he would have to return along this lane and no doubt he would be searching for her as he drove. A shiver of fear danced along her spine, and she tucked herself up into as small a position as she could manage while she waited for the sound of the car to return back along the lane.

After what felt like an age, she heard the car engine coming back towards her. This time, however, the car was being driven much more slowly and there were pauses as if the driver was stopping to look for something. Or, more probably someone, namely Kitty.

At least the heather colours of her tweed suit provided good camouflage and the bush growing over her head should shield her from anyone trying to look over the top of the walls. The sound of the motor grew louder, and she could smell the exhaust fumes as the car halted at the entrance to the field.

Kitty's heart hammered in her chest, and she prayed he wouldn't get out of the car to look inside the entrance. After a moment the car rolled further on down the track, and she breathed a sigh of relief.

She waited a few more minutes until she could no longer hear the note of the engine before crawling out of her hiding place and brushing off the dead leaves and bits of twig that had attached themselves to her clothes.

Kitty decided that it was unlikely that he would waste time returning to try to find her as the light was fading fast. The sun was almost gone from the sky now, the fiery red sunset had dissolved into rose gold and streaks of violet. The birdsong, which had been so loud when she had set off from the farmstead, was diminishing in volume as the day gave way to nightfall. She hoped that she wouldn't have to walk too much further before she found someone who might be able to help her. It would be difficult to travel in the dark on the unlit lane and she had no desire to fall into a ditch or sprain her ankle.

She walked as quickly as her footwear and the uneven surface would allow. The lane continued to lead up a gradient and the loss of light made progress difficult. By the time she had reached where the track met a wider road, darkness had fallen. A white-painted signpost stood at the junction, and she realised that she was some two miles outside Blackawton, a small village some six miles or so away from Dartmouth.

The direction she had walked from was signed Millcombe and she wondered if the boathouse had been nearer to the hamlet than she had realised. It looked as if she still had quite a way to walk before she had any hope of raising the alarm.

* * *

Matt stepped outside the interview room and lit up a cigarette. He needed to take a minute to calm his nerves. It was clear from Theodore Hawkes' testimony that they were dealing with a very dangerous man in Edward Forbes.

He continued to smoke, only half aware of the muffled sound of continued conversation in the room behind him. He glanced at his wristwatch. It would be dark soon and Kitty was still missing. Dolly and Alice would be frantic and Mrs Treadwell would soon be returning to the Dolphin unaware of Kitty's plight.

He finished his cigarette and disposed of the extinguished stub by tossing it from the window into the grass at the rear of the college.

'I've just telephoned the police station to see if there was any fresh news. The constable we dispatched to check on the property linked to Forbes near Millcombe has reported in. He says the farm is derelict and locked up tight with no sign of anyone having been there.' Inspector Greville had appeared at Matt's side.

Matt's heart sank at this unwelcome news. This possible link to a property outside Dartmouth was the only clue they had for where Forbes might have taken Kitty.

'What next then, sir? What of the other property Alice mentioned?' he asked.

'I have men looking on all the roads for Forbes' car. If it passes through a town or village then we'll know where he is. The constable also said he thinks that the farm he visited is only a part of the property all owned by the same family. He thinks the house that belonged to the same man is nearer to Blackawton than Millcombe. He's gone back to the village to enquire and see if his hunch is correct. If she's there, Captain Bryant, then we'll find her.' Inspector Greville's face was grave, and Matt knew that the policeman was as frustrated as he was by the situation.

'In the meantime, what are we to do with young Hawkes?' Matt asked.

'I suggest we take him back to the police station with us and he can repeat his statement to my sergeant. Lieutenant Faulkner intends to follow things up here. Billings, of course, will do as he's told and keep his mouth shut. At least the brigadier may discover the source of the leak before much longer.' Inspector Greville scratched his chin thoughtfully.

'Once we have deposited Master Hawkes we may have more information from the constable at Blackawton.'

Matt blew out a frustrated sigh. 'Very well.' At least this meant they would be doing something. He just wanted to be out there actively looking for Kitty. He had to hope that they wouldn't be too late.

They were escorted back through the rear corridors of the college by the lieutenant and Theo was stowed in the back of the inspector's car. They bade the officer farewell and drove back down the hill into Dartmouth.

'Could you let me out of the motor at the boat float, sir. I'll go to the Dolphin and let Alice and Dolly know what's happening. Kitty's grandmother may have returned by now too and she will be concerned at Kitty's absence,' Matt asked as they reached the bottom of the hill.

'Very well. I'll take Master Hawkes here along to the police station and will telephone you once I have more information,' the inspector agreed and pulled the car to a stop so that Matt could return to the hotel.

The sun was setting now over the river and the electric lights along the embankment had been lit. Matt was glad of the cool of the evening air as he made his way towards the familiar black-and-white hotel.

Mary had been replaced on reception by Bill, the night porter, when he entered the lobby. It was clear from his demeanour that the older man had been made aware of the day's events.

'Evening, Captain Bryant, sir. Any news of Miss Kitty?'

Matt shook his head. 'Not yet, Bill, I'm afraid. Are Alice and Dolly still here?'

'Yes, sir, they'm in Mrs Treadwell's apartment with your dog,' Bill replied.

'Has Kitty's grandmother returned yet?' Matt asked. He was mindful of Kitty's worries over her grandmother's health.

Discovering her beloved granddaughter was missing would be the most terrible shock.

'Not yet, sir. I believe she is dining out this evening and is not expected to return until after eleven o'clock.' Bill automatically glanced at the clock on the wall as he spoke.

'Thank you.' Matt hurried up the broad polished oak staircase to Mrs Treadwell's apartment.

Dolly and Alice were seated on the sofa as he entered the salon. Bertie immediately jumped up, his tail wagging to greet him.

'Any news, sir?' Alice placed the sewing she had been doing to one side.

'No, not yet. Inspector Greville has gone to the police station to see if any more information has been received. We are hoping the constable at Blackawton may uncover some more information.' Matt sank down on a nearby armchair and fussed the top of his dog's head.

Dolly had been occupying herself with the crossword in the newspaper, which she too now set aside. 'We hoped as you might have found her by now. Mr Lutterworth is out in the town doing some asking about. He seemed to think as some of the low places his nephew drinks at might have some kind of a clue about this Forbes man that they mayn't tell the police, but might tell him if he took a bit of money with him.'

'He's made his nephew accompany him to see if he can find anything out,' Alice added.

Matt appreciated Mr Lutterworth's ingenuity. 'That's good of him.'

'Let me get the kitchen to send you up something to eat and drink, Captain Bryant. You look as if you'm fair beat and if we'm to find Miss Kitty you need to keep your strength up,' Alice declared decisively. Before he could argue she was using the telephone to order cold beef sandwiches and a pot of tea.

He realised that it had been quite some time since he had

eaten anything and although he had little appetite, he appreciated her good intentions. When had Kitty last eaten? Did she have strength for whatever she was facing? The tea tray arrived at the same time as Mr Lutterworth.

'Captain Bryant, any news?' Cyril asked as he removed his cap.

Matt shook his head in reply, his mouth full of roast beef.

Cyril had clearly changed his attire in order to visit the public houses in the less savoury part of the town. He no longer wore his smart suit and rose, but had donned working man's apparel.

'I have made enquiries at some hostelries where it seems this man Forbes may have been. It was a bit of a long shot, but I felt it worth a try. My nephew let slip that the man who was murdered on the paddle steamer also drank in some of the same pubs.' Mr Lutterworth took a seat on the armchair opposite Matt, and Dolly immediately poured him a cup of tea in one of the extra china cups.

Matt finished his mouthful of sandwich and looked at the older man. 'Did you learn anything new?'

'A gentleman answering Mr Forbes' description had been seen talking to Herr Freiberg outside the public house. The landlord seemed to think that Mr Forbes' father's family came from near Blackawton and that he had inherited property there. His father's family were quite well-to-do. The landlord's wife is from Millcombe and she said that Mr Forbes' family had opposed his parents' marriage as there was a large age gap and the girl had a bad reputation. His father died when he was young, and the mother took off with Edward.' Mr Lutterworth took a sip of his tea clearly in need of refreshment. 'Edward only reappeared a couple of years ago when his uncle became ill. There was no other family.'

'Do you know what property?' Matt asked. The farm had

already been checked but the inspector had said the constable believed there might be another place.

'A farm closer to Millcombe that has gone to wrack and ruin and another smaller house in better condition closer to Blackawton itself. That one was tenanted until recently, but is believed to be empty again now. The landlord's wife was very helpful. I have made a note of the directions.' Mr Lutterworth reached inside the top pocket of his coat and pulled out a sheet of paper, which he passed to Matt.

Matt could have kissed the top of the older man's bald head. 'Thank you. I think this may be the property Inspector Greville was talking about.'

He was about to telephone the police station when the door opened once more and the inspector himself walked in.

'Mr Lutterworth has an address for us.' Matt gave the paper to the inspector.

Inspector Greville scanned the details. 'Come then, there's no time to lose.'

Matt collected Bertie's lead from the table. 'I'll bring Bertie. If Kitty has been anywhere near that property, I'm certain Bertie will let us know.'

Mr Lutterworth also rose from his chair. 'Might I also accompany you? An extra pair of eyes and hands may not come amiss.'

Dolly bustled out of the bedroom with her arms full. 'Take this blanket with you. If Miss Kitty has been outside, she might be a bit cold when you finds her.' She thrust the bundle at her sister. 'There's a little bottle of brandy there as well, for shock.'

'That's a good idea, Dolly.' Alice took the things from her sister and prepared to follow them from the room.

'Here, this is most irregular, Miss Miller. It's not a circus. This Forbes chap could be very dangerous,' Inspector Greville protested.

'And if Miss Kitty is hurt or something she might need the

presence of a woman with her. I'm coming as well.' Alice tipped her chin up and stared the inspector down. 'You stay here, our Dolly, and look after Mrs Treadwell when she comes back.'

Inspector Greville recognised from her determined expression that Alice was not to be deterred. He sighed heavily and appeared to resign himself to a full car and the group hurried away to the waiting police car.

CHAPTER TWENTY-FOUR

Kitty's eyes gradually became more accustomed to the darkness as she stumbled her way along the rutted lane. Fortunately, the moon was almost full and low in the sky and offered her some sense of where she was going. Small bats skittered about and once or twice she startled when a rabbit or pheasant suddenly popped out of the high hedges at the side of the road.

She guessed she must have been walking for at least thirty minutes or so when she caught a faint glimmer of light up ahead. Her spirits rose when she realised she could detect the faint smell of woodsmoke in the air. A house with a fire burning and lights at the window.

The thought of rescue gave added strength to her weary legs as she made her way towards the property. As she drew closer, she could see from the silhouette in the gloom that the house was large and set back from the road. Neatly trimmed hedges bordered a gravelled sweep of a driveway leading to the side of the house. The curtains were still open and yellow lamplight spilled out from the window at the far side of the front door.

Kitty could only hope and pray that whoever the occupants might be they would look past what must be her somewhat wild appearance and rescue her from her present dilemma. She limped past the white-painted gateposts and into the drive ready to head towards the front entrance.

Suddenly she noticed a vehicle parked almost in the hedge in the deep shadow at the side of the house and something made her pause. Her heart thumped as she drew closer. Forbes' dark-green sports car. She had almost walked right into the lion's den.

The front door opened sending another narrow beam of light spilling out onto the drive. Kitty looked around her frantically for somewhere to hide. There was no shelter to be found in the neatly trimmed privet hedge and she knew she would be seen and heard if she tried to escape back up the drive into the lane.

There was only one thing she could think of doing. She clambered on the running board and dived into the back seat of Forbes' open-topped car and curled down as low as she could go in the footwell behind the driver's seat. A tartan travel rug lay nearby next to a couple of leather suitcases so she pulled it over herself and hoped he wouldn't think to look in the back of his car.

She could hear Forbes talking to someone inside the house and guessed that he must be on the doorstep.

'Stop worrying. I'll find her, she can't have reached the village, or we would have heard by now. This is the most likely place she would find to try and get help. There are no other houses nearby. If she comes here, you know what to do.' Forbes sounded closer to the car now and Kitty's pulse raced.

The other speaker was female, but her voice was fainter and Kitty could only assume that whoever it was had remained on the step.

'I will deal with that little twerp Theo when he emerges from wherever he has gone to sulk. He's probably cooling his heels in some public house in Dartmouth. You look out for the girl, and I'll be back later once I've made the delivery and collected the money. The police may be looking for the car so it's better that I travel at night.' Forbes sounded very close now.

The driver door clicked open, and Kitty stifled a gasp. She held her breath as Edward climbed into his seat making the leather creak. She dared not risk looking out as any movement might make him realise that he had a stowaway.

It was quite sweaty under the rug and the wool prickled the sore spots on her legs. Her calves ached with cramp and her feet were throbbing from her long walk in her makeshift shoes. Kitty wondered where Edward was headed. She hoped it wasn't back to the boathouse or the derelict farm, or she would be right back where she started.

She made herself a small gap so that she could at least get a little air. The engine started and the powerful car was soon speeding along. She guessed they must be on a better road, or he would never dare to drive so quickly. He had mentioned a delivery and picking up money. Was this to drop off whatever he had received earlier from the man at Warfleet Creek?

If this were so, then she could have clambered out of the frying pan and directly into the fire. Even as the thought crossed her mind Forbes turned the car off the smooth surface of the road. Kitty was jolted and bumped as Forbes evidently took the car some place it was unlikely to be observed.

She winced and struggled not to cry out in pain as she was jolted and jarred in her cramped position. The car stopped and Forbes sat waiting with the engine still running. Kitty heard the rasp of a match striking and smelled the sudden acrid tang of cigarette smoke.

It seemed that he was waiting for someone. Perhaps this was the delivery he had spoken about. They had to be in a field or lay-by of some kind judging by the jolting and jarring she had experienced. She longed to move, to stretch out her legs and ease her discomfort.

Presently she heard the sound of another engine approaching. It didn't sound like a car though she decided. It reminded her of Matt's motorcycle. A tear leaked out onto her cheek. Poor Matt would be frantic with worry wondering where she could have gone. She would give anything she owned right now for this to be her fiancé riding to her rescue.

The other engine stopped, and it seemed brighter as light filtered through the fabric of the rug. Kitty guessed that the other motorist or motorcyclist had his headlamps on.

'You have the package?' A male voice sounded, clipped and harsh.

'Do you have the money?' Forbes' reply was almost languid as if he had no cares at all about this strange exchange.

There was a rustling sound and Kitty strained to try and work out what it might be.

'You do not need to count it. It is all complete.' The stranger's voice came once more.

Kitty held her breath. This must be the payment he had mentioned.

'Better not to assume, old chap.' Forbes sounded amused.

'Now for your part of the agreement,' the other man said.

There was more rustling, followed by the roar of the motorcycle engine restarting. 'We shall not do this again. We will be in contact for a new arrangement. The loss of Gunther was most unfortunate.' The stranger spoke again over the sound of the engine. Kitty thought he did not sound happy about Gunther's murder.

'Very well, but it's better to never leave loose ends. Dead men tell no tales,' Forbes said.

The motorcycle roared away. Kitty waited for Forbes to pull the car back onto the road bracing herself not to cry out at the expected jarring. The car moved slowly forward, and she bit her lip to stop herself from making a sound. Every movement hurt and she wondered where Forbes would go next.

He could return to the mystery woman at the house, or

perhaps he might venture into Dartmouth to look for the luckless Theo. If Theo had any sense, he would have returned to his parents' home and thrown himself on his father's mercy. Sir Montague would be angry and disappointed in his son, but at least he would be safe there as she doubted that even Forbes would dare return to the Hawkes' house.

A shudder ran through Kitty's frame at the thought of what would happen to the boy if Forbes found him first. It seemed clear to her that Forbes had murdered Gunther and he would have no qualms at killing again. If he were to discover that she was hidden in the back of the motor car she had no doubt that she would be next.

Forbes set off once more and Kitty waited to discover where he would stop next. If he returned to the house, then she would have to wait for him to go back inside and then make her way on to the village. It had sounded as if it were some distance away. If she was lucky, she might be able to find somewhere to rest and shelter overnight to give herself a chance to recover some of her strength.

Presently the car turned, and she heard the crunch of gravel under the wheels. She wondered if they were back at the house with the mystery woman. Forbes turned off the ignition, the driver's seat creaked and moved, and the door of the motor opened and closed.

Kitty heard Forbes' footsteps crunch on the gravel, and she slowly released the breath she had been holding. The blanket tickled the end of her nose and before she could stifle it a small sneeze escaped.

She froze in place. Had he heard her? Surely, he must have been by the front door and too far away. Nothing. Her shoulders sagged in relief. Then, without any warning the car door opened, and the tartan wool blanket was thrown off exposing her to the night air.

'Well, well, the enterprising Miss Underhay. And how long

have you been hiding back there, I wonder?' Forbes' eyes gleamed maliciously as he took hold of Kitty's arm and yanked her unceremoniously out of the car onto the driveway. 'I suggest you come inside for a little chat.'

He tugged her towards the house, his fingers biting into the tender flesh of her upper arm. The front door stood open spilling yellow light out into the night. Kitty had no choice but to accompany him.

He pushed her inside the hall then turned and locked the white-painted front door behind them.

'Do go on through, Miss Underhay.' He gave her another shove in the small of her back, so she was forced to enter the sitting room. A fire crackled in the grate and the room was comfortably furnished with plush upholstered seats and a fine Turkish rug. An older woman sat on the armchair beside the fire, a glass of sherry in her hand. She seemed unnervingly familiar and completely unsurprised to see Forbes accompanied by Kitty.

'We have a visitor, Mother.' Forbes gave Kitty another push forcing her into the chair opposite the woman.

Kitty's blood froze in her veins as she took her first proper look at the woman in the expensive dark-blue silk dress seated opposite her. She knew that face only too well. It was one that had haunted her nightmares ever since she had discovered the truth of what had happened to her mother all those years ago.

'Miss Underhay, you seem a little... dishevelled.' The woman's tone was as hard as the glint in her eye.

Esther Hammett looked at the remains of the sacking wrapped around Kitty's feet. 'And an unusual choice of footwear.'

Kitty swallowed. Forbes had addressed Esther as mother. Could that be possible? Forbes was Esther's son? Age wise she supposed he could be if he had been born when Esther was quite young. She knew that Esther had made several marriages, not all of them legal, but no one had ever said that Esther had children.

'Cat got your tongue, Miss Underhay? Most unusual for you. You always seem to have a lot to say for yourself.' Esther sipped her sherry.

'What do you want with me?' Kitty asked. She tried to keep her voice calm and firm despite her rising fear. This woman had threatened her and even tried to kill her in the past.

Esther shrugged and placed her crystal glass down carefully on the small, polished oak table at her side. 'Left to me on this occasion, nothing. Personally, I would like to see you dead and I would have rid myself of you in Dartmouth if I had been the one to find you snooping. You have a habit of being quite a nuisance. Edward, however, feels that there is some merit in keeping you alive at least temporarily as a kind of insurance should the police become too interested in his operations.'

Forbes was lounging now behind the sofa resting his arms on the back of it as he looked at Kitty. There was a leering amusement in his gaze.

'You do seem to have the most unfortunate gift, Miss Underhay, of popping up at the most inconvenient of times.'

'You killed Gunther Freiberg on the paddle steamer.' Kitty raised her chin and looked him in the eyes.

'Tsk, tsk, Miss Underhay, really that is not a very nice thing to say. I was present when he was killed certainly, but mine was not the hand that struck the fatal blow.' His lips thinned into a cruel smile.

Kitty's heart thumped as she tried to think who else could have been working with Forbes. It had to be either Theo or Flora. Surely, they were the only two people who had been below deck at the same time as Forbes who would have had the opportunity.

'But you don't deny that they were acting on your instruction? Was it Theo or Flora?' Kitty asked. 'Gunther was your middleman, wasn't he? He collected the information from your source inside the college and passed it on to you so you could sell it to the highest bidder?'

Edward's smile grew wider. 'I see what Mother means about you. Very good, Miss Underhay. Yes, that's true, except Gunther grew greedy and a little careless. He decided to do a few deals for himself. That meant that the information when I received it had a lower value or had already reached my intended buyer.'

'So, you wanted to get rid of him,' Kitty said. He hadn't confirmed who had struck the blow.

'My dear Miss Underhay, you are a businesswoman yourself. You know that you cannot keep a dishonest or untrustworthy employee. Sadly, we had to, well, let him go,' Esther said, raising her hands in a deprecating fashion.

'And it doesn't bother you that you are passing on secrets to a possibly hostile or unfriendly nation?' Kitty said.

'There is no room for sentiment in business.' The corners of Esther's thin lips turned upwards as if amused.

'And the necklace? Did you have anything to do with the Firestone being stolen?' Kitty asked, looking at Edward. She could see why and how Gunther's death fitted into Esther and her son's operation, but she still couldn't work out who had taken the necklace.

Esther raised a single elegantly pencilled eyebrow and looked towards her son.

'I rather wish we had been responsible for that, but since I expected dear Serafina to become my bride, I had anticipated acquiring the necklace via marriage,' Edward said. 'I'm afraid you will have to look elsewhere for that particular crime.'

'Yes, that was rather a pity,' Esther added. 'Now, where shall we stash you for the night until we decide what to do with you?'

'Somewhere secure I think, Mother. Miss Underhay has

already proved quite adept at escaping.' There was a glint in Edward's eye that sent a cold shiver along Kitty's spine.

'Perhaps the scullery? There is a secure lock on the cold store,' Esther suggested. 'She can cool her heels in there for the time being.' Her smile widened at her own pun.

'Good idea, Mother. In the morning I'll track down that idiot Theo and find out what's happening. We can decide then how best to make use of Miss Underhay.' Edward caught hold of Kitty's upper arm once more, tugging her up from her seat.

She cried out in pain as his grip tightened on the bruise that had begun to form from where he had mauled her before.

'Edward dear, don't damage the goods,' Esther reproved her son as he began to steer Kitty towards the hall.

Forbes released her arm causing her to stagger and half-fall against the cream-painted wall of the hallway. He pushed her hard between her shoulders once more to go through the door leading into a compact kitchen with a red, quarry-tiled floor.

Behind her Kitty thought she heard a noise outside at the front of the house and the hall suddenly seemed brighter as if a light were being shone through the frosted-coloured glass in the top of the front door.

'Edward, go with the girl and keep her quiet. There is someone outside,' Esther urged.

Forbes clamped his hand hard across Kitty's mouth preventing her from screaming or calling for help as he tried to drag her towards the rear of the kitchen and the entrance to the scullery.

Out in the hallway she heard a loud rain of knocks on the front door and a muffled shout of, 'Police, open the door.'

Edward hissed in her ear. 'One word and you are dead.'

Kitty was suddenly aware that there was something cold and hard being pushed into her side. Forbes had taken out his gun, and she knew he would have absolutely no compunction about shooting her.

He dragged her into the darkened kitchen and on into the scullery. Behind her she heard Esther opening the door.

'Police? My goodness whatever is the matter?'

There was a rumble of male voices as Edward forced her inside the cupboard in the scullery, his hand still firmly over her mouth as he pinned her there in the darkness as they listened to his mother talking to whoever had knocked on the front door.

In the distance Kitty thought she heard a dog bark. Esther seemed to have persuaded the visitors into the sitting room for a moment.

'Right, let's get out of here while Mother is keeping them busy,' Edward muttered and opened the back door as quietly as he could, ready to make their escape.

The rear of the house was in darkness. Kitty could hear more voices at the front of the house, and she wondered how many officers had come knocking. They had to be searching for Forbes and she wondered if they were also looking for her.

* * *

The house had been hard to find, lying back from the road on a small lane about a mile from the village of Blackawton. The inspector had requested another car to meet them at the address, but they had found the house before the other motor had arrived.

Inspector Greville had knocked on the front door with Matt following closely behind him. Forbes' motor car was parked in the shadows at the side of the house. Matt placed his hand on the bonnet and noted that the engine was still warm. Clearly someone had driven the car very recently.

A woman's voice answered the inspector's call, taking Matt somewhat by surprise. He had assumed that Forbes must be working alone now that Theo was in custody. Alice and Mr Lutterworth had climbed out of the car, with Mr Lutterworth holding on to Bertie's leash as the dog sniffed about on the drive.

Inspector Greville brushed past the smartly dressed woman who had opened the door to them and looked into the sitting room.

'What's wrong? How can I help you?' the woman asked.

'I'll check the upstairs.' Matt didn't wait for the house owner to give permission. Instead, he took the stairs two at a time. If Kitty was anywhere in this house, he was determined to find her.

The rooms were all empty. He opened and closed all the cupboard doors and peered quickly beneath the beds just to be on the safe side, before hurrying back down the stairs to the inspector. A cold draught of air alerted him as he entered the hall and he rushed through the door at the far end into the kitchen.

The back door in the scullery was standing open, and Matt groaned to himself. Someone had clearly gone out through the back of the house while the woman had delayed Inspector Greville in the lounge. He dashed outside and shouted to the inspector.

'Someone has come out of the house this way.'

Inspector Greville puffed up to join him on the small paved terrace, while Alice and Mr Lutterworth also appeared having come through the hall on hearing his shout.

'I'll take the bottom of the garden. It looks as if it may open onto the fields,' Matt said.

The sound of a car starting up made them all spin around, and Alice darted back inside the house as the car roared away.

''Tis the woman. She has taken Mr Forbes' car and driven off.' Alice ran back to meet them.

'Was anyone with her?' Matt demanded.

Alice shook her head. 'I don't reckon so, sir. I'd say as she saw her chance to get away and took it while we was out here.'

Inspector Greville muttered a curse under his breath. There was something familiar about her. 'Let's hope my colleagues encounter her on their way here. They can't be far away now, and they are looking out for the car.'

'We should search the area. That car engine was still warm, and I think Forbes was here very recently. We didn't pass another car in the lane on our way here and the map didn't show another way out.' Matt looked at the inspector.

'I agree. Take the bottom of the garden, Captain Bryant. Miss Miller go back inside and see if there is a telephone. Place a call to the police station in Dartmouth alerting them to the situation. Mr Lutterworth, if you could stay in hailing distance until the other police officers arrive, I shall take the other half of the garden.' Inspector Greville gave his orders and they all nodded in agreement before setting about their tasks.

Matt could have kicked himself for not checking the ground floor first before checking the upstairs. He could have prevented Forbes from fleeing if he had done so. He dragged the heavy rubber torch from his pocket. He had found it in the glovebox of the police car and hoped the beam might give him some clues as to where Forbes might have gone.

CHAPTER TWENTY-FIVE

Kitty heard shouting coming from the direction of the house followed by the sound of a powerful car engine driving away in the distance.

'Keep moving or I swear I will end you now,' Forbes cursed under his breath and prodded her with the gun, forcing her to keep stumbling forward through bushes and shrubs that tore at her hair and scratched her legs.

His hand was still clamped over her mouth, and he restricted her from trying to break free. Kitty did her best to try and slow their pace, breaking branches and trampling grass to try and leave some kind of trail in the hope that someone was following them.

'Kitty! Where are you?'

She recognised Matt's voice calling her and despite the danger of her predicament her heart lifted.

They had reached the perimeter of the garden and a low stone wall, and a ditch prevented their passage into the field beyond. Forbes paused as if taking stock and trying to work out an escape route.

The sound of a dog barking also seemed to be drawing

closer. Forbes momentarily slightly relaxed his grip on Kitty's mouth, and she took the opportunity to bite the flesh of his palm as hard as she could.

'Matt!' She barely had time to call out before Forbes had grabbed her once more, hitting her hard on the side of her head.

'Shut up, you little witch. Mother was right about you.'

Before he could say anything else or force her to attempt scaling the wall a compact, four-legged dark shadow burst through the bushes and launched itself at Forbes, knocking him to the ground. The gun he had been holding fell and disappeared into the bushes.

Taken by surprise, he released Kitty and she moved away from him as quickly as she could despite the pain in her head.

'Bertie!'

She realised that Matt's dog had come to her aid and was growling fiercely at her assailant. She looked around her for some kind of weapon, terrified that Edward might find the gun he had threatened her with and use it to attack the dog. She snatched up a broken branch and gripped it between her hands.

'Miss Underhay. Kitty!' Another familiar, but unexpected male voice.

'Mr Lutterworth!'

To her astonishment her hotel manager appeared through the shrubs like a bald middle-aged avenging angel. In seconds he had caught hold of Forbes and dragged him to his feet, twisting his arm up his back to force him to his feet.

'Miss Underhay, are you hurt?' Cyril asked as Bertie bounced up at her desperate to be petted.

'I'm much better now you are all here,' Kitty assured him, her voice cracked with emotion as she fussed the dog. 'Do be careful, Cyril. He had a gun, which I think has fallen into the bushes somewhere.'

'Kitty! Thank heavens.' Matt was out of breath as he arrived, shining the torch in his hand to light up the scene in the tiny clearing. His expression darkened when he looked at her and Kitty could see he was angry.

'What have you done to her?' Matt turned to where Forbes was wriggling like an angry fish in Mr Lutterworth's grip.

A stream of curses fell from Forbes' lips as he attempted to free himself.

'Nothing has happened to that nosey witch that she didn't deserve. I should have killed her back in Dartmouth,' Forbes spat, glaring at Kitty as he twisted away from Mr Lutterworth's grasp.

Matt drew back his fist and launched, hitting Forbes squarely under his jaw, sending the younger man sliding to the ground. Kitty gasped as her fiancé stepped back and rubbed his knuckles, before placing a tender arm around her waist.

'My poor darling. Are you all right, old thing?' Matt stirred the now unconscious Forbes' foot with the toe of his shoe.

'I'm much better for seeing you. Where is Esther? Do the police have her?'

Matt looked confused. 'Esther?'

'The woman in the house is Esther Hammett. It seems she is Edward's mother.' Kitty looked at Forbes who had already started to come around.

'She took off in his motor car when we came outside into the garden to search for you. I don't know if the police will manage to catch her,' Matt said as Mr Lutterworth dragged the now groaning Edward into a sitting position.

Bertie trotted off into the shrubs and returned dragging Forbes' gun in his mouth. Mr Lutterworth bent and swiftly retrieved it before it could accidentally go off. Inspector Greville arrived in the clearing and promptly took over from Mr Lutterworth, securing Forbes' hands behind his back with a pair of handcuffs.

He hoisted Forbes to his feet. 'I'll take this from here, Captain Bryant. The other police car has arrived now. There was no sign of the woman unfortunately, but we will continue to watch the roads for the Singer.'

'The woman was Esther Hammett, sir. She is Forbes' mother,' Kitty said.

The inspector's expression betrayed his astonishment at this revelation. 'I see, that's why she seemed familiar. This adds a whole new layer of complexity to our case. I suggest you go up to the house, Miss Underhay. Miss Miller is most anxious to see you.'

'Alice is here too?' Kitty looked at Mr Lutterworth.

'I believe she has a blanket and brandy waiting for you,' her manager said.

The inspector hauled the now protesting Forbes away and Mr Lutterworth followed after them, taking Bertie on his lead.

Matt gathered Kitty close to him and she breathed in the welcome familiar scent of his soap and the scent of his jacket as she rested her head on his chest.

'Oh, Matt, I was so scared.'

'It's all right now, darling. It's over, you're safe. Come, Alice will be horrified when she sees the state of you.' He dropped a tender kiss on her hair.

Kitty smiled. 'I'm sure she will. I've even managed to lose my shoes.' She waggled one of her sack-clad feet at him.

In response he swept her into his arms and carried her back up the garden and into the house, setting her down on the sofa in front of a startled Alice.

'Oh my stars, Miss Kitty, just look at the state of you. Am you all right?' Her friend enveloped her in a hug and a blanket. Matt disappeared momentarily to telephone the Dolphin with the good news that Kitty had been found.

The next few hours passed in a blur. Inspector Greville sent them all back to Dartmouth with a constable driving the police car, while he dealt with Forbes. After a hot bath, tea and copious piles of buttered toast and a tearful reunion with her grandmother, Kitty was dispatched to bed.

The sun was already quite high in the sky when Alice came to wake her the following morning.

'I brought you some more tea, toast and a nice boiled egg, Miss Kitty. How am you feeling now?' her friend asked as she set the loaded tray down on the top of the bedside cabinet.

Kitty sat herself up gingerly in her bed. 'Truthfully, Alice, I've had days when I felt much better.' She managed a smile at the maid as Alice set the strainer on the cup and poured the tea.

'I don't wonder at it. What a thing to happen and that dreadful Hammett woman at the back of it all.' Alice shook her head. 'Who'd have guessed as she was that Forbes' mother?'

'And it seems she has evaded the police yet again. Although there would have been very little that they could have arrested her for. The abduction was not planned and was all Edward's work. I daresay she would deny all knowledge of his espionage activities and about Gunther's murder,' Kitty said as she accepted her drink and made room for her friend to perch on the bed beside her.

'Nasty, dangerous piece of work she is. How she keeps getting away with everything defeats me.' Alice poured herself some tea and took her seat beside Kitty.

'I expect Inspector Greville will call later.' Kitty nibbled on a slice of toast. 'Oh bother.' She shook the front of her nightgown as a large crumb escaped and landed inside the lace-trimmed neck.

'Here, let me help you.' Alice set down her cup and rescued the toast crumb.

'Forbes said he didn't take the Firestone necklace.' Kitty picked up her toast once more and eyed it thoughtfully.

'Was he telling the truth though, miss? I reckon as neither

him nor his mother would recognise the truth if it bit them,' Alice huffed.

Kitty set the toast down again on the plate and picked up her spoon ready to take the top off her egg. 'I think he was, Alice. And I think I may have just worked out what did happen to the necklace.'

Alice sipped her tea. 'I heard as Master Hawkes has been sent home back to Priory Hall. I presume as he will face some kind of punishment. Captain Bryant didn't say what he had done exactly when we was driving to find you, but I gather it was something pretty serious.'

Kitty nodded. 'Yes, it was. I think there were a good many people caught up in Forbes' activities.'

Alice finished her tea and replaced her cup on the tray. 'Now, Miss Kitty, shall I help you get ready? You'll need some more ointment on your feet afore you tries to get any of your shoes on.'

Kitty finished her breakfast and allowed her friend to help her dress. She was quite sore and stiff after yesterday's events. Alice tutted over the bruising on her arms, legs and temple, before liberally applying cream to the myriad of tiny cuts on her feet.

Once she had finished and declared herself satisfied the maid gathered up her tray ready to return to her hotel duties.

'Now, please take it easy today, miss,' Alice warned her.

'I will. Thank you, Alice.' Kitty smiled at her friend.

After Alice had gone Kitty telephoned Matt to ask him to call. She had a theory she wished to explore with him about who may have taken the Firestone necklace and what may have become of it. She also needed to talk to Inspector Greville about Herr Freiberg's murder.

Matt arrived a little later and seemed relieved to see her looking more like her usual self.

'You look better today, old thing. I called the police station and Inspector Greville has gone to Sir Montague's home to talk to Theo again,' Matt explained, after greeting her with a kiss on the cheek.

'I think we should go to Sir Montague's home too,' Kitty said. 'I really want to talk to Theo, Saffy and Flora.'

Matt raised his eyebrows slightly at this. 'Are you well enough to drive or shall I telephone Mr Potter for a taxi?'

'My feet are a little sore, but I see no reason why I can't drive. Alice has taken very good care of me.' Kitty picked up her keys and made sure her second best summer hat was firmly fixed to her head. She was still rather annoyed that she had not only lost her shoes but also her favourite hat yesterday. At least her handbag had been recovered.

'If you are quite certain,' Matt said. Kitty knew that he was fully aware that once she had her mind set to something she was not to be easily dissuaded.

The weather, although fine and dry, was cooler than the day before. Kitty noticed that some of the leaves on the trees had also now started to take on a more golden hue. Matt directed her to Sir Montague's house as they approached Exeter.

Kitty couldn't help wondering if the police had apprehended Esther Hammett yet. The journey to Priory Hall held uncomfortable reminders of the one she had taken to see Ezekiel Hammett when he had been incarcerated in Exeter Gaol. A journey that had led ultimately to Ezekiel's demise and Kitty being unfairly blamed by Esther for his death.

She swung the crimson snub nose of her car into the drive of Sir Montague's home shortly before lunchtime. Inspector Greville's black police motor car was already parked outside the front door.

Matt got out and crossed around to offer her some much-needed support as she clambered somewhat stiffly from the driver's seat.

'Hold my arm, old thing. I think perhaps the journey here

may have been a bit much,' he said as she rested her hand on the crook of his arm to approach the front door of the Hawkes' house.

'I'll be all right in a moment,' Kitty reassured him as he rang the bell and they waited for a servant to answer the door.

A uniformed maid opened the door and accepted Matt's card as she showed them into the hall. Kitty looked around her with interest while they waited to see if the inspector and Sir Montague were happy to receive them.

'Please to come this way, sir, miss.' The maid led them along the hall to a spacious drawing room at the rear of the house. Sir Montague stood in front of the fine marble fireplace. Theo was seated on one of the leather armchairs, while Inspector Greville was at a small, polished mahogany writing desk with his notebook and pen laid out before him.

Theo glanced at Kitty as she entered the room and turned his gaze away quickly when he caught sight of the blue-black bruising on her temple. Sir Montague looked as if he had aged ten years overnight. Kitty could see that despite his stern demeanour his hand trembled when he held it out for Matt to shake it in greeting.

'Our apologies, Inspector, if we are interrupting, but Kitty wished to speak to you on some matters pertaining to the case,' Matt said as he shook Sir Montague's hand and tenderly ushered Kitty towards a vacant seat.

'Not at all, Captain Bryant, Miss Underhay. I need to complete Miss Underhay's statement about the events of yesterday anyway,' the inspector said.

Kitty took a seat feeling oddly nervous.

'Are you all right, Kitty? From what the inspector has told us you suffered the most dreadful ordeal at the hands of that man Forbes.' Sir Montague's expression showed his concern.

'I'm sure I shall recover quickly now that I am in the care of my family and friends, sir. It's not the first time that I've been injured in the course of an investigation,' Kitty reassured him.

'The whole affair has affected Rose dreadfully. She is unable to leave her bed at present she feels so ill. To think that Serafina might have become engaged to the man. Worming his way into her affections under false pretences. I cannot fathom how we were all so deceived.' Sir Montague's voice had a faint tremor.

'Forbes had a good tutor in his mother, Esther Hammett. The apple doesn't fall far from the tree, sir,' Matt responded.

'It seems Forbes' plan to win Serafina's affections was well thought out and designed to benefit both himself and his mother. Once established as your son-in-law, no doubt he would have felt that he had a degree of protection from the law and, of course, he used any information he could glean to aid members of his gang,' Kitty said.

'And presumably to also adversely affect the outcome of trials against his enemies too,' Matt said thoughtfully.

Theo kept his head low during the conversation.

'I presume, sir, that Theo has owned up to his part in Forbes' schemes?' Matt asked. He had told Kitty on the drive to Exeter everything that had happened while she was Forbes' prisoner.

Sir Montague paced up and down before the handsome marble fireplace before shooting an agitated glance at his son.

'Yes. He has made a full confession to Inspector Greville and to me.'

Theo's cheeks flushed a dull scarlet at his father's words.

Kitty cleared her throat. 'Inspector Greville, has Forbes told you what happened the night Herr Freiberg was killed?'

Theo's head snapped upwards, and she thought she saw a look of panic in his eyes.

The inspector sighed heavily. 'He has admitted being

present when Gunther was killed, but has denied dealing the fatal blow.'

'And you believe him? Good grief, man. We know him to be an absolute blackguard. He must have done it, who else could it have been?' Sir Montague wheeled around to glare at the inspector.

Theo buried his face in his hands.

Kitty looked at the boy and couldn't help feeling sorry for what she was about to say. 'Forbes told me that he coerced someone else into hitting Freiberg with that wrench. Someone he had a great deal of power over.'

A low moan escaped from Theo.

'Theodore?' Sir Montague looked at his son.

'I had no choice. It was either me or the steward. If I had declined, then I have no doubts that he would have harmed either me or Serafina.' Theo groaned and leaned forward burying his face in his hands. 'He lured the man into the engine room and handed me the weapon while Gunther's back was turned. I'm so sorry, Father.' The boy broke into sobs.

Sir Montague collapsed down onto a sofa and Kitty jumped up to pour a tot of brandy into a glass from the decanter on the sideboard.

'Here, sir, drink this.' She pressed the tumbler into his hand.

'Theo, my own son.' Sir Montague had grown so pale Kitty thought the man was about to faint and she urged the glass to his lips, hoping the spirit would revive him.

There was a faint knock on the panelled door to the drawing room and Serafina entered, with Flora following at her heels.

'Papa, are you all right?' Saffy rushed over to her father and took over from Kitty in administering the brandy. Her eyes were wide with alarm. 'What has happened?' She looked from her father to the inspector for an explanation.

Sir Montague seemed to recover a little of his colour after tasting the spirit.

'It was me. I killed Freiberg on the boat. Edward made me do it,' Theo confessed to his sister.

Patches of colour came and went in Serafina's plump cheeks and Flora bit back a gasp of astonishment.

'This is all my fault,' Serafina said. 'If I had not brought Edward here.' Tears ran freely down her face.

'You were not to know. That man is a monster. He looks for things that he can use against you. He is evil. Evil, I tell you,' Flora declared.

'You seem to speak from experience, Mademoiselle Rochelle. What hold did Forbes have over you?' Inspector Greville asked.

CHAPTER TWENTY-SIX

There was an awkward silence in the room after the inspector's question. Flora looked at Serafina, a mute plea in her eyes.

'Did he discover your plans for the Firestone necklace?' Kitty asked.

'The necklace? What about the necklace? Saffy?' Sir Montague stared at his daughter as she moved away from him to stand next to her friend.

'I don't know what you mean?' Serafina said hesitantly. She didn't, however, meet Kitty's gaze and her tone was unconvincing.

'You and Flora had a plan to steal the Firestone necklace. Technically once you had been gifted the jewels, I suppose the necklace was yours, but you were not free to do what you wished with it. Is that correct?' Kitty asked.

Flora clutched at Serafina's arm.

'It was just sat in a bank vault gathering dust to be brought out once in a blue moon. The necklace was mine. Why shouldn't I do something else with it? Why should it be kept locked in a safe? What good is that?' Serafina said forcefully.

'Edward knew you were due to inherit the necklace. He saw

it as a nice little bonus for him once you had accepted his marriage proposal. A proposal that he was certain you would not refuse. After all you knew he had the power to disgrace your brother and ruin his life even before Herr Freiberg was murdered. Theo had told you how much money he owed Edward and you were in debt to him too, weren't you?' Kitty said.

Inspector Greville's moustache twitched, and Kitty could hear the sound of his pen racing across the page as he took note of everything she was saying.

Serafina sank down onto the sofa beside her father. 'When I first met Edward at the exhibition, he was handsome, charming, intelligent. He seemed to understand what I wanted for my life and a friendship quickly grew between us. I am aware that I do not possess the kind of beauty that Flora here possesses, and I must confess that I didn't understand what the attraction might be for a man considered as handsome as Edward. He appeared wealthy and what Mama called a good catch.'

Tears rolled silently down Flora's face as she gave her friend an anguished look. 'Do not blame yourself, Saffy. I too was deceived.'

Serafina rested her hands in her lap and stared down at her fingers as she continued. 'It was some time before I began to realise that he had abused my trust in him to ingratiate himself into my family. Theo was in financial trouble and Edward had loaned him a considerable sum of money. Much more than Theo could ever hope to pay back without Father finding out. I gave Theo whatever I could, but Papa had cut my allowance since he disapproved of my desire to study.'

Sir Montague took another sip of brandy from the glass that Kitty had given him. She wondered if she should suggest asking a doctor to call he looked so ill.

'I must speak, Saffy. The Firestone necklace that was my idea.' Flora dabbed at her face with a lawn handkerchief.

Serafina shook her head. 'I did not have to agree, Flora. I needed money to free Theo and myself. Flora's father is also in financial difficulty and there was that stupid necklace, which was mine after all. Why should I not use it to free all of us? I knew Papa would never allow it to be sold. It would come out, shine for an evening and then go back to the bank. Flora's father had photographs and some drawings, so I decided to get a copy made.'

'And your plan was to switch it over during the ball? Keeping the original so that you could sell it?' Inspector Greville asked.

Flora nodded. 'I had discovered where the fuse was for the ballroom so when the time was right, I left and dimmed the lights.'

'And then in the darkness Saffy unclipped the necklace and dropped it inside the neckline of her dress. The gown she was wearing had a low front and a ruffle so the jewels could be concealed. She made the red mark on her neck herself to make the story of it being snatched more plausible,' Kitty said. 'I realised what she must have done this morning when I accidentally dropped a piece of toast in my nightgown.'

'I replaced the fuse and turned the lights back on and returned to the ballroom. I had placed the copy inside one of the plant pots earlier before I left the room,' Flora said.

'We didn't think anyone would look too closely at the copy. It was well made and once it was back in the bank vault no one would ever be any the wiser. I was only selling what was mine.' Saffy reached for her father's hand. 'I didn't think you would ever know, Papa. Then when we argued and you found out I thought well, the insurance money would perhaps help you.'

Sir Montague removed his hand from that of his daughter. 'Well, I seem to have raised a fine pair of criminals. A murderer and a thief. Inspector, I fear you must excuse me. I need to go and talk to my wife.'

The older man rose and walked stiffly from the room, leaving Flora to collapse in tears against her friend and the two girls to sob together on the sofa.

'I take it then that the Firestone necklace is safely in your possession, Miss Hawkes?' Inspector Greville asked.

'It's locked away in a box at the bottom of my wardrobe. I smuggled it back to the house rolled inside my stockings,' Saffy said.

'That was why you felt able to refuse Forbes' marriage proposal? You and Flora knew you would have some money from the sale of the Firestone and you hoped to extricate Theo from his clutches?' Matt asked.

Saffy nodded. 'I thought I could pay him off. Edward is very fond of money. I didn't know that he had suspicions about our plans and would force Theo into doing something much worse than delivering his odious packages.'

'What will happen now, *Monsieur l'inspecteur*?' Flora asked, raising her tear-stained face towards Inspector Greville.

The policeman frowned. 'The issue of the necklace is fairly clear. If it is returned and the claim to the insurance company is halted, then no crime has been committed. Miss Hawkes is legally the owner of the necklace. The only crime would be attempted fraud against the insurance company if the claim were to continue.' He gave Serafina a stern look. 'As for wasting police time, well, I think we shall let that go this time.'

He looked at Theodore. 'I have no choice but to arrest you, Mr Hawkes, for the murder of Gunther Freiberg.'

Saffy gave a loud sob and buried her face on her friend's shoulder.

'I have no doubt that given the circumstances that with a good barrister and testimony from Miss Hawkes and Mademoiselle Rochelle, coupled with Sir Montague's good standing, that the court may well be disposed to take a more lenient view than would usually be the case in such matters.' Inspector Greville rose from his seat and tucked his notebook and pen away inside his jacket pocket.

Theo also rose. His face pale and looking very young. Kitty blinked back her own tears. He might have killed Gunther Freiberg, but she couldn't help feeling sad that a life was to be ruined and potentially lost for his crime.

'If you would accompany me to the car, Master Hawkes?' Inspector Greville said.

'May I say goodbye to my mother first, please, sir?' Theo asked. 'You have my word I shall I not make a run for it.'

The inspector nodded and they went out into the hall.

Weariness swept through Kitty like a tide, and she wondered how many other families would be devastated by the tentacles of the Hammett family's empire before they themselves were finally destroyed.

Matt came around to her and placed his hand on her shoulder. 'Are you all right, old thing? Shall we take our own leave?' he asked quietly.

She nodded her acquiescence and they left Flora and Saffy in the drawing room to comfort each other.

Inspector Greville was at the foot of the stairs as they walked towards the front door.

'Are you off back to Dartmouth, Miss Underhay, Captain Bryant?'

'Yes, sir. Kitty is still a little frail and well, that was quite a trial.' Matt had his arm around Kitty's waist.

'Indeed. I suppose you will be speaking to the brigadier? The lieutenant telephoned me at the police station before I set off this morning. He said the matter had been sorted out at the college to the navy's satisfaction. There will be no more problems from that direction,' Inspector Greville said as he glanced up towards the floor above as the sound of a woman weeping could be heard.

'And Esther Hammett is still at large?' Kitty asked.

'There have been no sightings of her, although Mr Forbes' motor car was discovered in Exeter not far from the site of the old Glass Bottle public house early this morning,' Inspector Greville said.

Kitty swallowed. The Glass Bottle brought back terrible memories for her as it was where she had finally discovered what had happened to her mother all those years ago.

'I see. Thank you, Inspector.' She allowed Matt to guide her outside where the cool autumnal air helped to relieve the wave of nausea that had engulfed her at the mention of the Glass Bottle.

'Would you like to take a short turn in the gardens before we return to Dartmouth?' Matt asked. 'I know that mention of the Glass Bottle was distressing.'

She could see his concern for her written in his deep-blue eyes. She leaned on his arm, and they walked for a few moments on the finely manicured lawns. The quiet of the garden and the fresh air helped to restore her equilibrium. Despite Esther and everything that had happened in the last few days she had so much to be grateful about.

'I expect Sir Montague will offer his resignation over this affair.' Matt pulled at the yellowing leaf of a cherry tree.

'It will be very difficult for him to continue in his post, especially when the press find out that Theo has been charged with murder. I suppose retirement would be an honourable and acceptable way to go. Poor Sir Monty and Lady Rose, none of this was really their fault. Grams and Mrs Craven will be dreadfully upset.' Kitty gave his arm a gentle squeeze.

'Do you feel able to drive now, my dear?' Matt asked tenderly.

'Yes, I think so. Let's go back to the Dolphin. I have still to thank Mr Lutterworth for all his bravery yesterday and I know that Grams will be fretting that I've gone out in the car.' Kitty smiled up at her fiancé.

'Cyril is certainly full of surprises. He tackled Forbes with the spirit of a much younger man.' Matt smiled back at her. 'At least you can be certain that the Dolphin will be in safe hands with him at the helm after we are married.'

Kitty leaned on Matt's arm as they walked towards her car. 'Yes, indeed. I think we have made a good choice.'

Matt opened the driver's door for her and kissed her cheek. 'Then let's go. Our wedding is only weeks away now and we need to put all of this behind us.'

Kitty slid into the driver's seat and smiled at her fiancé. 'Until my father arrives before the wedding and then I'm sure there will be drama of a different kind.'

She turned the key in the ignition as she spoke, drowning Matt's amused chuckle as he crossed around the front of the car to take his seat beside her for the journey back to the Dolphin.

A LETTER FROM HELENA

Thank you for choosing to read *Murder on Board*. If you enjoyed it and want to keep up to date with all my latest releases, just sign up at the following link. Your email address will never be shared and you can unsubscribe at any time.

www.bookouture.com/helena-dixon

If you read the first book in the series, *Murder at the Dolphin Hotel*, you can find out how Kitty and Matt first met and began their sleuthing adventures. I always enjoy meeting characters again as a series reader, which is why I love writing this series so much. I hope you enjoy their exploits as much as I love creating them. This one was a tricky one to write with two mystery puzzles to solve. You can take a trip on the paddle steamer today and also book tours of the Naval College, which is very much a working building.

I hope you loved reading *Murder on Board* and if you did, I would be very grateful if you could write a review. I'd love to hear what you think, and it makes such a difference helping new readers to discover one of my books for the first time.

I love hearing from all my readers – you can get in touch on my Facebook page, through Twitter, Goodreads or my website.

Thank you,

Helena Dixon

KEEP IN TOUCH WITH HELENA

www.nelldixon.com

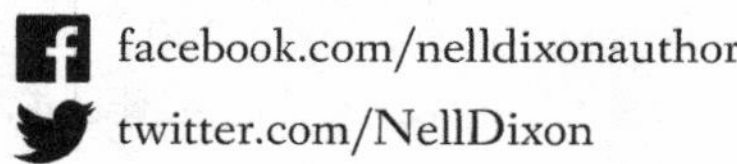

facebook.com/nelldixonauthor

twitter.com/NellDixon

ACKNOWLEDGEMENTS

My thanks to the staff and former graduates of Dartmouth Royal Naval College for all their information, photographs and assistance. Any errors are entirely my own. I have the greatest admiration for our naval service. My thanks also, as always, to the people of Dartmouth and Torbay for their assistance. I'm so grateful that you are all not completely fed up by now with my endless questions.

Special thanks to everyone who supported me during the writing of this book during a very difficult and emotional time. My family and friends who kept me going with coffee, cake and messages of encouragement, I love all of you so much.

My lovely agent, Kate Nash, and my wonderful editor, Emily Gowers, and everyone at Bookouture for your unstinting kindness and support. Special hug to Kim Nash, Phillipa Ashley, Georgia Hill, Elizabeth Hanbury and the Tuesday morning zoomers. Also huge love to the wonderful ladies of Galmpton WI and Viv our lovely chair.